God Touched

A novel of the Demon Accords

John Conroe

This book is a work of fiction. All of the characters, organizations, and events portrayed in this novel either products of the author's imagination or are used fictitiously.

GOD TOUCHED

ISBN: 978-0-557-38473-0

This book would not exist without the help of a lot of people. Thanks to my beta readers : Deann, Jessica, Elaine, Kaylie (my niece) and my sister, Laurie. Thanks to Jack for listening to improbable ideas and offering creative names. My brother Scott provided invaluable editing and advice.

My parents need to receive my thanks for teaching me to enjoy reading (no reading – no writing). Most of all I need to thank my wife, Robin, and my girls, Emilee and Allison for living with a mid-life writer. Thanks for putting up with all the hours I snuck away to write.

Chapter 1

I had to admit it, these vampires really knew how to run a club. It had to be the most bizarre place in the Big Apple, and that's saying something. I wouldn't have chosen a vampire/Goth club myself, but Henderson's ravings about Plasma had won over Pella, and so I went along. Now, I had to confess to some curiosity, myself.

Of course the vampires weren't real, but the owners had done a great job capitalizing on the current nationwide love affair with all things vampire—movies, books, and dance clubs. The Brooklyn building had once housed a newspaper, and the center of the building, where the printing presses had operated, was open all the way to the ceiling, three stories above. The club's entrance brought you in on the second floor, and a labyrinth of stairs provided passage to the top floor or down to the bottom where the dance floor and band stage were.

I sipped my Corona and took in the atmosphere. The walls were black, and most of the lighting came from red neon that bathed everything in a bloody glow. Dark nooks and corners abounded, occupied with a strange mixture of serious Goth and trendy night clubbers. The staff was uniformly pale and etheric looking, an effect that puzzled me to no end. Our *vampire* waitress had visited our table four or five

4

times, and I hadn't been able to detect a trace of white makeup on her face. Likewise, the club appeared to only hire professional dancers as staff, since they all moved entirely too gracefully to be regular clods like the three of us.

"Hey Chris, dude, here's to six months on the Force and the end of probation!" Pella exclaimed for the dozenth time, his slurring getting more pronounced with each toast. I clinked my bottle to his glass, having to first steady his hand. Pella and I had just finished probation with the NYPD and were now eligible for full benefits.

Our host for the evening, veteran officer Scott Henderson, single and ever the playa, was charming a pair of young ladies at the bar. He had waved me over several times, but that wasn't gonna happen. Bad enough that I was out with my brothers in blue, there was no way I'd involve a girl in the minefield of my life.

Pella had jumped into the celebration with both feet, pounding Bacardi and Coke like water. I, on the other hand, was having a tough time relaxing, only just getting to the bottom of my second beer. Something had me on edge, maybe just the strange nature of the club. Any club would be strange to me, having grown up at the top of New York State, right on the border of the six-million-acre Adirondack Park. Not much opportunity for clubbing up there, although I had been exposed to a little nightlife during my college years in Albany. But nothing in my college career had prepared me for a nightclub where accountants and lawyers, bond traders and stockbrokers flocked for the thrill of pretending to be in the company of vampires.

Plasma's resident vampire staff carried the whole thing off with surprising realism. Our pretty little five-foot-nothing waitress acted the part, with sly smirks and hungry glances at our throats. Spiky black hair and excellent green contact lenses gave her the full effect. For some reason, even knowing everything was fake, it raised the hair on the back of my neck—obviously the effect that kept bringing hordes of people through the door. The lines outside were two blocks long and we would probably still be out there if the head bouncer hadn't recognized Henderson as a regular and a cop. Now, that guy had set the tone right from the beginning. Well over six feet tall and built like a professional wrestler, he had been dressed in leather pants and python-skin vest. His bald head gleamed in the sodium light, and a large gold earring hung from his right lobe. Eerie yellow contact lenses had added to his formidable appearance. But despite the theatrical nature of his costume, his movements and carriage screamed serious fighter. Having spent most of my twenty-two-plus years in mixed martial arts, I am a pretty good judge. Friendly enough when he greeted Henderson, he had given Pella a glance and then spent an uncomfortable amount of time evaluating me, before letting us through without waiting in line. Henderson had called him Vadim, which sounded Russian. Rumor had it that the club's owners were originally from Moscow, with possible connections to the Russian mob.

"Falling behind your friends a bit there, ay North boy?" a silky voice purred in my ear. Somehow I kept from jumping, but my heart lurched in my chest. Turning my head, I found our spooky waitress with her mouth inches from my neck. She had introduced herself as Lydia when we first claimed the table overlooking the dance floor. Now, her bright green eyes glittered in the low light. Where do you buy contacts like that? I wondered as goosebumps covered my arms.

"How do you know I'm from the North and not Canada?" I asked, almost shouting to be heard over the band.

She shrugged, "Your accent. Kinda like a Canadian, but still not exactly like it. Ay, ya hoser." Her smile was sly. "So you look like you could use a shot to catch up with your pals."

"No, one of us needs to keep his wits about him in this wicked nest of vampires," I shot back, half joking. I was beginning to have serious questions about this place.

"Oh, you'll be safe enough, Officer. We don't eat our civil servants."

She smiled, spun in place, her tray of empties not even clinking, and swished gracefully away, glancing over her left shoulder once to catch me watching her walk. Entering a pool of darkness, her eyes glowing, she swerved to miss a drunken ass grab from a patron on her right, her eyes still locked on me. Okay, she was officially weirding me out. This place had a serious commitment to creepy. I'm fairly comfortable with creepy. You could say that it's pretty much been my life, but this was outside my realm of experience. Gramps always said the other supernatural creatures (vampires, witches, and werewolves) were real. I always thought he was kidding me. Hard to tell with him sometimes. The existence of other supernatural beings was not a big stretch from what I normally dealt with. But vampires wouldn't advertise as a vampire club if they were real, would they? Actually, Plasma didn't bill itself as vampire-owned at all, but every ad featured shots of the ethereally beautiful, preternaturally pale staff. The vampire part was mostly spread by word of mouth. Clever!

The vision hit me as I put my head back to take a long pull on my beer. Thankfully, my visions never hit while I am driving, because I can't see a thing until the vision passes. This one hit really hard, about three seconds of movie-image violence involving a girl, a corridor, and, of course, one of the demon-ridden. My eyesight returned as I choked on my mouthful of Mexican beer. Coughing the rest of it out, I immediately scanned the room for the source of my blackout.

We were on the second floor, so I moved to the railing. Pella had joined Scott and the two girls he was hitting on. My new view covered most of the dance floor, stage, and main bar. At about that time, the band finished their song and the lights dimmed, shrouding the stage in blackness. Fantastic! I need every feeble sense I have to find the monsters I hunt.

Some of the more serious Goth types started to chant a name, but it was too indistinct to make out. I stopped my scan, getting caught up in the club's theatrics. More of the crowd by the dance floor started to pick up the shout, repeating something that sounded like *tat*. Still in darkness, the band began a new song, one with a really heavy beat. The regulars went wild, and now every floor's railing was crowded with screaming people as the female lead added her voice to the burgeoning song. A punky girl and her acne-ridden boyfriend shoved up against me, trying to see the dance floor. As if by common agreement, the center of the dance floor cleared, leaving two indistinct figures standing motionless in the dark. The song suddenly paused, music and vocals both stopping dead for three heartbeats, and then suddenly exploding in full sound. A pool of light blasted into being, illuminating the lead singer but centered on two female dancers in the middle of the dance floor.

It was like nothing I had ever seen or heard of before. More than anything else in the entire club, these two women pushed me over the edge of belief. It didn't seem possible that any human could move the way these two did. One was blonde, wrapped in a curve-hugging red dress, cut low in the front and high on the side. Her bright eyes scanned the crowd as she spun and wove around her companion. The other was raven haired, wearing white, spinning with her head down, lost in her own dance. She finally lifted her head, and electric blue eyes knocked the breath out of my chest. The blonde was gorgeous, but the brunette had to be the most beautiful woman in existence. She was also the girl in my vision. I can't begin to describe their dancing, not in any way that would portray it accurately. It was alluring, primal, sensual, and utterly captivating. Fluid, athletic, and well beyond the grasp of any ballerina on earth.

I was reluctant to tear my eyes away, but now that I had found the victim, the Hellbourne couldn't be far away. Pretty much the entire club had stopped to watch the show, crowding the rails three people deep all the way around. Closing my eyes for a moment, I opened my mind, just a little, feeling for the vile, oily essence of the Hellbourne. After a moment, I got it— below—near the dance floor. Opening my eyes, I scanned the main bar, skimming over the people crowded there, then back a second time.

One man caught my eye on the second pass, mainly because he was exceptionally unexceptional. Bland. Average height, dirty blond hair, slim build, and plain, ordinary face. He stood out to my Sight because he was so unnoticeable. That and the greasy blackness of his aura.

The people around him paid no attention to the thing in their midst. Most stood with their backs to the most dangerous creature I knew.

Shoving my way through the crowd by the rail, I moved to the stairs. Movement near me caught my eye. Sometimes Hellbourne travel in pairs, and it wouldn't do to get blindsided. It was just the waitress, watching me with a puzzled look on her face. I snapped my attention back to the bland man, panicking when I didn't get a visual on him immediately. But he was still there, watching the show from the bar. A support post gave me a place to lean, pretending to watch the awesome display on the dance floor while I kept my attention squarely on him. Much harder to do than it sounds, because I felt a real compulsion to watch the brunette dance, but looking away could be disastrous. A Hellbourne in Albany had almost gutted me once when I let my attention drift in a bar. That scar was still on my stomach, a reminder to pay attention.

The dance ended almost as suddenly as it had begun, and the bland man moved from the bar in a fast, jerky manner that was inhuman and went unnoticed by the people around him. Hellbourne have a powerful ability to cloak themselves, forcing people to forget them on sight. Except me... I always see them. Part of the tool kit of talents that for some Godforsaken reason, I was born with. Yeah, me.

The demon moved toward the back of the stage area and ahead of it, I spotted the beautiful brunette leaving through a metal door. The Hellbourne followed her, walking right past several large bouncer types. I hurried to catch up, knowing that the demon's bubble of forgetfulness could cloak me, too. The bland man opened the door and followed the dancer. I slid through just a whisper behind him. The door opened into a long, institutional corridor, stacked on the sides with cartons and crates of supplies, the lighting white florescent. The air was musty and cool. Footsteps pattered ahead of me, and I ran to catch up. A sharp left brought me to another metal door, this one just closing. Instinct made me rush through... right into my vision.

A split-second glance laid it all out. The girl was backed up to the cinderblock wall, pinned in place by a silver bolt through each shoulder. A strange two-barreled gun was clattering to the floor as the Hellbourne drew a long, silver blade from the back of his plain tan jacket. I was unarmed, but my vision had given me an advanced sight of the fighting area. My right hand fell on an empty crate that I knew would be there. I swung it at the man-shape as it spun to face me. I missed the torso but hit my target—the demon's knife hand—knocking the blade flying.

Hellbourne have blinding-fast reactions. The demon snapped a wicked roundhouse kick at my head without any pause. Despite the slim build of the body that housed it, it was stronger than I. That kick would break my neck if it landed, but again, foresight gave my reactions a boost, allowing me to block the kick in time. Its force knocked me into the wall and before I could recover, the demon had turned and run down the hallway, slamming through a crash-bar-equipped door. It was gone—but the girl needed my attention.

She was thrashing like a feral cat caught in a trap, her fast, jerky spasms ripping huge wounds in her chest and shoulders. Her reaction wasn't remotely normal, at least human normal.

"Whoa, easy, easy. You have to stop so I can get these out." I tried to calm her, at least so I could pull the bolts. She was injuring herself so much trying to get free that she would bleed out long before help got there.

Her motions slowed a bit; those blue eyes locked on mine. I moved closer, grabbing the bolt in her left shoulder with my right hand, yanking it hard and fast. As it came out, I grabbed the other bolt with my left hand. That one was deeper in the wall, and it took a few tugs to get it free. She had been hissing in pain, but as the bolt slid from her chest, she stopped, frozen in place. I was thinking that she would die in the next few seconds. The blood was gushing down her front in crimson waves, staining her white dress red. I reached out to steady her, but she just suddenly moved. She sort of blurred, then I felt a sledgehammer hit my left arm. She was biting my wrist, a sharp pain lancing up my arm. The force was stunning, like getting an arm caught in an industrial machine. I tried to pull away, but she didn't budge. Not even an inch. She couldn't weigh over one-twenty, but I couldn't move her.

It took a second to realize that she was sucking my wrist. I could feel blood spurting into her mouth in great gushes. Her heart, which I could see through the hole still in her chest, didn't seem to be beating. The rest of her wounds were healing so fast that most were gone in seconds.

I was getting dizzy, but the big wound over her heart wasn't healing and when I peered close, a bit of silver gleamed. A tiny part of my brain offered up a tally of current events. I was in a night club that was supposed to be run by vampires, a demon had tried to kill the most beautiful girl on the planet, and said girl was now draining my body of blood, through my wrist, killing me with her mouth. And she had a big hole in her chest.

I don't know why I did it. By all rights, I should have just jammed that silver bolt right through her still heart as hard as I could. It's possible that part of me considered the fact that the Hellbourne wanted her dead. Doing anything that screwed up their plans was generally a good idea. It could have been that she was trying so hard to live. I've always admired survivors.

It may have been that I'd never had a hot girl suck on my arm—or any other body part for that matter—before, and I just wasn't gonna ruin the experience. It would be a hell of a way to die, I decided. I could hear the boys at the Precinct talking about it. "Hey, did ya hear about Gordon? Sucked to death by a super hottie!"

"Really? And here I always thought he was gay!"

Dropping the bolt, I reached my thumb and forefinger into her wound. The blood made it almost impossible to grip the chunk of silver that was left in there, and I was getting dizzier by the second, but I got it. My index finger actually touched her still heart, and a shock jumped between us. Her heart beat once, hard.

Her eyes, which had been shut, snapped open and met my own as I pulled the piece of metal from her body. It pinged on the floor when my jittery fingers dropped it. The wound began to close instantly. Then my vision started to swim, swirling around two blue pools of light.

But the shock had snapped her frenzy, and she raised her head from my arm, watching me. When I started to fall, her arm slipped around my waist, holding me up without effort. It felt like rubber-covered steel. She looked at me for a moment, her head tilted to the right, like she was listening to something. She then leaned toward my wrist and licked it. She lapped it daintily, like a cat with a saucer of milk, cleaning the blood from it, revealing two pink dots, healing shut as I watched. Over the coppery stink of blood, I could smell her scent, jasmine and lilac.

I leaned woozily against a stack of crates behind me while she continued to watch me. After a moment, she wiped some her own blood from her front with a finger. Before I could react, she stuck the gore-covered digit in my mouth, depositing the load of cool blood on my tongue, then pulled her finger free. She clapped her other hand over my lips, stopping me from spitting it out.

"Sssswallow!" she ordered. Dizzy, cold, and confused, I did as she commanded, gulping to clear my mouth and throat, even as the thought of AIDS and other diseases crossed my mind. Laying her finger across her lips in the universal sign for silence, she turned her head to look at the metal door to the Club.

For a second, nothing happened, and then the door slammed free from its hinges, rocketed across the hallway, and crunched into the wall.

The corridor was suddenly filled with a large number of very serious vampires.

Vampires. That's what they were. It was all that they could be. Part of my brain had already added up the individual parts of the equation and arrived at that conclusion And the beautiful young girl in front of me was most certainly one as well. Gramps was right. Damn! He was so going to say he told me so... if I lived.

My sight centered on the big bouncer leading the pack, Vadim. His right arm was cocked back in a punching position, his hand stiff and flat in a spear hand. Dizzy and confused, I idly noted that his fingernails glittered like they were razor sharp. I'll bet he can jam his hand right through me.

He started forward, but a sharp "Nyet!" sounded from the girl in the crimson-stained dress, and everyone froze. They were all watching her with varying degrees of astonishment. The blonde girl in red pushed through along with the waitress, Lydia. Then the whole group parted down the middle and a brown-haired female walked through, taking charge with her presence. She spoke in what sounded like Russian to Vadim and the blonde, but it was my black-haired friend who answered in the same language, speaking haltingly at first, then faster. Now it was the newcomer's turn to look shocked, but as the dark-haired dancer spoke, some of the males blurred down the hall to the door. The blonde moved up to look at me, stopping a few feet away. I just sat back on the crates, shivering, trying to stay upright. "He's lost a lot of blood. He needs fluids, like now!" the blonde said.

My vampire stopped her narrative in mid-sentence and spoke again, speech still not smooth.

"Lydiiia?"

"I'm on it," Lydia replied, zipping out of the corridor.

"Who are you?" questioned the leader, staring holes in me with blue eyes that were much lighter than the dancer's.

"Chris... Chris Gordon." I answered once I was able to remember my name.

"He's a cop," Lydia supplied as she reappeared, handing me an open bottle of Gatorade. It was the red kind, which struck me as funny. Oops, did I just chuckle out loud?

"He's here with some cop friends. I watched him follow some guy who was following Tanya."

I sipped my Gatorade, thinking about what to tell them while the blonde watched me. The irony wasn't lost on me. Demons and vampires...what next? Zombies? How much should I tell them, what would they believe? They probably thought I had attacked the girl. What if vampires don't believe in ghosts and demons? I had a sudden image of me arguing with bloodsuckers over proof of the demonic while they fanged me to death. The demons could obviously cloud vampire senses as easily as human senses. Tired, I was so tired. Maybe getting bled out would be a good thing. I wouldn't have to fight anymore, and it wouldn't be like I was giving up the demon hunting business. The blonde's eyes widened as I was thinking this, and it was suddenly her turn to start speaking in Russian. That was getting really annoying. I've always hated when people speak other languages around me. A French-Canadian father and son vet team back home used to do it to me all the time. Assholes.

"Well, you people don't need me for your private conversations, so I'll just be going."

I stood up, wobbled a bit, and then started for the door. One of the males moved to block me, snarling. "You go nowhere, human blood bag," he growled.

His fangs were two inches long; his eyes were black from rim to rim. He scared me. I don't do well with being scared.   I started my career in being scared pretty early in life, and now it just pisses me off. The memory popped up unbidden.

I was jammed in the hiding space that Marcus had built in the back of his closet. He had shoved me into that space when the stranger had attacked Mom and Dad downstairs. "Don't you move, Christian! You stay here till it's clear! No matter what!" He shook me to make his point, the same way he had shaken me when he caught me in his room, leafing through his comics. With one last look, my twelve-year-old big brother picked up his baseball bat from the closet corner, shoved the panel shut, and rushed from the room. Huddled on the floor, my hands over my ears to block the awful sounds, I tried not to breathe, not make a sound. Too scared to move.

The silver spike from the dancer's shoulder was on the ground by my feet. I scooped it up, wiped her blood off on my sleeve and took stock. Dizzy, check. Vision blurry, check. Hands shaky, check. Perfect for taking on a vampire. Good night to die. Be with ya soon, Mom and Dad. I've had about enough of this ride. Time to get off. Of course, the conversation would be different at the Precinct house.

"Hey, did ya hear about Gordon? Sucked to death by a creepy Russian dude!"

"Well, I always knew he was gay!"

Screw it.

"Fuck off, Fang! Why don't you come over here? I'll show you where I keep the good silver." My balance shifted half an inch forward and just like that, the black-haired vampire was in front of me, facing the male. A low growl was coming from somewhere. I couldn't quite place it. The male's snarl disappeared, replaced by a look of fear, his attention centered on the small girl.

"Enough! Arkady, get the clean-up gear and get rid of this blood. Tanya, calm down. No one will hurt him."

The female leader never raised her voice, but her orders lasered through the tension. The male vanished and Tanya turned to me, the growl cutting off as she examined me curiously. The others looked at me like I was certifiable, not an unreasonable conclusion based on my behavior. The blonde was watching me differently, her eyes wide. Like I had spoken my thoughts out loud. I hadn't, had I?

"My apologies, Officer Gordon," the leader said. " Arkady is a trifle overzealous. But where are my manners? I am Galina Demidova; you have met my daughter Tatiana. This is Nika," she said, pointing to the blonde in red. "You have already met Lydia. This is Vadim, our head of security."

It took a second for the names to register. Galina Demidova, reputed to own more NYC real estate than Trump, but much more secretive. Never any pictures, lots of donations to charities, hospitals, and even one to the Police and Firefighter's Benevolent Association.

And she was a vampire. Then her other words hit me. Daughter? I looked at Tatiana or Tanya or whatever her name was and then her mother. The resemblance was unmistakable.   Vampires have daughters?

Nika smirked at me, and another thought occurred to me. Can vampires read minds? She smirked again. "Some can," she said. Great! Can't keep secrets, can hardly stand up, surrounded by predators. I glanced Heavenward, wondering for the ten thousandth time what I had ever done in this life or the previous one to deserve this.

"So, is your daughter Tatiana or Tanya? I'm confused... more confused."

"Tatiana is her formal name, Tanya is her short name. Like Jennifer and Jen," Galina answered. "Officer Gordon, would you be so kind as to tell us what happened here?"

What the Hell, why not. Maybe it would move things along and we could get to the part where I shuffled off this mortal coil. I gave them my narrative of the past ten minutes, although I didn't mention the part where Tanya stuck her blood-covered finger in my mouth. For some reason, I got the impression she wouldn't want me to. While I talked, I used my shaky right hand to pull my ever-present pencil from my back pocket. It's always one of those little pencils like you get for scorekeeping at miniature golf. A clipboard hanging nearby gave me both paper and a writing platform. Flipping to the clean back of one piece of paper, I started to draw, not bothering to look at my work.

It's not necessary for me to look, mainly because I don't believe that it's me doing the drawing when this happens. The pictures just come on their own, kind of like physic writing, I suppose. Each time I have a vision, a drawing follows, a snapshot from the vision. I finished my story but was still drawing. The vampires were watching me, openly puzzled, and when the drawing was done, I handed it to Tatiana. Even though she had half-killed me, I liked her best. Maybe they'd let her do the killing. The image was still in my head, as it always would be. It would be graphically cartoonish, with the Hellbourne's eyes overly large and Tatiana's figure exaggerated. I could recall and draw the first vision I ever had. The drawing would be artistically perfect. Myself, I can barely draw a stick figure. Galina and the others moved over to look at the picture in Tatiana's hands.

"That's your guy... er... demon. Demon ridden, if you want to get technical. I call them Hellbourne. The body is just a shell." I was babbling.

"How do you know all this? How can you know all this?" Lydia asked, and then glanced apologetically at Galina, who gave her an exasperated look.

Good question. A real good question. I pondered how to answer, worried about giving away too much. Then it occurred to my foggy brain that it was a moot point, what with the mind reader, Nika, nearby.

"The clergy say that I'm God Touched. Personally, I think He bitch slapped me. We have agreed to disagree on that point."

"Clergy?" Galina questioned, one eyebrow arched.

"Yeah, well, the various churches come to me for their tougher exorcisms. The prayers and holy water routine doesn't always work," I answered.

"And you do?" she asked. At her side, Tatiana was just staring at me, eerily motionless.

"I don't use their techniques. I'm more of a hands-on kinda guy." I shrugged. "The entities that make up most possessions are pretty easy to yank out and send back to Hell. Plus I'm nondenominational."

They all looked at me like I was crazy. Great, a room full of vampires questioning my sanity. After a moment, I continued, "You all seem to be having a lot more trouble believing me than I'm having believing all this." I waved my hand at all of them and at Tatiana's blood-covered form. Her catlike stare was starting to bother me. I was feeling distinctly mousy.

Galina took in my comment, then abruptly changed direction.

"I'm afraid we need to ask you for your clothes, as we must burn all of Tatiana's blood that has been spilled. Nika, please get Tatiana cleaned up. Lydia, would you find Officer Gordon some new clothes?" New clothes? Why did I need clothes at all if they were gonna kill me?

The blonde vampire grabbed Tatiana's hand, leading her up the hall to another door marked *Dressing Room*. Lydia looked me up and down, ostensibly measuring me for clothes or maybe a coffin, a sardonic grin on her face. The hulking Vadim stepped over to me, holding out a plastic bag for my clothes. I sighed, beginning to empty my pockets. That done, I stripped off my ruined shirt and pants, trying not to fall over, shivering in just my boxer briefs.

"That's what it wanted, you know. Her blood." I nodded at a plastic water bottle lying on the concrete where the Hellbourne had dropped it. Galina and Vadim both started at my words, then exchanged a wordless glance. Lydia danced back into the room, mere minutes after leaving, a stack of clothes in hand. "Damn, Northern! Do you live at the gym or what?" she asked, not unfriendly.

I'm only average looking, but my body is not so average. Can't help it. My grandfather had received custody of me after the death of my family. I lived most of my life on his four-hundred-acre farm. First hard farm work, then after my talents appeared, heavy-duty workouts and martial arts training had left their mark on my physique. I was probably twelve the last time I had more than ten percent body fat. Baggy clothes help me to hide my build, as I don't like to draw attention.

I struggled into the black leather pants that she provided, much to her amusement, and was just buttoning the waistband when Tatiana reappeared from the dressing room. Holy shit! She must have taken the world's fastest shower, as her long black hair lay in a damp, twisted rope down her back. She was wearing a blue cutoff tee with the word PINK across the chest. White designer sweats and flip-flops completed the outfit. She looked like a dressed-down rich girl, which, actually, she was. I knew I was staring, but couldn't seem to stop. The others took in my expression and then turned to look at her. Tatiana ignored all of them, her shocking blue eyes locked onto mine.

I had a hard time deciding where to look first. Her exposed stomach was ripped, her arms well-muscled, as were her legs where her sweats clung to them. She was apparently braless and cold, if in fact vampires could get cold or excited. But ultimately, I came back to her piercing eyes. They were curious and measuring. Her gliding walk was graceful even by comparison to the other vampires, and she was right in front of me before I could quite gather my thoughts. The smell of lilac and jasmine flowed over me. Her eyes were now locked on my bare chest and after a second, I realized the talisman that hung 'round my neck captivated her.

It was an interesting piece. The arrowhead, made from flint, was probably early Mohawk. I had found it my first week at my gramp's farm. The rawhide thong had come from a buck harvested from the farm. The broken eagle feather behind it had its own story. The Mohawk reservation of Akwesasne lies on the U.S./Canada border and comes equipped with a casino. My gramps has almost no vices, but he does like to play the blackjack tables from time to time. On one of his forays to the casino, we encountered a tribal elder of Gramps' acquaintance. It was he who identified the arrowhead as Mohawk and, after examining both it and me, had reached into a small leather bag that had hung around his own neck and pulled out the rounded tip of the broken eagle feather. Smelling of pipe tobacco and leather, he had explained that he had found the partial feather and recognized that it was looking for a proper home. While he spoke, he fastened the feather behind the arrowhead, making it both a background for the flint point and a cushion for my eight-year-old chest. That necklace had been with me for every demon hunt and banishment that I had ever been on. It had absorbed some of my power each time.

Tatiana reached for it tentatively and as she did, an idea occurred to me. Again, I don't know why it mattered, but for some reason, I still felt like I needed to protect her from the Hellbourne. In between struggling in and out of various clothes, my dizzy brain had been worrying at the problem of leaving Tatiana unguarded. I was either dead soon, or, if the clothes were a sign that I might see the morning, then I needed to go home, soon, blood loss making me completely ineffective for fighting the Hellbourne. The vampires seemed to be useless at noticing the demon that wanted her blood. The necklace was the answer. While she was holding it, I took the leather thong from around my neck and slowly slipped it over her head, her big blues widening as I did it. Arkady chose that moment to come back down the corridor, three SCUBA-sized tanks strapped together and held effortlessly in one hand, the other hand holding a sprayer wand. "Aww, is cute that we are giving friendship gifts now," he said sarcastically.

I didn't look up as I responded, "Well, seeing as the Hellbourne walked within two feet of your blind ass on his way to kill Tatiana, maybe you don't have a friggin' clue what you're talking about?"

"You call me Tanya. Not Tatiana," the black haired girl said, a bit forcefully.

"Oh, er, sorry. No offense," I said quickly. I'm so not good with girls.

Lydia spoke up. "She wants you to call her by the name her friends and family use, not her formal name."

Her meaning was clear: Tanya wanted me to speak to her as a friend. Not dinner. Things might be looking up.

I backed up and examined her with my Sight, which made me even dizzier. She now stood in a sphere of purple-hued light, her own soul and aura blazing brilliant white. Humans tend to shade toward blue, and I'm told my own aura is violet in the same shade as my odd eye color. It looked pretty strong, but it occurred to me that I could strengthen it.

"Explain please," Galina requested, just shy of a command.

"Well, when I banish demons, I give off a lot of... power. Objects made of stone tend to absorb some of that power and sort of store it, like a battery. I usually carry a piece of carved soapstone with me when I exorcise a house or apartment, Indian fetishes. I leave it behind as a protection. If any other demons come around, they will shy away from the stone. They've helped a few people who, for one reason or another, tend to draw demonkind."

"Is that arrowhead such a fetish?" she questioned.

"Better. I've had it since I was a kid, and it's absorbed some power every time I have kicked Hellbourne ass. Which would be something like, oh about.. thirty-seven times or so. Not counting exorcisms," I answered, still studying the violet sphere. Yes, I could definitely up its amperage.

"Why?" Tanya asked. I didn't understand.

"Er, what?"

"Why do you give it to me?" Her eyes were still wide and, oddly, there was something very vulnerable in them. Vulnerable vampire? I tried to shake it off, but her eyes mesmerized me.

"Well, the demon that wants your blood will be back. If it is during the day tomorrow, I'll probably be able to nail his ass. But this should protect you if I'm not here. It will make you invisible to him and it will repel him, as well. But I want to boost it if I can. I'll feel better if it is ramped up a bit more."

I hesitated. Galina looked at me expectantly and said, "So do it!" Okay, that was definitely a command.

Ah shucks. Stop. Your profuse thanks are embarrassing me. It seems the rich all feel the same sense of entitlement, be they vampire or human. Fucking rich people!

Nika snorted as I thought this and covered her mouth to hide a grin.

"Well, I'm gonna spill a drop of my own blood and I'm just wondering..."

"Go ahead. We can probably control ourselves," Galina said sardonically.

I nodded and grabbed my folding knife from the pile of pocket junk and flicked the blade open. After pooling my aura in my right hand, I pricked my trigger finger. I push power out of my right hand and draw power in with my left. The reason for this isn't clear, but that's just how it works. I squeezed a fat drop of blood onto the tip and then dabbed it onto the back of the arrowhead. "Ah, that needs to be against your skin, um, like under your shirt," I explained with all the composure of a three year old. Tanya tucked it into her shirt, between her breasts, her eyes watching me the whole time. The view momentarily snuffed out my feeble thoughts. I wiped my finger on my pants and tried to ignore the way they all stared. I rechecked the necklace. The purple sphere was now twice as big as before and much denser in color. I don't see auras like Reiki masters do. No different layers, just solid hues, sometimes with streaks of other colors.

"I don't know what you people do during the daytime, whether you go to sleep or lie in coffins or whatever, but you two," I pointed at Nika and Lydia, "might want to hang close to her. It can probably protect all three of you. You can leave Arkady out by the door as bait," I suggested, putting my knife in my pants pocket. A hiss sounded from the big male vamp, spraying the blood-covered wall and floor with some chemical cleaner. With nothing else to do, I wrestled myself into the white Plasma long-sleeve tee shirt that Lydia had provided. It was a tight fit, but I immediately felt a little warmer.

"Officer Gordon, you are remarkably blasé about this situation. Most of your kind are scared witless by our presence, if in fact they live through the introduction. How is it that you aren't?" Galina asked.

I snorted. " You mean the vampire part? Most humans haven't been hunting Hellbourne since they were twelve, either. Actually, I don't think any other humans do what I do. Compared to demons, you all aren't that scary. Plus I'm too damn tired at this point to give a crap."

They all went spooky still and blank faced. Ooops, wrong thing to say. I held my hands out in a placating gesture.

"Oh, you're scary enough, all right. Top predators and all. I'm sure that Lydia there could twist my head off before I got done blinking, but really, what's the worst you can do? Kill me? Torture me, then kill me? Big whup! Hellbourne can trap or foul my soul, haul me to Hell. "

Their faces reflected disbelief. Nika spoke first.

"You really aren't afraid of dying, are you?"

It was more of a statement.

"You tell me mighty, Kreskin," I replied. "Hell, I've outlived my death by about fifteen years. Actually, I was on borrowed time from the moment of birth, twenty-three years ago. Well, twenty-three in seven more days. If I get there."

Vadim did the math first. "Halloween? You were born on Halloween?"

"Yeah. Spooky, isn't it?"

They all looked at each other, except Tanya, who was giving me the cat stare again.

"Do you know the time of your birth?" Galina asked. What the hell did that have to do with anything?

They were all interested, kinda of like wolves circled up for the kill.

"Well, I'm told it was midnight. But I don't really remember, being pretty young and all," I answered. They were all silent, processing that piece of info, or maybe deciding if my wiseass mouth was pissing them off.

Arkady spoke suddenly from across the room. "Killing is not the worst. We could Turn you."

"How is that worse? Let's see, if the legends are true, I would be stronger, faster, tougher, and live a lot longer. The downside would be what, exactly? Liquid diet?"

"Soul is lost when Turned," he answered.

I stared at them, dumbfounded. "My soul... lost? Why would my soul be lost? Yours aren't!"

Silence. No one made a sound for at least fifteen seconds. It was the mind reader who spoke first.

"He believes we all still have souls," she said.

"Yeah, because you do. I can see them." I started putting the rest of my stuff away.

"You can see souls?" Tanya asked.

"Yes. Yours all look white to me. Humans usually are some shade of blue."

"Let me get this right: you think you can see souls, and you think you can see ours?" Galina asked.

"Yup. I see all kinds of shit, some of which you apparently don't. How else can I see Hellbourne? They can only occupy and use bodies that are soul-free. Meat shells."

"What does the white mean?" Lydia interjected.

"I don't know. Probably that you are a different species or something. You're each slightly different. Tanya's is wicked bright."

I swigged down the last of my Gatorade.

Tanya looked troubled. "White means evil!"

"What? Since when did white mean evil? Why would you think that? Black means evil. Oily, greasy, stomach-turning black. I don't think you're necessarily evil, any more than wolves, bears, or tigers are evil. I'm not gonna lie, though. You're all pretty damn eerie though."

Her expression was suddenly angry.

"You lie! You are a liar! You know we are evil!" she said.

To say I was taken aback was an understatement. Up until this moment, I had assumed some sort of bond or connection to her. Which, when you think about it, was really stupid. Mind-numbing stupid. The whole save, defend, heal thing. The rest of them, I had no illusions about. But I had fooled myself into thinking that somehow we were friends. Idiot! Suddenly, I was just as angry; at her, at myself, at all the stupid vampires in the room. My life sucked on a regular basis; now I was a liar? Fuck that!

"Righhht." I set the empty bottle down. "Well, thanks for the clothes and Gatorade and shit. Unless you're gonna eat me, I'm leaving." I shouldered past Vadim and staggered through the ruined door, none of them moving to stop me. The club was jumping as I entered the main floor, the deep bass of the music pushing on my ribs. I had to grab the doorframe to steady myself for a moment. I looked for Pella and Henderson, but when I got to our table, it was occupied by some black-garbed, chain-strewn Goths. My coat was still on the back of one of the chairs and I grabbed it with a quick, "Excuse me. Just getting my coat."

One said, "Dude, no prob."

They all looked at me oddly, and one of the girls asked, "Do you work here?"

I could hear the disbelief in her voice and I realized that I was wearing the same tee shirt that the staff wore: big, blood-red *Plasma* spelled out diagonally across the torso. I was dressed the part, but my tan skin and lack of grace didn't fit.

"Oh hell no! Just wearing the colors."

I turned away before she could answer and put on the jacket to avoid any more questions. "Your friends left with the girls they were hitting on." Lydia was suddenly standing by the stairs.

"Lucky them. Did they pay the tab?" I asked. She shook her head.

"Bastards! How much?"

She shrugged it off, but I persisted. "How much?"

"One ten, but it's on the house."

Screw that! I wasn't going to owe them anything. I handed her three fifties from my money clip and left.

Chapter 2

I fumed the whole cab ride home. It was a little past eleven-thirty when I climbed the stairs to my second-floor apartment, still berating myself for thinking this time might have been different. Fifteen years of keeping myself distant from anyone but Gramps, and I get all giddy over the first gorgeous female vampire I happen to save. Moron. Asshole.

When I got inside, I only paused long enough to drop three raw eggs into a glass of orange juice and swig it down, Rocky style. I needed the iron and protein, but I had no energy left to cook. Couldn't be any worse than a mouth full of vampire blood. After that , I crashed into bed, not even bothering to undress.

Something was making a banging sound. Banging by the door. Banging on the door. I staggered over and peered through the peephole. My two neighbors from across the hall, Paige and Kathy, were standing there. "Ah, hi, Chris," Paige greeted me when I got the locks undone and the door open. I knew them enough to say *hi* in the hallway, but that was it.

"Hi. What's up?" I didn't know them very well, but they had been very nice whenever I bumped into them. They didn't speak for a moment, both taking in my attire, which I realized was the Plasma shirt and leather pants I had fallen asleep in.

"Do you work at Plasma?" asked Kathy, who was the taller of the two brunettes by about two inches. That made her about five nine, or an inch shorter than me.

"No, these are borrowed. They ruined my clothes last night and they gave me these to get home in," I explained.

"Too bad! You oughta keep 'em," she said, her roommate nodding in agreement.

"No, I can't stand the place. I'll be sending them back," I stated.

"You didn't like it? I heard it is the best club in the city. Maybe we could all go sometime," Paige gushed. She was really cute, with short brown hair and brown eyes. She possessed a slim runner's build that looked great in the jeans and tees she seemed to favor. Kathy was rail thin and pleasant looking, in a mousy kind of way, with curly brown hair and hazel eyes. They smelled like peaches and kiwi. Must be their shampoo. I shuddered to think of these two alone in the vampire den.

"I don't think it's a real safe place. But what's up?" I brought the conversation back on point.

"Oh, we're heading over to Chico's for breakfast and thought you might like to come along?" Paige supplied.

My initial reflex was to decline, but now that I was up, my stomach was demanding immediate attention. In fact, it growled right on cue.

We all laughed and after noting that it was only eight a.m., I said, "Okay, let me change real quick."

"Oh, you should leave the Plasma shirt on..." Paige said, but I had it off before she could complete the sentence. "Or not."

"I'll just be a sec," I said, backing from the doorway with my shirt off. I headed to the dresser as the two followed me in.

"If you went like that, Chico might give us breakfast," Paige commented. Chico was known to prefer shirtless men to a shirtless women.

I grabbed some jeans and a tee shirt and my North Face Jacket, ducking into the bathroom to change and brush my teeth. I threw on my favorite hat, a Springfield Armory black ball cap emblazoned with the words *Fear No Evil*. Of course, it means something different to me than to most people.

When I came out, the girls were looking curiously around my tiny studio pad. It's small, but bright, with a high ceiling, hardwood floors, and a clawfoot tub in the bathroom. That tub had soaked many a bruised and sore muscle during my short residence. Two big windows look out to the Northeast, and I get a great view if I step out on the fire escape. My place is uncluttered, as I have a minimalist approach to possessions. Just one leather chair, a futon that doubles as my bed, flatscreen, compact stereo, dresser, small bookshelf, and several lamps. A small table just outside the tiny galley kitchen doubles as a desk, and I had two chairs that went with it. One of my walls was hung with a Native American rug, in deep reds, with the silhouette of a standing bear. Another bear, this one a large soapstone fetish from New Mexico, stood guard over the apartment from the bookshelf. I have no Native American heritage, but I had decided as a child that my spirit guide animal would be a bear. We were both loners and fighters, at least that's how I looked at it. I don't know how the Great Bear felt about it, as I never gave him the option to say no.

The girls looked up as I came out, their curious expressions changing quickly to smiles, and we headed out.

If you had told me that an Adirondack north-country kid could be reasonably happy in the Big Apple, I would have laughed in your face. But my neighborhood of Bay Ridge in Brooklyn is really pretty nice. It's mostly single-family homes, with a five- or six-story apartment building sprinkled here and there. Lots of small trees line the street and there are tons of restaurants, bars, gyms, and small shops. Brooklyn is the most populated borough in New York City, with a population of right around two-and-a-half million people. Our building, on the corner of Bay Ridge Boulevard and Eighty Third Street, is a prewar elevator building, and the owners keep it up to date and very clean. Still, I miss my forests.

Chico's is a small corner restaurant run by a flamboyant bundle of energy who looks Hispanic but sounds Italian. The owner was behind the counter, wearing a hot pink tee with his own name across the front, and he greeted the girls by name and me with a nod. Chico's is a seat-yourself kind of place, so we found a booth and settled in. Rich coffee and bacon smells were driving me crazy. I made sure that I got the seat that faced the door, not leaving enough room for either of them to slide next to me. The waitress swung by and brought us coffee. During the walk over, we had all decided on omelets, so we ordered immediately. I ordered two three-egg spinach and cheddar omelets, toast with peanut butter, and a large orange juice.

"Hungry much?" Kathy teased, her eyes mock wide at my order.

"Starving!"

"Sounds like you're craving iron, too. Spinach? Six eggs? You do look a little pale today. You're not anemic, are you?" Kathy asked. I remembered that she was a nutritionist at Sisters of Mercy Hospital. Paige worked for a television production company.

"Er... not that I know of. But I haven't been eating right, with the job and all. Too many donuts."

They laughed, and the topic changed to plans for the day. "We thought we'd go to Owl's Head Park today. Wanna come... along?" Paige asked.

This was the part I hated. The rebuff. When I took up Hellbourne hunting, I pretty much gave up on friends, and particularly girlfriends.

I had had exactly one date in my life. The end of eighth grade, I finally got up enough courage to ask Mary Chauffey to go out. Shy, smart, and pretty, Mary was universally liked, but for one reason or another hadn't dated many of the class boys. I had crushed on her all year, and when I asked her to pizza and the movies, she had said yes. The date had been great. She had the same sense of humor that I did, but we were both too shy in school to display it. On top of that, she was very intelligent, conversant in a lot of the science subjects that I liked. I learned later that she had studied those topics just because I liked them. The real problem came three days later, when I was banishing a minor house demon in Ogdensburg. Just before I tore the vile thing from its roots and threw it to Kirby, the Collector, it whispered her name to me. Then it was gone, plucked from the air by Kirby's shadowy claws, hauled back to Hell. I sat in the dark house for thirty minutes, horror struck. It knew her name. The implications were immediate and horrific.

I went to school the next day and broke up with her. It was truly awful. She had really liked me, and I trashed it. But the alternative was unthinkable. Her older brother and his friend jumped me several days later. The fight lasted twenty minutes and the cops, called by a housewife who was witness to the whole thing, broke it up. We were all pretty beat up, but the brother had a cracked rib, his friend lost a few teeth. My face and body were black and blue for a month. Because the witness had seen them jump me, I didn't go to jail, but if I had been on the social fringe before, I was a true outcast from then on.

So I had to turn Paige and Kathy down easy.

"Aw, I've something I have to do today. It's gonna take me most of the day." I wasn't lying. I would be lucky if my project didn't go into nighttime.

"Really, all day? Isn't this your first day off in, like, forever?" Kathy asked. Paige didn't say anything, but I saw a flicker of disappointment cross her face.

"Yeah, I know. But it's a commitment I can't break. Believe me, I would rather not do it."

"You know, Chris, you work way too much. You're like, never home." Kathy was still carrying the conversation, but her tone was crisp.

The waitress brought our food, and I tucked in. The girls started a two-way conversation that excluded me, punishment for not accepting their invite. I understood. I was being a jerk, and they knew it. Hell, I had been rebuffed myself, just last night.

We finished breakfast and I excused myself, receiving a cold goodbye from each of them. Better that way.

Back at the apartment, I got set for the day. Changing into running clothes and equipping my runner's chest pack, I paused to consider the events of the previous night.

Vampires were real. Not that big of a shocker to someone in my line of work. But there were a thousand mysteries around Plasma's resident coven.

First, Tatiana was obviously Galina's daughter, but how did that happen? Was Galina turned after Tatiana was born? Did she turn Tatiana?

The other vampires treated Tatiana very deferentially. At the same time, the hulking Arkady had been genuinely afraid of the tiny girl vampire when she had protected me. Which was also a puzzle: why had she interceded? But the number one question had to be the mystery of the Hellbourne's interest in Tatiana. Galina and Vadim hadn't contradicted my theory that it had wanted the young vampire's blood. Why would it want her blood? Why did Galina have our clothes burned to destroy her blood? It all revolved around the quiet, raven-haired vampire. Truth be told, she hadn't been far from my thoughts since I woke up.

I shrugged into the Civilian Labs chest pack, which was packed with my badge, wallet, cash, cell phone, and issue Glock 9mm and one spare magazine of ammo. Hellbourne are tough, but a hollow point bullet in the brain will ruin their day. Tying up my Asics, I headed out at a jog.

My plan was to patrol the area around Plasma for the day, evening, and night if necessary. The Hellbourne would be back; all I could hope was that it happened within the next twenty-four hours. I was a little concerned about my ability to fight. By best estimation, based on the dizziness, cold shakes, and lack of mental focus last night, Tatiana had drained me of something like fifteen percent of my blood supply. Oddly, I wasn't appalled by that. She had needed it to survive. I should have been terrified by it. Despite her sudden anger at me the previous night, I hoped she was all right. Her beautiful face hung in my mind's eye, her expression vulnerable and innocent. Idiot! I shook my head to clear and focus. My arm was completely healed, and I felt good—really good, in fact. My vision, hearing, and sense of smell all seemed extra crisp. And as I started to jog, my legs felt great and my breathing was steady and even. It made me wonder about the small amount of blood she had made me ingest.

Plasma was on Third Ave., about ten blocks north of my apartment. The smells from all the restaurants immediately drove me crazy. It was like I could almost pick out the individual spices and foodstuffs. The single best part of living in the City has to be the incredible array of food. Turkish, Thai, Japanese, Chinese, Scandianvian, Hungarian, Russian, Italian, German, French, Jewish, Middle Eastern, you name it and I'll lead you to the restaurants that serve it. If gambling was Gramps' vice, food was mine. Gotta have something to fill in for all the sex I wasn't ever going to have. And with my workout schedule, I burned it off as fast as I ate it. Although it did strike me as odd that I was already hungry forty minutes after that huge breakfast I had scarfed down.

Finally, I stopped and grabbed a shawarma sandwich from a Middle Eastern place. Hot, spicy beef and lamb strips in pita with tahini. Yum. I ate it in five bites while running, the spices bursting on my tongue.

Plasma occupied an unassuming two-story brick building with almost no exterior features of interest. Before I got near it, I swung down a side street and ran a circuit behind it on Fourth Avenue. I couldn't see the back of the building, so I stopped running and walked down an alley between a news store and kosher deli. As I walked, the thought struck me that the vampires probably didn't live in the club. The Demidovas were sure to have a big, expensive residence someplace, but I didn't have a clue where. Suddenly panicky, I visualized the Hellbourne breaking into some huge brownstone and slaughtering Tatiana as she slept.

Idiot. I hadn't even thought it through. Now what the hell was I gonna do? Oddly, I flashed to a memory of Gramps teaching me about survival. We were with the Search and Rescue group that he helped regularly, and he was instructing me in how not to panic. "What do you do if you're lost, Chris?" he had asked. One of the other guys, a local sheriff's deputy, had chimed in, "Drop your pants and start to jerk off! Someone's bound to see you!" When the laughter had died down, Gramps had pushed me for an answer.

"Stop and take stock? Then prioritize?" I said.

"Very good, Chris. Always prioritize. Think your way out. Use your big brain. Not your little brain, like Steve over there." He said, pointing to the deputy.

So I thought about the Demidovas and who might know where their house was. Michel St. James was a freelance society reporter whose articles appeared in *The New Yorker*, *The New York Times*, and half a dozen other publications. He sometimes hosted a cable station show of similar ilk, and that was how he knew Paige. I met him one night when Kathy and Paige threw a party. A couple of acquaintances had crashed the party and were giving Michel a hard time. Abrasive and condescending, he had an irritating effect on people. Coming back from a house cleansing, I interrupted the unpleasant scene and threw them out. It would be worth a phone call. 411 had his number, and he picked up on the third ring. "Hallo, theeeese is Michel." His accent was very affected.

"Michel, this is Chris Gordon, Paige and Kathy's neighbor."

"Yes, I remember," he drawled nonchalantly, but I could hear curiosity in his voice.

"I'm trying to get to Galina Demidova's place, and I wondered if you knew the address."

"Why would you be going to Galina's place?" His voice was a subtle mix of condescension, disbelief, and wariness.

"Look, I am supposed to do some security work there and none of the other guys that are working are picking up their phones," I lied. Michel knew I was a cop, and it would make perfect sense for me to be acting as security. Certainly there could not possibly be any other reason. It was also a not-too-subtle reminder of my help with his own security.

"Weell, of course I've been to her place. Brooklyn Heights, Willow Street, if I recall. Let me look it up."

I hailed a cab while he rustled up the street number. No way was I gonna run all the way there. Not enough time. I told the driver Willow Street in the

Heights and then Michel's fake French accent came back on the cell.

"Ett is 119 Willow, Christian." I thanked him roughly and hung up, repeating the number to the driver, whose name was Ismahel, according to his cabbie card.

The Demidova residence was a five-story brownstone in the glitzy, nose-in-the-air neighborhood of Brooklyn Heights. There was also a basement below street level. It probably went for four to six million and must have had over seven thousand square feet of space. I had the taxi drive past it and then got out on the opposite side of the street, eyeballing the place for detail. The front would be well guarded, as would the back.

A vision hit just then. A deck, a French door, and a bland reflection in the glass of the door. I broke into a jog and ran around the block. Of course, the house was located right in the middle of the block, giving me the longest possible run to get behind it. Immediately, I spotted the deck, on top of a bump-out from the first and second floors. The deck was likely accessed from the third floor, but I could see how easy it would be for a demon-ridden meat shell to climb the exterior after first getting into the first level's walled garden space. Discreet security cameras were visible to my trained eye, but the human security guards would not likely notice the Hellbourne. Not wanting to get shot, I pulled my badge from my chest pack and dangled it around my neck. Then I studied the garden wall.

About eight feet high and clear of any climbable objects. Piece of cake for the eerily-quick demonkind, but a pretty good obstacle for me. Backing up, I visualized a big Rottweiler chasing me for inspiration, then ran hard at the wall, bounding off my right foot. The fingers of both hands caught the top, fingers scrabbling on the crumbly brick of the old wall. Just like that, I was up, feeling pretty pleased with myself.

Then two things happened simultaneously.

The whirring of a security camera spinning caught my ears, and the oily, dark presence of Hellbourne pressed on my aura like a bowling ball on a trampoline. It was here, close and moving. I jumped to the stained concrete surface of the garden, knocking over a potted cedar tree as I landed. The outer walls were lined with fruit trees and bushy conifers. An ornate yellow-metal trellis was centered over a pair of sitting benches, the top curved like the golden arches of McDonalds. Ahead of me, I could see the brick wall of the bump out that held the deck as its roof. The back door opened and two burly men in dark suits came out, their steady stares glued to me like frat boys watching a beer truck. "Sir, stop right there. This is private property," said the first, a wall of crew-cut beef with pale blue eyes rolling toward me in a great impersonation of an Abrams main battle tank. The second, even bigger, black with black eyes, hove into sight behind him like a naval vessel. Where did they grow these guys? I ignored his comments, as a rustle-smack sound announced the bland man-thing landing ten feet from me and moving toward the bump-out wall. I raced to intercept it, the security guys completely ignoring it. The Abrams tank guy held up a salad-plate-sized hand , but I swerved around him like he was in slow motion and grabbed the ankle of the Hellbourne as it climbed the wall. It climbed with my full weight hanging from it for a moment, then fell back to the garden, its grip slipping. The two security hulks had stopped to process the unexpected sight of the demon. Once my hand touched it, its cloak was shot and it had become visible to them. I couldn't be bothered. I was busy getting a modified arm bar on it to hold it just long enough to rip it loose. Jujitsu and wrestling are heavy components of my own style of unarmed combat, as much of my time is spent getting my prey into position to rip them from their shells. Its left hand was under my right armpit, my right hand pressing the center of its back, my left on its chest. Time is short in these encounters, as Hellbourne are not put off by things like broken elbow joints or choke holds. A lifetime of practice made it easy to force my will and aura through the demon's body from my right hand and pulling the foul thing free of the meat shell with my left. Noxious sulfer stink burned my eyes, nose, and mouth like a hunting camp full of overweight beer drinkers after a night of cheap beer and pickled eggs. The demon made an audible wet, ripping sound as it pulled free from the body, and I was left holding a roiling blob of greasy blackness in my left hand. Quick as thought, I flung the noisome thing straight up while calling >Kirby<

in my mind. The dark shadow-hawk form of the Collector popped into being above us, gripping the black form of the Hellbourne in both smoky talons. Two flaps of car-hood-sized wings, and it popped back out of our plane of existence, hauling the demon to who-knew-where. I lay there panting like I had run a marathon, tangled in the limbs of the suddenly dead body.

Chapter 3

By the time I could get untangled and sit up, a forest of beefy legs, all dressed in cargo pants and dark blue polo shirts surrounded me. The original set of security guys had drawn sidearms, and my view of them was obscured by the Holland tunnel muzzles of twin Sig Sauer .45s. "Benson, Hedges—holster those weapons! Now!" barked a voice that would have made my Academy instructors cower.

A compact block of muscle shouldered through the crowd. Short blond hair, tan weathered face, and a *Semper Fi* tattoo on his right forearm. He watched me warily, taking in the scene. "Officer Gordon, I presume. I was warned you might appear." He looked at the meat shell. "Is that secure?" I nodded. He detailed the two giants to haul it away, the body starting to smell like a Porta Potty. He surveyed the area, noting the ripped and shredded ivy where the Hellbourne had tried to climb to the deck above, the knocked-over cedar tree, and my generally scraped-up appearance.

"My name is Deckert. I run the daytime shift." His voice was level, not friendly, not hostile, all business. A straight-forward, mission-first operator. I wanted to be just like him when I grew up. "I'm gonna go out on a limb here and surmise that was a demon?" he asked. I nodded, still trying to catch my breath. "It didn't show up on the monitors," he stated.

"They can cloak themselves," I panted. One eyebrow raised, but that was it. Just another day at the office for him.

"My employer would like you to hang out till she... arrives," he stated, making it sound like a real good idea.

Right then my chest, started to vibrate. "Wait one minute, please, Mr. Deckert," I replied. My cell was lit up with a text message from Peter G.

r u free for cleansing t-nite?

Peter Gillian ran a local paranormal investigation group. He obviously had a problem entity that normal exorcism had failed to remove. Pete acted as my clearing house for these kinds of things, only bringing me in when it was really bad.

I texted a reply: How bad?

He came right back: Kid in danger!

Kids were often the target of demonic entities and always commanded my immediate attention. My response was immediate. Needs be tonite. shift change t-mrow.

8 p.m.?

With Bells on!

He sent me an address on Second Avenue, not too many blocks from my apartment.

Deckert was watching, arms crossed, evaluating me.

"Mr. Deckert, I'll have to decline your employer's request at this time. I have another matter to attend to."

He didn't say anything for a moment, just stared at me as he considered my response. His men closed in around us. Many private security types in the City are ex-cops. Not these guys. Deckert and the rest of his guards were blatantly ex-military types. Marine Force Recon, SEALs, Spec Ops, Army Rangers, and that ilk. Growing up to be a demon hunter, I had fantasized about getting that kind of training. Learning to kill bad guys with drinking straws and camel patties, improvising explosives from twenty dollars' worth of convenience store items, rappelling down 30-story buildings on a Batman utility belt. Useful stuff like that. The problem had always been one of time commitment. Military basic training was like six months, twelve months for more specialized stuff, three- and four-year tours of duty, that sort of thing. It added up to some real time. I get two to four visions per month, each requiring a foray into the stuff of nightmares, hunting down things that inspire serial killers. Near as I could figure, most military units frowned on trainees popping out of camp to cap some monster in a meat shell. So, Gramps and I did the best we could with what we had. When I was thirteen, I shut down a minor demon that was haunting a family in Potsdam. The dad was an ex-Ranger who had been totally helpless to protect his own family. He threw himself into training me with everything he could, calling in favors to have other guys come by and help educate me. I enrolled in every martial arts school in the area, wrestled on the high school team, and played football. In football, I played safety, and the guys I hit went down hard enough to lose memory. I was playing only to learn how to take down stronger, faster people. To me, it was life or death.

The local cops were on board after I helped with a Hellbourne who wounded two cops and slashed a housewife. I was the only fourteen-year-old who regularly had firearms training with the sheriff's department Special Response Team.

Deckert's men moved in to restrain me, and my adrenaline ramped up. This would be interesting. The group opened a bit and a guard came through with about a hundred and ten pounds of German Shepherd straining its leash. Dogs don't scare me. Mostly 'cause they haven't made one that will bite me. I think it must be God's consolation prize. Here Gordon , you're gonna live a short, brutal, loveless life, but at least dogs will always like you.

The Shepherd pulled his handler right up to me, sniffed my hand, licked it, and sprawled at my feet. Deckert snorted in disgust and held up his hand to wave his guys back, nodding to me. "My employer indicated that we were not to harm you or restrain you in any way. Vadim made that point particularly clear." He gave me a curious look. I shrugged.

"Probably want to save me for dinner."

None of them thought that was very funny. Tough audience.

Turning, Deckert led me through the first floor of the house, which was tastefully decorated with antiques that probably cost more than my whole Precinct's annual budget. When we got to the front door, he paused.

"Vadim was adamant about keeping my guys from harming you. Seemed to think it would be bad for our health if anything happened to you. Any thoughts as to why that would be?"

I could see that Deckert didn't like mysteries, particularly those that posed a threat to his men. I just shrugged, not able to answer his question, although the image of Tatiana facing down the hulking Arkady came to mind.

"I helped the black-haired one last night. Tatiana. Maybe she told him not to hurt me."

"She doesn't talk," he said, frowning.

"She did last night," I said, staring right back.

Our little stare down went for about ten seconds before he finally sighed.

"Gordon, you're leaving me with nothing to tell Ms. Demidova," he said mildly.

"Well, I'm sure she'll track me down if she is interested, but you could tell her that I have to help a kid with a problem. Of the demonic type," I replied and then trotted down the steps and out into the warm October day.

The encounter with the Hellbourne had left me drained. I'm not sure what my power is or where it comes from, but sometimes I use up a lot of it. Getting away from the Demidovas' house was the first step in recharging before tonight's house cleansing party. My stomach was demanding attention again, so I stopped at an Italian deli and got a panini sandwich, cup of pasta fagioli, and an ice-cold Diet Pepsi. I eat a lot, but my metabolism seemed a little overboard, even for me. The deli had a few tables and chairs outside, and I decided to sit and indulge two of my favorite pasttimes: eating and people watching. My life is hunting, work, working out, and hunting. There is a certain satisfaction in helping people with unholy problems, but that has worn thin over time. It would be appropriate to consider the tapestry of my life to be woven from chain mail. Hard and unyielding, protective and coldly pragmatic. But I really wished to have some cotton and wool interwoven with the steel links to soften the feel and warm my soul. Family, friends, relationships, and emotional bonds all seem normal and commonplace, unless you don't have them. I had Gramps, five hundred miles away. Other than him, I had no one. I liked music, to listen to and try to play on my guitar; I liked reading; I loved New York's museums—mostly of science and natural history—and bad sci fi movies are fun. At home, I had the woods, a place where very few

Hellbourne ever go, not because they can't but because they thrive on the despair and agony of people. The woods are relatively empty of people and are therefore a wasteland for the demonkind. So, to try to fill the empty spots in my chainmail tapestry, I like to watch people. Couples, families, joggers, kids on bikes, gangs, street performers, bums, the old, the young, and the busy. All fascinating, all potential stories that I could imagine and try to understand. High school had been hell, but it had taught me to go relatively unnoticed, and I was able to observe fairly discreetly. It isn't much of a hobby, but it keeps the dark clouds that hang over my life at bay. A little.

As I ate my sandwich, I watched a young couple with a toddler, feeding, wiping, playing, holding, reassuring, chasing, and protecting, all within twenty minutes.

It was intriguing and a little scary. Facing Hellbourne was often terrifying, but ultimately, if I screwed up, only I felt the pain. Raising children meant much wider consequences for others. All your actions, both good and bad, would impact another's life, even after your own was over. I admired the couple's bravery.

I was finishing my soup when I noticed a couple of girls walking a dog and automatically watched them. Attractive, fashionably dressed, requisite toy dog on leash—a fairly common sight in Brooklyn. Chatting away as they walked, their gazes passed right over me without pause. I wondered if it was my lack of expensive clothes or other signs of social status that relegated me to the ignore bin. Almost as effective as a Hellbourne's cloak. Most likely just not putting out the right signals. It's another aspect of people watching: assigning motives, personalities, observing social behaviors. I had noted over the years that men were invariably drawn to looks, and women to status. The two material girls had almost passed me when the little dog caught my scent, me—God's gift to dogs. It was one of those little ones, possibly a Pomeranian or Shiatsu (or is that a massage?). Gramps calls them kicking dogs, as he sees no earthly use for them. I'll admit to being partial to a more robust canine, but little dogs are still dogs when you get through all the manicured fur, bows, and bling-bling collars. This little thing just beelined for me, pulling the rhinestone-encrusted leash right out of the blonde's hand. Both girls whirled, panic stricken, only to find Fluffy or Pierre or whatever-its-name-was swarming around my legs in a wiggly happy dance. Catching the leash in my hand, I patted the little beast until the girls arrived in breathless drama to reclaim him/her.

"Oh, Brutus, you naughty dog. Come back here to Mommy," the blonde baby-talked. Brutus? What the hell was she thinking? There were squirrels in the park that weighed more than Brutus did.

"Thanks for grabbing him. He usually doesn't like men at all. How odd?" she continued. I just nodded and handed her the leash with a smile. Her friend, a brunette, stood back a few feet, giving me a reappraisal to see if maybe something may have been missed that might suddenly make me more interesting. Like a fancy watch or platinum card—or maybe a brokerage account statement showing millions on deposit. Actually, I had one of those, back in the apartment, for the trust fund that was created from my parents' estate, but it wasn't evident here. Their eyes darted over my build with some interest, but alas, no other signs of potential worthiness were apparent. So after a lot of thank you's, smiles, and with a few looks back, they continued on their way, picking up their chatter without pause. My lunch over, I jogged home, careful to avoid women with dogs.

Chapter 4

I keep a large cardboard box under my futon, which holds my supply of fetishes. A doglike wolf caught my eye. He looked like something that would appeal to a little girl. Peter had emailed more information regarding the case tonight.

The problems began about a month ago, with strange noises, then progressed to objects moving, foul odors, and apparitions. The final straw was the appearance of claw marks on the couple's seven-year-old daughter, Libi.

The wolf/dog was carved from tan-hued soapstone with little flecks of red. Twisted plant fiber of some type held a feather and a miniature turquoise arrowhead to its back. A small, pointed stick protruding from between its hind legs announced it was a boy wolf. I placed it in the pocket of my coat and pushed the box back under the futon.

The day had been warm, but the weatherman was calling for a cold front to sweep in during the evening, and it would get cold and windy. I layered an Under Armour turtleneck with a thick NYPD hoodie and cargo pants. Hiking boots over wool socks and my heavy canvas Carhartt jacket finished my preparations.

The address was in a predominantly Jewish neighborhood of single-family homes. The house that needed cleansing was white with green shutters and a black door. A dark blue van was parked in front, white letters NYPRT printed on its side. I ignored the van and looked the house over. The house looked back. Yup, I was getting a definite vibe from it. There was an additional feeling of being watched from somewhere else in the neighborhood, but it didn't feel unfriendly like the house did, so I ignored it. The sound of the van's door opening brought me around to find Peter striding toward me.

"Hey Chris. Boy, am I glad to see you," he said. And he was. Peter was one of the few people that knows about me and is still always happy to see me. The New York Paranormal Research Team is his baby; he co-founded it with his girlfriend, Melissa Turner. She was still getting out of the van by the time Peter had reached me.

He shook my hand, his big mitt engulfing my own. Peter is about six-foot-four, and Melissa is just a little above five feet. He looks like a football captain, and she could be an eighth grader. "What's the deal, Pete?" I asked. Melissa was walking toward us with two others from the van. One of the two was Carlton Sinclair, the foppish overly dramatic medium who provided the group's psychic heavy lifting. He was surprisingly effective. The other person was unknown to me. I frowned at her. My participation in these events is not a spectator sport. In fact, I would be entering the house alone or not at all.

I turned to Peter. "Who is that?" I demanded. He looked, apologetic. "Ah, Chris, this is Gina Velasquez. She's with another paranormal group and she actually called us in on this case. She insisted on being here tonight and the family backed her. I didn't get a chance to tell you. Sorry about that," he said.

The other three had reached us in time to hear all of that, but I wasn't paying them any attention. I was staring at Peter and making him uncomfortable.

Good! I was pissed. He knew better! All I needed was the wrong person talking about me, and my cop job would be history. The girl was tall, about five nine, dressed in a gray hoodie and jeans. She would probably be pretty if she didn't have such a pissy look on her face. "Peter, you know better. I'm gone." I turned to leave, and the girl, Gina, snorted in disgust and said, "So much for your big gun, Pete."

"Chris, wait," Peter said.

But I was already walking. Then the door opened at the house next to the haunted one and a young, scared family came down the steps, an elderly couple standing in the doorway. The father and mother were small of stature, and their terror was easy to read. Painful to read. One look in their eyes, and I could see the anguish of parents unable to protect their child. Clutching the mother's hand was a living doll, one of the absolute cutest kids I've ever seen. Seriously, she could have been on the front cover of an American Girls catalog. Brown ringlets and the darkest brown eyes I've ever seen. They were very sad, scared little eyes, and they froze me in my tracks. All right, I'd have to stay. No way was I letting that little girl deal with demonkind. Peter sensed an easy victory and swooped in.

"Chris, this is Mr. and Mrs. Klein. And this is Libi."

The father nodded hello while shaking my hand. Mrs. Klein gripped my hand hard and spoke for the both of them: "Thank you for helping us, Mr—"

"Just Chris will be fine," I said.

"Thank you, Chris. Peter says you can get rid of this thing. Nothing has worked. The Rabbis can't do it, and nothing Peter's group does seems to have any effect."

"Well, Ma'am, I shouldn't have any problem. But I do need some help." I reached in my jacket and pulled out the wolf fetish. "You see, I need someone to help me name this little guy." I looked at Libi as I said this, then dropped to one knee and set the little wolf down in front of her. "Libi, this is a guardian wolf. His job is to protect families like yours from scary things like the thing in your house. He's going into the house with me, and together we'll throw that thing out. And after, he is going to stay here and live with you and your mom and dad. But he needs a name first. And I'm afraid you're the only one who can name him," I explained to her wide brown eyes.

I can't tell you why this works, but whenever I take a fetish that's been named by a haunted child in with me, the resulting guardian is much more formidable. I suspect it has something to do with the power of a child's belief.

"Do you have any ideas for a name?" I asked her.

She looked at me very seriously, thinking it over. "Malachi."

"Malachi is perfect," I said, standing back up with the newly named Malachi in my hand. It was perfect, the newly named fetish taking on an almost palpable presence against my skin.

"Okay, everyone settle in for a little wait and I'll go clean it out. You'll hear noises and yells, but just ignore it." I turned to Carlton. "Did you get a name?" He sometimes will see a demonic entity's name. Sure enough, he handed me a scrap of paper with a neatly printed word. Azamogtath.

Don't say that out loud as you read this. It's generally a pretty bad idea to speak their names... unless... you happen to be me.

"Perfect." I nodded my thanks and then headed in, thinking as I always do, of my first time.

The house is old, a small two-story, wood shingle affair, long neglected. Its decay is a result of active avoidance by whoever owns it rather than forgetfulness, laziness, or lack of money. The owners simply want nothing to do with it, and it isn't likely to sell. On either side of the dull brown door, broken windows look out at us like the eyes of a monster, bracketing a rectangular maw.

The three of us stand by our bikes, one bullying, one uncertain, and one resigned. Carl, Eric's fat, red-faced cousin, is pushing him to get on with it. It's well past dinnertime and the late August day is rapidly aging, approaching its natural death. Carl is beginning to show signs that the house is getting on his nerves. In fact, I would say he is scared shitless, based on his increasing rants and insults. Eric, my only real friend, hasn't fully committed himself to the quest for his pre-teen honor. And I'm just waiting for him to decide to go in, as I know he eventually will.

"Come on already! I'm growing a fucking beard here!" Carl says.

"All right, all right, I'm going," Eric says. "But I'm only going as far as the kitchen!"

"Whatever. Just get on with it, pussy."

Eric started up the steps and after a moment, I followed.

"Where the fuck you think you're going?" Carl asks.

"With him," I replied.

"Like fuck you are! He's gotta go by himself," Carl says.

"He is. I'm just following."

I'm not about to let Eric go in alone, for three reasons.

First, because the house is hostile and dangerous. Anyone can tell that with one glance. Five people died in this wreck eight years ago. Old Man Miller shot his kids, his wife, and finally himself. The house had never sold, the stories of haunting had grown, and countless kids had tested their courage in the same way we were. I'm not willing to let my only friend go in without backup.

Secondly, Carl is once again manipulating his cousin. If Eric chickens out, which Carl is betting he will, he could lord it over him for years. That's not going to happen.

Third, the house scares the crap out of me. So I'm going in.

Eric tugs on the door handle, perhaps hoping it will be locked. It opens surprisingly quietly, no spooky haunted house creak or groan. The late-day sun casts beams of dust-moted light in pools on the floor and faded furniture. We have entered directly into a small living room, complete with couch and flower-

upholstered chairs. Everything is coated in a thick
blanket of dust, the floor directly in front of us littered
with old footprints. The trail leads through the gloomy
doorway ahead, sunlight not quite reaching that far into
the house. It smells moldy and stale, like clothes left wet
for days. Eric pushes ahead and the house stays quiet,
like it's waiting. The dark hallway leads to the back of
the house where it empties into a dining room. The
kitchen lies off to the right, the stairway to the left. A
small bathroom is straight ahead. I'm up close to Eric's
back, unwilling to let him move away from me. We
round the corner into the kitchen, tension fading fast as
we see it is empty of anything overtly threatening. A
tiny table and chairs, ancient refrigerator—door open
and empty, sink stacked with old dishes. The stove is
pulled away from the wall, uplugged and left, as if in a
hurry. A tiny window looks east, the unkempt yard now
gray with the afternoon growing old. Above the window
hangs an electric clock in the shape of a cat, the kind
with the swinging tail and eyes that move back and
forth with each tick. It's not plugged in.

     "Grab a fork or something and let's get out!" I
whisper. The tableware is a trophy, proof of his ordeal.

     "Ookay." He reaches toward the pile in the sink.

     The whirring sound makes us both jump, looking
wildly for its source. It takes a second to realize the cat
clock is swinging its tail and flicking its eyes—without
apparent need of electricity. The air is suddenly,
impossibly cold, shocking after the humid summer heat.
Eric bolts and I start to follow, only to catch a glimpse of

a figure on the stairway ahead. It's Marcus, my brother, turning and climbing the stairs almost in the same moment that I catch sight of him. I follow him, aware that Eric is thundering down the hall on my left, but unwilling to lose this chance at seeing Marcus. As I start to climb the stairs, numbed by the sight of my older brother who looks the same as my current age of twelve, he glances at me and rounds the landing halfway up. I hurry to catch him, my brain not yet realizing he can't be here. I climb as fast as I can, rounding the landing and gaining sight of the upstairs. Marcus is gone. The tiny hallway has a bedroom to either side, and I turn to look into the left first. A rustle of cloth brings me around in a whirl and I freeze. My mother is looking at me sadly, her pretty face and neck, marred with bright red ax wounds. I am suddenly terrified and certain this is not my mother. My natural cowardice takes hold, and I turn to run. The thing masquerading as my mother makes a mistake.

"Christian, why didn't you help us?" it implores in my mother's voice. My terror turns to rage, and I change my retreat to a charge, running full out without thinking about my action. My mother's face changes to something else, something that my mind can't quite grasp. Then I'm right in the middle of it, flailing my arms in angry boy fight, violet light flaring up around me, and the thing spins up into a greasy blot of blackness that sticks to my left hand like coal miner's snot. My hand flicks on its own in disgust, and the black blob flies

upward. Something huge, smoky, and birdlike snatches it, and then both are gone.

Gramps finds me on the front porch, responding to a garbled message of hysteria translated by Eric's mother. He looks me over and then sits next to me. We say nothing for a while, then the words flow and not long after, so do the tears. He takes me home, my bike in the back of his big red pickup.

The first thing I like to do when I go inside is say the thing's name. I speak in a clear, loud voice, and I mock it. Like a cat unable to stop from chasing a string, Azamogtath comes to its name. Like a coward, it comes from behind me and, like I guessed that it would, it comes with Tatiana's face. Or at least a pretty good imitation of it. But my Sight always shows me the reality, and my left hand caught it like a Yankee fielder catches a pop fly. It struggled and cursed me, but I'm pretty smooth at this part of the job. I think this must be my one hundred and seventh cleansing, each just like the rest. I toss it up and think >Kirby<, and my giant smoky, hawk-winged friend snatches the nasty thing from the air and pops back to whereever it is that he goes.

The house stinks of sulfur and brimstone as I trot down the front steps and hand Malachi to Libi. "You're gonna want to air it out. Smells like Hell's Outhouse. But it's gone and Malachi will keep anything else from bothering you."

Carlton leads the family and the others in to check my claim, Peter giving me a high five as he heads in. Gina just looks at me, her face unreadable, before I turn away and head into the dark.

Chapter 5

The predicted cold front had moved in, and the dark autumn sky swirled with bulbous gray clouds, the wind rushing alongside me, brushing the painted leaves of the small maples that lined the street. The air temperature had dropped a good ten degrees, and I was glad for my fleece-lined jacket and the thick, cottony feel of my NYPD hoodie as I hustled down the sidewalk. It was blustery and Halloween spooky, and I enjoyed it immensely. Fall is my favorite season, as I welcome the change from the wet, tropical heat of August to the cool of September and October. I love warm clothes and heavy jackets, although I am usually happy to put them away come spring. And I'll admit that I like feeling the mystic veil between this life and the next thin appreciably as Halloween draws near.

The sensation of being watched was still with me, in fact, stronger than before, almost palpable. Something or someone was pacing me, and I had the oddest feeling that I knew who it might be. An extra gust of air brushed my right cheek, smelling of jasmine and lilac, and I turned to find Tatiana walking next to me. She glanced at me once, her blue eyes glinting in the low streetlight, before she turned to look ahead. A second rush of air on my left announced Lydia's arrival, smelling of rose and musk, her Cheshire cat grin bright in the dark. "Hello ladies," I greeted them, trying to project calm. "Love the outfits." They were both wearing skintight black leather catsuits that blended with the night but failed to hide their charms. Think Kate Beckinsale in *Underworld*, times two.

"Hiya Northern. Nice night," Lydia said, her voice amused.

"Hello Christian," Tatiana said, her accented voice wrapping around my name like smoke. Nobody calls me Christian, but the way she said it had physical weight, like a warm hand pressing on my chest.

Whatever smartass comment I was gonna make next flew right out of my head.

"Are you well? Your heartbeat sounds... erratic," Tanya asked, concern shadowing her voice.

Lydia choked back a laugh as I replied, "I'm fine. It's nothing." Just you, your voice, and that damned catsuit. Any annoyance I still felt from the night before was gone, destroyed by her impossible presence.

"To what do I owe the honor?" I asked, trying to center myself.

"You were at our house today. You were injured when you struggled with the... thing. I wanted to make sure you were all right." It was the longest speech I had heard Tanya make, and her Russian accent was much less noticeable than before. But what was she talking about? Injured? I turned to her and found her looking at me, apparently not needing to see where she was walking. Me, I need to keep eyes forward to walk uneven sidewalks at night, so I stopped, both vampires stopping instantly as well. I marveled at the reflexes that produced such an immediate reaction. "Er... what injury?" I asked, puzzled.

Tanya reached out and brushed my left cheek. I felt a slight sting, and, touching it with my own hand, found some small scrapes where my face had met the patio.

"This? It's just a scrape. I didn't even realize it was there. How could you even know about it?" I asked.

Lydia looked between Tanya and me, a small smile on her face.

Tanya answered shyly. "I could smell your blood. I was concerned. I asked Mr. Deckert about it, but he didn't seem to think you were hurt." Lydia snorted at this final comment, like she was remembering something funny.

The amount of blood spilled was smaller than the drop I had pressed into her amulet, and she had noticed it in a house full of humans—and at least one dog. But her concern, which twisted something inside me, seemed excessive.

"Thank you for checking up on me, Tatiana. But I'm fine. I'm more concerned with how you are. Are you completely healed?"

"Tanya, you must call me Tanya. But yes! Your blood did a marvelous job!" She pulled her suit zipper to her stomach and bared a dangerous amount of creamy white skin. My face was instantly radiating at a thousand degrees Fahrenheit. Lydia almost collapsed in laughter.

"She's laughing at me, not you, Tanya," I explained to her puzzled and slightly hurt expression. "And yes, you certainly look great!" This set off a second burst of uncontrolled mirth from the spiky-haired waitress—who was apparently much more than a waitress. Tanya was quick, though. A slow smile of understanding spread across her face as she took in my expression, tone, breathing, and heart rate. Hell, I probably gave off pheromones that she could detect. I hadn't seen her smile before, and its effect was just as powerful as her unzipped jacket. But something she had said finally penetrated my hormone-addled brain.

"What did you mean about my blood? Wouldn't any blood have healed you?"

Lydia stopped laughing at this and was suddenly serious as she answered my question.

"That's a real good question, Northern. One we would like to understand as well. Normally, even Tanya, who heals the fastest of all of us, would need an enormous amount of blood to repair half that much damage. Yet she healed completely with only about a quart of your blood. You can bet that Galina is very interested in how that is possible."

Suddenly, I had visions of long lines of injured vampires waiting to get a hit from a tap plugged into my chest as my body shriveled and shrank, like a prune.

Tanya was fingering the arrowhead, drawing my attention back to her aforementioned gloriously healed torso. She started when she realized I was looking and began to take off the amulet.

"I must give this back, as you have destroyed the demon," she said reluctantly. I stepped closer to her unzipped self and touched her hands to stop her from taking off the necklace.

"Tanya, I didn't lend it to you, I gave it to you. Plus, I think you still very much need to keep it on." She smiled again, stunning me.

Lydia looked a little stunned too, like she had never seen Tatiana's smile before. Then she asked, "What do you mean by her still needing it?"

I shrugged. "I don't think the Hellbourne will give up trying, not with all the effort they put into this attempt. I'm afraid you'll have to put up with my presence for the foreseeable future."

Lydia frowned at this news, but Tanya lit up even brighter, if that was possible. The soft purr of a well-tuned motor announced the arrival of a huge Mercedes stretch limo pulling alongside us. The door opened and Vadim ghosted out, giving us a cursory glance, then scanning the darkness for threats. Galina leaned out of the open door and smiled at me like a cat smiles at a bird.

"Ah, Officer Gordon. I see the ladies have found you and in good health too. See, Tanya, he's fine. Chris... may I call you Chris?"

I nodded, and she continued, "I wonder if I might have a few moments of your time?" she asked, indicating that I should step into the limo. I sighed, figuring that it was inevitable, and walked over to the big car, my sexy escorts gliding along beside me. The inside was cavernous, capable of holding a small party. Nika was there also. I stood aside to let Tanya and Lydia in first. I eyed Vadim, who was eyeing me. When I did slide in, the only obvious spot was next to Tanya. Somehow, upon sitting, there wasn't as much room as I had thought, and she was suddenly pressed against my side, setting my heart pounding again. I briefly hoped that the vampires would attribute it to my fear, but Lydia's smile and Nika's knowing gaze said otherwise.

"For the second time in less than twenty-four hours, I find myself thanking you for protecting my daughter. In fact, my coven," Galina began, her voice and face expressing gratitude, her eyes devoid of emotion. "You are really quite the most interesting person, human or vampire, that we have come across in many years." I felt the big car move powerfully forward, like gravity. A different gravity seemed to have pinned Tanya's shoulder, arm, hip, thigh, and calf to mine. Coulda sworn the seat was bigger. She was warmer than I would have guessed.

"Did you know, Chris, that you share the same birth day, year, hour, and even minute with my daughter? Also that you each had a life-altering, traumatic experience on the exact same day, fifteen years ago." Tanya stiffened next to me while my mind tried to fathom the odds of our mutual birth... moment.

"You, of course, lost your whole family to an ax-wielding stranger. Possibly a demon-ridden one, as you might say?"

My teeth clenched as I had a sudden image of myself, like an out-of-body experience, huddled in a cowardly heap on the floor of my brother's closet. I couldn't help but be aware that Nika was studying me like a bug.

"Tanya lost her nursemaid that same day. It left her absolutely speechless for fifteen years. Until last night. When you found her and saved her."

Speechless? What could cause that? How had she lost her nursemaid? Why would she start talking now? I would have glanced at her but I could feel the emotion and tension radiating from her, and I sensed that she did not want me looking at her at that moment.

"I happen to hear you speaking with Lydia about the abnormally fast healing that Tanya achieved with your blood In fact, she is arguably stronger and faster today than she was yesterday. And most unsettling of all, you have an ability to see, sense, track, and destroy dangerous entities that we, for all of our admittedly superior gifts, cannot."

I finally answered one of her points, if only to clarify. "Er... I don't destroy them. I don't think that is possible in this.... realm or dimension. I just send them back."

She nodded at this piece of information. "But you send them back quite... forcibly. The video we watched from earlier today was fascinating. What was that dark form that appeared and snatched away the entity? It appeared again at the house back up the street, if I'm not mistaken."

So they had been watching me.

"Ah, I just call it Kirby." They all looked at me with blank stares. "As in the vacuum cleaner. I named him when I was twelve. It seemed to make sense at the time," I explained.

Galina was nodding again.

"Yes, I imagine it has been difficult. There doesn't seem to be anyone else with your... talents, so to speak. You've had to make it up as you go, haven't you?"

You have no freaking idea!

"In fact, you are just about as unique as Tanya. I'm uncertain of your understanding of vampires, Chris, but my daughter is in fact my actual daughter. The only known vampire to be born of two full vampires. She is completely unprecedented. As near as we can ascertain, she was conceived the night her father and I were Turned. She apparently remained in some sort of stasis for something on the order of two hundred and fifty years or so. The tiny fertilized egg finally started to develop nine months before she was born. About the time you were conceived. But at the risk of changing the topic rather suddenly, what did you mean about the demons still hunting Tanya?"

I tried to align my thoughts to answer while I reeled from the overload of information she had just dumped in my lap.

"Well, the Hellbourne that was sent was one of the most powerful that I've come across. Most demonkind tends to avoid daylight, yet this one was able to fully cloak in the middle of the day. Sooo, I can't imagine that this setback will stop them completely. I think I'm going to need to protect Tanya as long as I can. But we'll have to do some serious planning for what you will do if I'm no longer around," I added thoughtfully. Maybe I would have enough time to empower another couple amulets. Hmm.

I suddenly became aware of total silence in the car. All five were staring at me with puzzled expressions, although Tanya's was slightly alarmed. "What?" I asked as I tried to think of what I had said.

"Where will you be going that you would leave Tanya unprotected?" Lydia asked.

"Huh? Oh, well, I'm not actually leaving, but you have to understand that my life expectancy is not what you could call robust. I'm only human, and the things I fight are almost always faster and stronger. So it's only prudent to prepare for the most likely outcome. It's actually something of a wonder that I've lasted this long. Not to mention that my day job has its own risks."

I tried for a light tone but no one was smiling, although Vadim was nodding in appreciation at my line of thought. Lydia and Nika were a little wide-eyed, Galina was tapping her ruby lips with a single ruby fingernail, and Tanya... well, Tanya was looking rather angry. Alarmingly angry, in fact. The soft pressure against my side had turned titanium hard, and she literally thrummed with tension. Everybody became still. I learned then that when vampires freeze, they're like department store mannequins. I, on the other hand, can't stay still very long. Finally, I sighed and very softly said her name. "Tanya."

No response.

"Tanya, what's the matter?" There, just a flicker, but still noticeable. Her eyes had moved. They first flickered, then locked onto mine. I was alarmed to notice they were black. Completely, from edge to edge with no iris or white showing. I have to admit that she was scary. But I felt no danger from her. The other vampires were stone still.

I took a chance. Gently, I covered her velvet-over-metal hand with my own warmer, human hand and just let it sit while staring into her pitch black eyes. Her hand wasn't cold, but it was cooler than my own. Her skin warmed to my own temperature as my hand lay over hers. After a moment, I noticed a speck of light, deep in the celestial center of her eyes. Gradually it grew, becoming first a blue star, then finally her normal, exotic blue peepers. The steel in her hand softened perceptibly as she came back to herself. Her expression wavered between anger and sadness, and even an idiot like me was able to discern that she was upset at my very limited prospects for life.

I smiled at her, squeezed her hand gently—not that I would be able to hurt her—and said, "Tanya, I promise you that I will do my best to protect you and keep myself alive. We can talk about this another time." She said nothing, just kept staring into my eyes. I probably could have spent the night doing nothing else, despite the audience, but at that moment, the limo slowed to a stop and the driver's partition came down enough for Arkady to mention that we were at my building. The vampires were all watching her avidly, not bothering to breathe. I gently disengaged my hand from Tanya's and moved to the door of the limo. Vadim shook himself into motion and opened it for me, and I slid out into the night with a murmured goodbye.

The door closed and the limo started away, only to stop a few feet further on. Again, the door opened and this time, Tanya emerged like a dancer. She flitted to my side and the limo drove off. There wasn't a whole lot to say. I knew she wasn't ready to say goodnight, so I led her into my building and into my life.

Chapter 6

She was curious about everything. Why a girl who grew up in a seven-thousand-square-foot brownstone would find my four-hundred-square-foot studio fascinating, I don't know. She studied every minute detail of my tiny space. And she asked questions, lots of questions. How much was the rent? Why did I live here? Was I poor? Many would have bordered on offensive, but I couldn't seem to find any offense. She was asking in complete innocence, her worldview very narrow and contained.

She loved the bear in the tapestry. The photo on the bookshelf of Gramps and me generated twenty or thirty questions on its own. Where did he live, how was he related, what did he do? Pretty quickly, I was laying out my life story, which I had never done for anyone. I sat in my leather chair and she held the bear fetish in her lap as she sat on the futon. When we had first entered the studio, I had switched into host mode without much thought.

"Would you like something to drin...k? Er... oops. Sorry about that. Habit," I had said.

"I would like some water," she answered.

"You drink water?"

"Of course. We are mostly water, just like you. We get lots from blood, but still need a little from time to time," she said.

I got her a glass while I thought about this. "Are you hungry? For blood?" I asked.

"Are you offering?" she asked, smirking and obviously amused.

Was I?

"Yeah, I guess I am."

She smiled. "No thank you. I am still working from what you gave me last night."

"It doesn't seem enough. I can't seem to stop eating today," I babbled.

"I make you nervous," she stated.

"A little. I'm not used to being alone with girls. Especially really pretty girls," I admitted, cursing myself for my lame attempt at a compliment. Like she was just pretty.

"But you are not nervous that I am vampire?"

I thought about that before I answered. "No."

"Why? Why are you not scared or nervous or bothered?" she asked, with intensity.

I shrugged and struggled to organize my thoughts.

"Well... first, because of what I deal with—demons—I guess finding out that vampires are real isn't that much of a shock. Then, I don't get any kind of scary vibe from you. And finally... I... like you... and I guess that outweighs everything else." I paused and threw caution aside. "I also think that you like me... or at least think I'm interesting... or something." My courage floundered a bit at the end.

She sipped her water, watching me over the edge of her glass. Her feet were tucked up on the futon, the bear under her hand. She was seriously cute as hell.

"You like the way I look," she stated. "You are attracted to this." Waving a hand up and down herself.

"Yes, but actually that's part of what makes me nervous. The parts that don't make me nervous are the things like the fact that you cared enough about my being hurt to track me down. Or that you protected me from the others last night. Even facing Arkady down when I provoked him. I like the way you dance, I like that you are quiet, and I really liked that you stopped last night, when you could have drank me dry... so to speak."

She didn't say anything, just stared at me like I had either said something important or crazy. I kept going.

"And yes, I think you are the most beautiful girl I've ever seen, but I like you in spite of that."

She frowned at that.

"What?"

Suddenly nervous again, I busied myself with my uniform and gear, getting it ready for work tomorrow, answering as I worked, my face turned away from her. "Well, I don't know much about girls. I have always avoided them. The Hellbourne always know if I have a friend, and they will attack them or use them against me. But I like girls... I mean... I don't want to be alone. It's just not fair to endanger someone just because I'm lonely or something. But I watch them... girls, that is. And it seems that the really pretty ones, the beautiful ones, are usually not so much the kind of people that I like. Not all of them. But most. You don't seem to even know that you're beautiful. And you're definitely the kind of person I like."

I finished babbling and finally turned to read her expression, figuring to find the window open and her long gone.

Instead, I found her only about ten inches away, staring intently into my eyes.

"Ah... hi!" I said, shocked at her proximity. Her eyes looked back and forth between my two. I held still. She blurred a bit, and I felt a soft kiss on my lips. She was back on the futon, looking down at the bear as she petted it.

"I asked Lydia about kisses. She said I would know when I should kiss you. That was a when," she explained, still not looking up.

I was frozen in place, trying to think of something to say, but my brain wasn't in gear. Finally, she looked up bashfully and I automatically smiled at her. She smiled back, and my brain slipped out of gear again.

"What is that?" she asked, curious again. She was looking at my feet, where my vest was sitting on the floor.

"It's my body armor. You know... to protect me from bullets and knives," I answered. She was back at my side in a split second, examining the vest from all angles but not touching it. I picked it up and handed it to her. The weight meant nothing to her; she held it like a sheet of paper.

"Is it good?" she asked, a little dubious.

"It's the best. Dragon Skin, made by Pinnacle Armor. Top of the line."

"Put it on... please," she said. I shrugged into the vest and sealed it up. She poked the vest, fingered the exposed areas around my armpits and neck.

"It does not protect the big veins in your neck or inside of your thighs," she pointed out.

"No, it's a concealable vest, so it doesn't protect the neck. I don't think anyone makes armor for the thighs, but I've never checked into it."

Next, she wanted to see all my gear and what it did. She snorted at my cuffs, but allowed that they would probably hold a human. She sniffed the pepper spray, flashed the flashlight, and twirled the baton. That was illuminating, as she handled the stick expertly, at least during the moments when it wasn't a blur. Tanya was no stranger to weapons. Next, she wanted to test my flex cuffs, which are basically giant plastic zip ties like electricians use. We use them when we have lots of people to restrain. So I zipped a set closed on her, interested to see the result. She simply flexed her wrists lightly and the heavy plastic broke. I made a note not to zip tie any vampires. Finally, we got to the gun, and I slipped into instructor mode, teaching safety as I had been taught. I expected derision or flippant disregard, but she took it very seriously. I showed her how to clear the chamber and drop the magazine. I explained the Big Four rules: keep your finger off the trigger, keep the muzzle pointed away from anything you don't want dead, know your target, and treat every gun as if it is loaded. She was a natural.

I started to ask my own questions. Does sunlight hurt her? No, it makes her sleepy but it could give most vampires a burn, like bad sunburn, but quicker. How often does she need to eat? Depends on activity. Usually one unit of blood a day. My blood seemed to hold her longer. Odd. Where do they get the blood? Turns out the Coven owns its own blood bank, but there are lots of humans who love to be bitten. Does she have any powers? Not yet, but she was really young in most ways.

I asked her what that meant.

"Well, vampires get stronger and faster with age. We tend to develop new abilities as we get older. I'm only twenty-three, like you, but I'm stronger and faster than most vampires. Maybe like a six hundred year old."

That shut me up for a while. I decided to change into sweats and a tee shirt. When I came out of the bathroom, Tanya was holding my discarded hoodie in both hands, sniffing it.

"Careful. Any clothes you find on the floor might have a serious stink to them."

"No, it smells of you," she said.

"Tanya, are you cold?" I asked.

"I don't really feel the cold... wait... if I am cold, I can wear the sweatshirt?" she guessed.

"Yup, or you can wear it even if you're not cold," I suggested.

She smiled and sort of wriggled and was suddenly wearing the NYPD hoodie. It was huge on her, and it just made her look even cuter. I smiled at her, then covered a yawn.

Instantly she was adamant about me sleeping, thinking of my work tomorrow.

"Tanya, tomorrow is a shift change for me. I was on seven to threes last week. Tomorrow starts three to elevens. So I don't have to go in early. And I do need to get used to staying up later." Of course, that resulted in a new round of questions about my shifts and what I actually did. "So, you just walk around the City? With your partner? Who is your partner?" I explained about eight-person squads, run by a sergeant, and rotating partners for us rookies. I thought that I was partnered with Bernice Hughes for the week.

"Is she pretty?"

"What does that have to do with anything?" I asked.

She frowned. "That means she's pretty."

"Actually, she's not. But I still don't see why that matters."

She changed the subject. "When will you get home?"

"Oh, usually eleven-thirty to twelve or so."

"May I come by?" Her voice was quiet as she asked.

"Sure. It always takes me some time to settle down after a shift. If you're especially bored, I'll show you pictures on my laptop."

Apparently, she was bored right then, 'cause she slipped off the futon and snagged my laptop from the little table by the kitchen. So we looked at pictures of the farm, the woods, the Search & Rescue guys, my town, Gramps, lots of tracks—I collect animal tracks with both photos and plaster casts—and, eventually, my parents and brother. She asked a ton of questions, of course, from things like, "What was your mother like?" to "how many kids in your high school?" She must have been really bored but she kept at it gamely, right up until I fell asleep.

Chapter 7

I woke abruptly the next morning, my mouth metallic and my pillows scented with lilac and jasmine. Starving again, I whipped up scrambled eggs and toast with a half pot of home-brewed Dunkin' Donuts coffee. While eating, I fired off a quick email to Gramps to keep him in the loop.

Hi Gramps,
Just a quick note. Took out daytime Hlbrn yesterday and cleaned house in neighborhood. Switching to evenings this week. Miss the farm. Anything new up there? Can't wait to get up there at Thanksgiving, which was approved by my Sergeant. Not much else to report.
Chris

After sending it, I cleaned up and then headed to the gym. It was heavy weight day, and I spent all morning kicking my own butt. I broke through four personal bests for bench press, squat, dead lift, and clean and press. Lunch was a seafood sub and soup that I grabbed on the way home. I spent the afternoon cleaning up my uniform and gear, not going overboard or I'd stand out as a rookie, and researching Galina Demidova.

There were bits and pieces from twenty years back or so, but not much. The last ten years, however, provided a much greater amount and variety of articles. Building dedications and construction projects were most common, with a fair amount of charitable donations mentioned. Only two photos showed up, both from charity balls from ten years back. Actually, it was for the same charity, The American Red Cross. How's that for ironic? That article mentioned the private blood bank and research into synthetic blood, which her company was funding. Her backstory was very sparse, but from what I could glean, she was reputed to be single, had one daughter, was publicity shy in the extreme, and possessed a scary, sharp business mind. No mention of scary, sharp teeth.

Gramps emailed back while I was Googling.

Hi Chris,
Daytime Hlbrn is concerning. Any idea of goal?
Farm is good, harvest in although the old John Deere
(the 8450) is on its way out. I'll be shopping soon. Let

me know on the Daytimer? Can't wait to see you at
Tkgiving. Oh, Benningtons are selling. He'll give us first
shot. $600k for 600 acres. What do you think?
    Love,
    Gramps

I knew he would get concerned about the Hellbourne that attacked Tatiana, but I was hoping he'd let it slide. I didn't want to lie to him, and I had already omitted the whole vampire thing. I wouldn't answer him immediately, and I needed to get ready and head to work. Although the sale of the farm and land next to ours was a no-brainer—land was almost always a good investment.

I elected to drive to the Precinct, as it's a good distance from my apartment and, getting off at close to midnight, I wouldn't feel like walking, especially at the thought that Tatiana might be around to see me. The light of day brought a whole truckload of self-doubt regarding the vampire girl. Did she really like me? Was I just an interesting experiment? Was I just caught in some artificial vampire attraction, drawn like a minnow to the snapping turtle's wiggly tongue? She was the first girl of any species that already had a demon-kind bull's-eye on her back, freeing me from worrying they might use her against me. I didn't arrive at any answers, but I did arrive at work, parking my bright Tonka-toy-yellow Nissan Xterra in a rare open spot near the Precinct house. After checking in with the Desk Officer,

I headed to the muster room and hooked up with my squad.

"Yo, Gordon! What happened to you Friday night? I looked up and you were gone. I was gonna hook you up with one of the girls, but I hadda let Pella in on the deal," Henderson said as I came up on the group.

"As if he had a chance with me there!" Pella rebutted.

Henderson snorted. "Hell, Pella from what that blonde said the next morning, your chance was shot after your seventh drink! Whiskey dick!"

Pella scowled as the others laughed, and I tried to slide by without answering. Luckily, Sergeant Scazoli stomped up and started shouting out assignments.

I was paired with Bernice as I had suspected. Not a real hard prediction, as either Pella or I was usually with her and the Sarge, being the only rookies in the squad.

Bernice Hughes was black, short, wide, and tough. She took no crap from anyone and could swear to make a sailor blush. She also mentored young rookies like a mama grizzly. Bernice could take charge of any situation and solve it with nothing but her mouth. She never drew her gun and rarely needed backup; instead, she understood the root cause of the problem and dealt from there. Hardened street criminals would submit without a fight if Bernice was involved, simply because they respected her. I learned early on to stay back and observe, learning more in a shift than I did in the whole six months of Academy Police Science or Behavior classes.

Most of the job in foot patrol is just talking to people. Handling complaints, solving problems, offering suggestions, gathering information. This last was important, as the Muster Room lecture had been all about a new designer drug, N'Hance—or Hance, for short. It was reputed to provide the user with sharper senses and increased reflexes, the stories hinting at a secret military origin. The main side effect was a fairly common PCP-like rage that usually ended in injury to all involved. So Bernice and I were handling the normal stuff and keeping our ears open for any Hance-related intelligence.

The only excitement during the shift was a mugger who grabbed a pocketbook without noticing two cops behind him. He was pretty quick, but I was on my game and caught him within a hundred feet of the victim. I collared him in an alley between a pizza shop and a locksmith, taking him down in a righteous tackle that would have made my old coach proud. I cuffed him while Bernice called a squad car, and we sent the perp in to get booked, then worked our way back to the Precinct to fill out the paperwork. As soon as we checked in, the Duty Officer told me to see the Lieutenant in his office. I had never been near Lieutenant Tredont's office, or Deputy Inspector Pelossi's office, for that matter. DI Pelossi ran the Precinct, but he would generally be home at ten-thirty at night.

The blinds were open on the glass walls of Tredont's office, and I could see the back of a brown-haired woman sitting across from him. Tredont, himself, was sitting almost at attention, a highly unusual position for a veteran officer. I knocked on the door and he waved me in, relief flashing across his face. Tredont was in his late thirties, a tall, rawboned kind of guy with the beginnings of a paunch. He stood up as I announced myself.

"Officer Gordon, sir!" I reported at attention. The civilian turned to look at me, and my quick glance told me it was Galina.

"Ah Gordon, Ms. Demidova was just telling me how you helped her daughter Friday night. Trouble with a drunk, was it?" He was nervous and completely in her thrall.

"Yes sir," I answered. I had a suspicion he was holding his gut in.

"Oh it was much more than that. If Officer Gordon hadn't intervened, I don't know what that awful man would have done to my little Tatiana," Galina gushed. Yeah, right. Good one.

If she had seen him in time, *little Tatiana* could have thrown him through a wall or dropped a car on him or something. I controlled my reflexive snort.

"Anyway, good job, Gordon! This will go in your service jacket, and Ms. Demidova has graciously donated ten thousand dollars to the Widows and Children's fund!" the Lieutenant continued, holding up a check.

"That's wonderful, sir!" I tried for the right degree of enthusiasm, but didn't quite get there. Tredont gave me a level look, which was broken when Galina spoke up. "Lieutenant Tredont, do you think Chris could walk me to my car? I'm not sure I could find my way out on my own."

I had to control a second snort. Hell, she could probably smell her way out, if her predator's mind hadn't kept a perfect map of the route.

"Of course, Ms. Demidova. Gordon, see Ms. Demidova out and to her car."

"Yes, Sir!"

I held the door for her and followed as she swept out. She correctly chose the route without my guidance. She was wearing a snug gray sweaterdress that was classy and sexy at the same time. Her perfume was floral, undoubtedly expensive, and not overdone. No one was up on this floor, and she got right down to business.

"Just so we're clear on this, as much as I appreciate your help in protecting Tatiana, do not for a moment think that entitles you to anything else," she said. "Tatiana may feel a small amount of... gratitude at the moment, but I guarantee you that will change. Do not delude yourself into believing otherwise. Stay away from her. If you have difficulty remembering this, I can have someone explain it to your grandfather. St. Lawrence County is not so far away."

My feet stopped on their own, my mind flooded with rage, fear, despair, and doubt. She stopped and looked back at me with a smirk, waiting to see if I was stupid enough to attack her. Almost. My fight brain wondered if my trick at pulling demons out of a body would pull a vampire's soul free before she could kill me. Shaking, I pulled back from the red rage that threatened to control me and continued on without talking, walking her past the Front Desk, ignoring the stares of my fellow officers, and out to her limo, where Vadim was holding the car door open. I couldn't say a word, my jaw clenched so tight that my teeth should have shattered. The car absorbed Galina like a sponge, and with one last dead-eyed look, Vadim joined her, and the big limo powered off into the dark.

Chapter 8

The rest of the shift went by in a fog of anger and self-doubt. I knew what she was doing, but the problem was, she was probably right. Tanya's interest was most likely fleeting, at best. I headed to my car, deep in thought, unlocking it with my keyfob as I approached it. I slid in and slammed the door, which sounded like both front doors closing, and became aware of someone sitting next to me.

"Jeeze, Northern, you look like someone shot your puppy," Lydia said in greeting.

I stared ahead, clenching my jaw, and finally said, "You can tell Galina I got the message! Your reinforcement isn't needed."

"What? Whoa there. You talked to Galina? When?" She was puzzled.

I sighed. "A couple of hours ago. You two need to communicate better. She already warned me off."

"She did what? She didn't? Oh, the old hag is really scared!"

I studied her expression, trying to ferret out if she was acting or not.

"Okay Chris, take it from the top. Tell me everything she said." Lydia didn't appear to be lying, but who knew how good an actress she was? I noted that she had never used my name before. I decided it didn't hurt to play along, giving her the rundown of my meeting with the Lieutenant and Galina and our private conversation. She processed that for a moment, then turned to me, her green eyes bright with sudden understanding. "You believe her, don't you? I mean, about Tanya?"

I shrugged, then nodded. Her face softened in sympathy for a moment, then hardened into a fiercer expression. "All right, listen up. Class is in session. Welcome to Tatiana 101. Here are the facts of life. You drive, I'll talk."

I started the Xterra and pulled into traffic as she began to speak.

"Vampires are not flighty as a rule. Our emotions, likes, dislikes, and habits run longer and stronger than they do in humans. They have to, because we live so much longer. When we make up our minds on something, it usually stays that way, etched into stone. Tanya is no exception. If anything, she's even more rock solid in her ways. And we don't take forever to make up our minds. It can happen faster than you can blink."

She paused to make sure I was up to speed. I nodded, and she continued.

"Tanya hasn't spoken for fifteen years. Not one word! And she has not fed from a living being in that entire time! Until you reached into her chest and touched her heart! You had every opportunity to kill her to save yourself and you didn't! Her first word in fifteen years was 'nyet'." She paused.

I must be a double moron, because I decided to correct her.

"Actually, her first word was 'swallow,' " I said.

Her palm slapped the dashboard like a gunshot, making me jump despite myself. "I knew it! She gave you her blood! Hah!" She was really excited now. "Don't tell anyone else that! And don't even think about it near Nika!"

"Why?"

"Because, my slow-to-understand friend, no one... NO ONE has ever tasted Tanya's blood. No one but you! That proves it! Absolutely proves it!"

"I'm not following any of this," I admitted.

"Vampire blood, when shared with a human, does a lot of things. If the vampire has taken blood from the human, then shares their own, it creates a bond. The human also gets improved health, better senses, faster reflexes, greater strength, and other stuff.

Depending on how much blood is taken, it usually wears off anywhere from several hours to several days, unless more blood is shared. Tanya, as the only born vampire... the only Full Blood, has probably the most potent blood of any vampire, even the Elders. It has been guarded, her whole life, like gold, better than gold. And she chose to share it with you. She's never given it to anyone."

That explained the extensive cleanup efforts and burned clothing. It also explained why I had recovered so quickly without a transfusion. And probably why I had broken so many personal weight lifting records today.

"How much did she give you?"

"Just what she wiped onto her finger. Maybe a couple of CC's?" I answered.

She looked at me blankly.

"What? I watched the tape of your fight with the demon yesterday. You moved a lot faster than most humans, but that amount of blood should not have affected you so much. Hmm... I wonder?" She tapped one long black fingernail against her bottom ruby lip in thought.

"It's like you two were made for each other..." she mused. "Anyway, back to my original point. Tanya has Chosen you. You're it! She's not going to change her mind... ever."

We were at a stoplight, and I was so overwhelmed by the conversation that she had to remind me to drive.

"What does that mean... chose me?"

She sighed. "Tanya has decided that you are her life mate. Her beloved. You are hers, now and forever."

"What? You can't choose a lifemate after knowing someone for twenty minutes! That's crazy!"

"No, Chris, that's vampire. And I know Tanya, probably better than even her mother."

"I knew you weren't a waitress, but what exactly is your role?"

"Galina made me. Turned me, if you will. But fifteen years ago, she gave me to Tanya. So I am hers. I used to be more a keeper, but now that you woke her up, I'm her assistant, her confidant, sister, friend, and all-around right hand."

"Galina gave you to Tatiana?"

"Chris, you have to understand: vampires belong to their sires, the ones who turned them. The vampire world is all about relationships, covens, and families. There are very few unaffiliated vampires in existence. We simply don't thrive or survive without support systems and networks. Living for centuries is not bearable without close connections with fellow beings. Not to mention being caught alone by our enemies. Tanya is of her own line, due to her unique nature. Galina gave me to her to give her that anchor that we all need."

"What happened to Tanya? Fifteen years ago? She killed her own nursemaid by accident, didn't she?" I guessed.

"Oh, Northern, I have to apologize. You are quicker than you look. Yes, Tatiana's vampire minder wasn't paying attention and she was feeding on Belina, her human nursemaid. Something frightened her, we don't know what, and she never stopped her feeding. She was devastated. She really loved Belina."

"That's why she thinks she's evil, isn't it," I guessed again.

"Yup."

"What happened to the vampire who was minding her?"

"She was me. I volunteered to be her minder."

Another question occurred to me. "Lydia, what were you doing waiting table last Friday night?"

She smiled in the dark interior, the instrument lights reflecting off her teeth.

"Nika heard Vadim when he saw you in line. Something about you caught his attention," she said. " I checked you out myself when you came in with your friends. There was definitely something that caught my attention, as well. So I took the table to keep an eye on you. Looks like I was right. You've really shaken things up."

After a moment, I pushed on. "So Galina is... threatened by me?"

"Tatiana Demidova is viewed like royalty throughout the vampire world. Born vampire. Abilities from birth that take centuries to develop. Galina's position has more to do with the status of being her mother than anything else. She's only about two hundred and seventy, or so."

Lydia explained, "Suddenly, her little girl is awake and learning again, making decisions, growing mentally, interested in business, life, and chasing boys. Well, just one boy," she teased. "And the Elders are coming to see for themselves. She's panicking. Kinda stupid, really. If she drives you away, Tanya will only follow you. She must be in denial. Hmm. Don't worry about it. Let me handle it. You just keep the demon things away from Tanya."

Watching me, she continued, "Now it's my turn to ask a question. How do you feel about Tanya?"

I couldn't answer; my emotions were too raw and unfamiliar. Elation, wonder, sun-hot happiness mixed with fear of disappointment into a confusing jumble. Lydia was watching my face, and she nodded. "Yeah, that's pretty much what I thought.

"Okay, my original mission, before we got sidetracked, was to give you some Tanya pointers. First, she's extremely worried about you. Protective AND territorial. Her feelings are cement, but she is worried if you will feel the same way. I think you do. But just keep doing what you're doing. She came home floating this morning and hasn't taken that damn sweatshirt off since."

She paused in thought, and I threw in a question.

"When you say protective, is that why she got in Arkady's face? What if he had pushed it? She might have gotten hurt."

Lydia snorted in amusement. "Please! Arkady would never attack her. He worships at the altar of Tatiana. But if for some reason he lost his mind and did? He wouldn't have lasted a nanosecond."

"She's a good fighter?"

"Chris, I don't think I have the vocabulary to describe just how good a fighter she is. For the last fifteen years, all she has done has been to study and to practice fighting. She's a natural, and she's faster and stronger than any other vampires except the Elders. Every day, she fights as many fighters as Vadim can plead, bully, and bribe into sparring with her. Whips all of them. And now that she's got a boyfriend, she kicks all their asses in half the time. Like she's been holding back, but now has places to go, a guy to see. Matter of fact, I think she's been on hold for awhile and now is making up for lost time. She even cracked a joke yesterday; at least, I think she did."

"No way. What was the joke?" I asked.

"Well, when dusk hit, she shot straight outta bed and raced downstairs. She knew you had been in the house. When I caught up to her, she had cornered Deckert and four of his guys, demanding to know who had hurt you. She smelled your blood and was ready to go to war. I got her calmed down, and Deckert reassured her that you only scraped your face fighting the demon thingy, but by then, one of Deckert's guys had pissed himself. Pretty understandable, really, 'cause she was scary as hell. Never seen her do that before."

She grinned in the darkness.

"Anyway, Tanya apologized and then offered to buy the guy new pants, but they would be black or navy so the next time, the piss wouldn't show up so much. Then she smiled. Of course, they didn't know if she was joking or not, but I laughed."

"That is sorta funny. The guy pissed himself? Really?"

"Oh Northern, you have no idea what she was like. Do me a favor and don't get hurt. And don't flirt with other girls!"

"Ah, I don't flirt. And girls don't flirt with me."

"Hmm, I'm not so sure about that, but don't be surprised if they start."

"Why?"

"Never mind, just trust me."

I was already trusting her with my life, what more could I do.

We were at my building and I found a spot to park not far from the door. Lydia leaned over and pecked my check, then was out of the SUV in a blink. "All right, go be nice to my girl." I started to nod, but she had faded into the dark.

Tatiana was sitting in my leather chair, wearing jeans and the NYPD hoodie, paging through one of my books, The Hobbit. She bounced to her feet when I came in, a little smile on her face.

"Hi *zayka*," she said.

"Hi right back at ya," I replied with a grin. "Er, what's a *zayka*?"

"It is a bunny."

"A bunny?"

"Is term like... honey," she said.

I guess that was okay. Then I studied her some more. She was paler, circles under her eyes and a nervous sort of edgy look about her. She froze while I thought about it for a second.

"You're hungry, aren't you?" I guessed.

She didn't answer for a moment, then gave a little nod and said, "A little."

I couldn't believe I was about to do this, but it seemed natural.

"Okay, let me change and then you can... err... feed?" I wasn't sure how to phrase it.

She started to shake her head, but I jumped back in. "No really, Tanya... *zayka*, if you're hungry and my blood is especially good for you, then we feed you. Simple as that. I got lots."

I tried for light, but it was such an odd thing to say that I didn't get it quite right. I changed out of my uniform and gear, putting on nylon wind pants and a red Fall Out Boys tee shirt.

She was nervous, but I had settled myself down while changing and I just asked, "Okay, what's the best way to do this, or maybe I should say, what's your preferred way?"

Her eyes got wide, her pupils fully dilated, and she licked her lips nervously.

"Oh, you haven't done this in a long time, right? Why don't I sit on the futon and you can lean back on my chest and feed from my wrist?" I suggested, holding up my right arm. She nodded, so I got into a comfortable sitting position, my feet on the floor. She sat next to me, her legs out on the futon, my right arm around her.

She looked at me and asked, "Are you sure?"

When I nodded, she gently pulled my arm to her mouth, her eyes on mine, and bit. I felt a sharp pinch, like the doctor always says you'll feel, just before he jabs you with a spear-sized needle. The tiny pain was gone in a flash, and I felt heat radiate up my arm and through my chest, down my torso, pelvis, and legs. It was nothing like the night at the club. Waves of feeling rolled from my wrist through the rest of me, the sensation completely pleasurable. Really pleasurable. In fact, I was glad she was only leaning on me and not sitting on my lap, or she would have instantly known just how much I liked it.

I could thoroughly understand how vampires could find willing donors. Thinking back to my one night at the club, I could now see that some of the clubbers had been there just for that reason.

Tatiana was drawing blood very slowly, and while I could feel the blood flow out, it didn't create the panic I had felt the other night. It seemed like a long time, but it was only four or five minutes when she finished, licking my wrist. I was breathing hard, my pulse racing. Her saliva healed the punctures instantly. My left wrist didn't even have a pink spot from her first feeding. Her cheeks were flushed and she smiled and stretched, arching her back in a lithe motion, and then kissed me.

Soft at first, the kiss built its own momentum, and we spent quite a bit of time exploring each other's lips. She smelled of jasmine, lilac, and musk. She tasted clean and coppery from my blood. It was entirely new for both of us, and I think that mutual lack of experience kept us from being self-conscious. Suddenly, she popped up with an "Oh!" and zipped into the tiny kitchen, returning with a big glass of orange juice. Nothing would do but that I had to drink the whole thing down before she would return to her previous spot.

We were having the teenager experience that we had both missed out on. The kissing continued, and she seemed pretty good at it. I mentioned that. "Oh, Lydia showed me how." That image stuck. She asked more questions, this time about Hellbourne, so I filled her in.

Basically, I knew of two kinds of demon. The ones that settled in a location, like a house, and then went to work on the inhabitants. Feeding on misery, pain, and anguish and then creating more by manipulating one or more inhabitants. I opened the browser on my laptop and found a recent article about a guy that suddenly went nuts, killed his wife and kids, then himself. They happen daily and almost always are the result of a house-bound demon.

The second kind inhabited a body and moved through the world creating chaos and mayhem with direct action. They were the more powerful of the two kinds. "How do they get the bodies?" she asked.

"Sometimes a person will invite them in willingly, not realizing that their own soul will be tossed aside like trash. Some are the result of Wyrms."

"Worms?"

"That's what I call them, but with a *y*. Hellbourne will toss them on people as they move about. If a person is weak-willed or despondent enough, the Wyrm will get a hold and start to dig in. Mindless and brainless, the Wyrm weakens the person's hold on their own body. When the time is right, the Wyrm becomes a doorway for a demon to take over the body. Most people fight them off without ever knowing they were at risk. Friends and family can really help. But enough people succumb to make my life interesting."

"And these demons know about you?"

"Yeah, they would love to take me out, but just as they can cloak from humans and vampires, I am cloaked from them." I didn't add that it was what had protected my eight-year-old self when I cowered in my brother's closet. Because I was too afraid to tell her just how cowardly I was, which, ironically, proved my cowardice all over again.

"Why don't they hire a human to kill you? Why don't they go after your Gramps?"

"Both good questions. I don't know the first, although I have been expecting something like that for some time. Gramps is pretty protected by a whole bunch of fetishes. My turn for a question. Are there other types of paranormal beings besides vampires? You know: like werewolves, zombies, ghouls, witches, and chubacabra?" I asked.

She laughed, a warm throaty kind of laugh that made me want to laugh with her. "Of course. It only makes sense that if vampires are real, so are a bunch of other legends. Certainly weres are real, with the wolves the most numerous. But others, too. Werebears, were-panthers, weretigers."

"How about weredeer?" I asked.

"What? Of course not! Only carnivores."

"Okay, what about wereweasels?" I joked.

She nodded without smiling. "Yeah, they're pretty dangerous. Really quick."

"As quick as you?" I asked. She just smiled and shook her head. I had a feeling that there wasn't much out there that could match her.

"Wererats?"

"Eww, don't be gross."

Sweet! I managed to gross out a vampire princess.

"How about zombies?"

"Well, I've heard rumors in the vampire world of some who can temporarily animate the dead."

"Can you animate things?" I asked.

"Oh, I'm pretty certain I can animate you!"

She was right.

Chapter 9

Monday dawned cold and wet, which, of course, meant that it had to be my day for an outdoor workout. One of the local parks has a series of body-weight exercise stations—chin up bars, dip railings, wooden posts—and I use them as the basis for a workout. Most times, my hands would be ice cold by the time I finished the last set of pull-ups and began the run home, but today, I managed to stay warm.

I stopped at a corner deli for an order of chili and corn bread with a big cup of hot tea. All morning, I had been noticing odors: the wet leaves, dead worms, diesel fumes, garbage, pipe tobacco, women's' perfume, and a thousand separate foods. By the time I hit my apartment door, I was too hungry to shower, opting to eat my takeout first. I emailed Gramps after my shower.

Gramps,
Count me in on the land purchase (if you can talk my Trustee into it). I'll fill you in on the daytime thing when I visit at T-giving. Hlbrn interested in a girl. Too complex for email. Work is going well. Weather down here is cold and damp, but I see from the weather channel that you've already had snow. Can't wait to see

the farm, the dogs and of course your old curmudgeon self.
 Love,
 Chris.

    Seeing as Gramps was my Trustee, it was as good as a done deal that we would buy the adjoining farm and its six hundred acres. He would take half the money from my Trust, which had been funded after my family's murder. During the last fifteen years, the principal had grown from just over six hundred thousand to slightly over two million, although the market crash had knocked it down a bit. Gramps had about half the account in Treasury bonds that had gained in value as the market declined, and so offset some of the stock losses. Now we would get a great deal on a large chunk of land, which to Gramps' way of thinking was always a good investment.

    I layered my uniform over a solid base of synthetic Under Armour, grabbed my heavy rain gear and patrol bag, and headed into work. The Muster room smelled like a moldy locker room, the result of changing through two shifts of wet cops. "Hi Bernice, whaddya we got today?" I greeted my partner.
     "I got prisoner detail, you gotta see the Sarge about an interview."
     "What? What interview?"
     "Sugar, you got some suits from the Plaza to talk to. Sooo, I get to stay dry and move bad girls around."

She looked at my expression and added, "Don't sweat it, Chris. It ain't a bad thing."

Before I could answer, I heard the Sarge calling my name, and I turned to find him almost upon me.

"Gordon, get your ass up stairs. Some suits from Police Plaza wanna see you. You been up to anything I should know about?" he asked.

"No Sarge, not a thing. Who are they?"

He eyed me for a moment, then answered. "Inspecter Roma, Special Situations. Now why would Special Situations be interested in you?"

"What the hell is Special Situations?"

"Hmm, never mind. Just get your ass upstairs and don't embarrass us."

He turned away before I could ask any other questions, leaving me nothing for it but to climb the old stairs to the second floor. This was the domain of the detectives: Homicide, Robbery, Narcotics, and Vice. The Robbery detective at the first desk sent me back into the Homicide division's realm at the back of the building. An overweight plainclothes officer saw me enter the bullpen and turned to his right, nodding at a muscular blond guy in khakis and black turtleneck. The blond immediately approached me. "You Gordon?"

"Yeah," I answered.

"Come with me." He turned and led me down a hall to a conference room, where he knocked on the door once and stuck his head in. "Sir, Gordon's here."

"Send him in, Steve."

The blond guy pushed the door open and waved me through. As I took in the room, I could feel Steve follow me in and close the door, standing directly behind me. In front of me was a small table with four chairs, one of which was occupied by what had to be Inspector Roma, who was making a show of studying my file. That it was my file was obvious from the photo conspicuously displayed on the inside cover. I'm not sure how I noticed that, as most of my attention was centered on the female detective standing just behind the Inspector's left elbow. My heart sank into my shoes as I realized that the hard brown eyes in the dark suit belonged to Gina Velasquez, Peter's observer from Saturday night.

The badge and gun clipped to her belt told me that my career in the force was over and Special Situations was a smartass name for Internal Affairs.

Roma finally looked up and after a moment announced, "We're not Internal Affairs." He stood up and held out his hand. I took in his details as I shook his hand: strong grip, about five nine, trim cyclist's build, short dark hair peppered with gray, mustache and trimmed goatee, expensive suit and a pair of penetrating gray eyes. He looked more like a hardened corporate attorney than a cop.

"I'm Inspector Martin Roma. I head up the Special Situations Squad, which is a subgroup of Special Operations. We handle... unique cases. You've already met Detective Velasquez, and behind you is Detective Steve Sommers."

Special Ops is the unit that holds Emergency services, the NYPD Harbor unit, NYPD Aviation, and a host of others—essentially the largest SWAT force in the country. Whatever this Special Situations group was, it was headed by a full Inspector, which was unusual to say the least. Most precincts are headed by Captains or higher ranked Deputy Inspectors. Inspectors are the next rank higher.

"Officer Gordon, this isn't a witch hunt."

Sommers snorted behind me in amusement as Roma said this.

"It's a job interview."

"Ah Sir, there must be a mistake. I haven't been on foot patrol long enough to change jobs."

"Well, that's normally the case, Chris... may I call you Chris? But Special Situations has a certain degree of latitude to select personnel that other departments don't. Gina has told us about your activities of Saturday night. Meeting you was the natural next step."

I glanced at her once, noting her hard stare, and returned my puzzled attention to Roma.

"The Special Situations Squad doesn't appear on the Department's org chart, Chris. The Department will not admit or deny our existence, but we have strong funding and a free hand to handle our mission. As you are fully aware, there are many things that go bump in the night and, sometimes, the day. Our modern society doesn't officially recognize them, but a city of eight million people attracts more than its fair share of them and always has. The NYPD created this group over fifty years ago to investigate and deal with those things that are a danger to society but aren't recognized by that same society. Which brings us to you. You see, we've been hearing through our contacts in the clergy about a young man that could exercise any evil entity without fail and without religious means. Gina, as the Squad's Parapsychologist, has been quietly looking for you, and when she brought NYPRT in to check out that demonic entity, lo and behold, your name popped up."

I was trying to keep up. NYPD had a group that dealt with the supernatural! Velasquez was a parapsychologist, and Peter had thrown me under the bus.

After a moment's pause, Roma asked, "You have questions?"

"NYPRT told you about me, Sir?"

"Don't be too hard on poor Peter. The lion's share of their funding comes from us, as we use their personnel and equipment to help our investigations where appropriate. Gina really did find that case and call them in. It was only when they had exhausted their normal exorcism channels that he was willing to bring you in. Can't blame him, really. A Class Five entity is nothing to sneeze at, although Gina tells me it took you just a little under four minutes to completely eradicate all trace of the vile beasty. How does that work?"

I stalled for time as I tried to figure out what to say. "Er, *Class Five entity*, sir?"

"We classify demonic entities on a ten-class system, Gordon, with five being middle of the pack and ten being Linda Blair type situations. How do you classify them?"

"Ah, either geographically bound or corporeal, Sir."

"What the hell is corporeal, Gordon?"

"You know... ambulatory... occupying a body... ah, sir."

He just looked at me for a moment. Velasquez's mouth was hanging open a bit till she shut it and looked to Roma in question.

"Gordon, are you telling me that there are entities that can move about on their own... in a person's body?"

Oops. My stalling technique had let out more than I had planned.

"Well, yes, in an empty body, sir. I... ah... call them meat shells... as the person is long gone."

From behind me, Sommers threw out the next question. "How do you rank the house-bound ones, then?"

I turned to answer: "I don't. They're pretty much all the same, as far as I'm concerned. Not much trouble, although they throw stuff and play mind games. It's the Hellbourne... the ambulatory ones that are the challenge."

"And you don't use any religious methods?" Roma asked.

"God and I aren't on speaking terms, sir."

"Does your odd violet aura have anything to do with it?" he asked.

"You see auras sir?" He nodded, so I answered. "Yes sir. I use it to, ahh... rip them from their meat shells and then I... well... I guess you could say I banish them. Sir."

They all looked at me for a moment, but the silence was suddenly broken by three cell phones ringing at the same time. Roma read the text that came through on his, then dialed a number and identified himself. After listening for a moment, he answered, "Have the rest of the team meet us on site." He hung up and turned to me. "Gordon, we have a call. I want you to come with us on this. I'm interested in your reactions. Consider it part of the interview."

We moved quickly downstairs, with me pausing to grab my rain gear and patrol bag. A stack of sub sandwiches caught my eye as I passed through the Muster room, and I grabbed one in a plastic bag and stuffed it in the cargo pockets on my navy blue BDU pants, not knowing when my next meal would come.

I rode in the backseat of the dark Ford Explorer, next to Velasquez. Roma had shotgun and Sommers was driving. We headed north out of Brooklyn, crossing the Brooklyn Bridge into Manhattan. The city street view suddenly gave way to green trees, and I realized we were entering Central Park. In the twelve months I had been in the city, I hadn't made it to Central Park.

Sommers parked in a cluster of official vehicles near the north end of the park, after entering through the gate near 102nd Street. I jumped out of the vehicle and followed the other three as they beelined for the center of activity, which was the middle of a bunch of ball fields in a wide meadow. Cops and Emergency services personnel, dressed in rain gear, were all over the place, treating wounded, taking statements, photographing bodies, with some obviously searching the grounds for something. Roma was met by some Homicide types, and I could just hear the conversation over the pouring rain.

"About an hour ago, six to eight perps attacked a group of ball players trying to get a game in between showers. There are eleven wounded, six dead, including four of the attackers."

"What weapons did they use?" Roma asked.

"The attackers? Just hands and teeth. The bystanders? Anything they had, mainly umbrellas."

"Teeth?" Roma asked.

Gunfire suddenly erupted at the north end of the field, causing most of us to grab our guns. Roma just turned to look, and the rest of us holstered after seeing the officers at that part of the field put away their guns and move to the downed individual.

"Make that five of the attackers," the Homicide officer added.

Roma turned to look at the three of us. "Have a look around and see what you can find out."

Sommers joined the group that had just done the shooting, and Velasquez headed to where the EMTs were treating the wounded. I moved across the field, trying to read the tracks in the torn-up, muddy field.

I could see that a group had moved in a straight line from the entrance we had just come through to one of the ball fields. It looked like several attackers had peeled off to assault bystanders on the way. A blanket-covered body lay off to the side, a bare foot poking out from under. At least four of the attackers had continued straight on. A body lay in front of me, eyes open, lips drawn back in snarl, head bent back at an impossible angle. One of the four, I guessed. A pair of woman's shoes were lying a little further on, and the tracks showed female-sized feet moving away from the dead attacker and a pair of child-sized shoe prints moving parallel. I paused, confused by the next pattern. The small female-sized feet disappeared, covered or obliterated by some really large dog tracks. Where the hell had the dog come from? I shifted around a couple of Crime Scene types who were photographing another body, this one with its throat ripped out. Same snarl on the face, though. Okay, first attacker gets his neck broken... by the woman? Second gets his throat ripped out by one hell of a big dog. I picked up the tracks again, heading slightly northwest. At least the dog's tracks and the child's. What happened to the woman's? I couldn't find them, so I kept on with the ones I had. Which brought me to body number three, also with its throat ripped out. The rain was coming down harder, and a normally difficult crime scene was fast becoming impossible. The daylight, already muted by the storm clouds, was almost gone, and I broke out my Surefire LED light to help pick out the tracks. I could smell the blood and feces of the dead attackers, mingled with a wet dog smell and a salty, coppery blood smell that was different from the dead bodies'.

How the hell was I smelling all this, especially in the rain? I spotted a dot of red in the dog tracks, then another and another. The red splotches got bigger as I moved out of the field on a path headed into a wooded area. Most of the other cops and emergency personnel were back in the field, and nobody was paying me any attention. Just another uniform searching the park. The woods got thicker and the tracks disappeared on a paved path, but the red splotches kept on. Abruptly, I came to a stream running out of a rough rock arch, the front overhung with yellow forsythia. Instinct made me slow, as the wet dog smell got stronger. A low growl stopped me in my tracks, and I realized I was all alone, well out of sight of the field. A pair of red-rimmed eyes watched me from a rocky hollow on the left side of the arch, the forsythia partially blocking my view. I edged slowly closer until I could make out a pale face watching me from next to a very large, very disturbed canine face. So here was the kid and the dog, with the dog being wounded. Where had the woman gone?

"Hey kid, you all right?" I asked quietly, trying not to spook him or his dog.

He didn't say anything, his expression a mix of fear and determination. Brave kid.

"Is your dog hurt?" I asked.

He glanced at the dog and looked back at me, undecided. I kept edging closer, and the growls gradually subsided, although the red eyes never left me. The kid looked about eight or nine, dark hair, dark eyes. The dog was huge, reddish brown and, if I didn't know better, more wolf than dog. I could see wounds on the dog's neck and as I studied the two of them, I realized that the wounds were looking better as time went on. It brought to mind an image of Tatiana, her wounds healing as she drank my blood. I also noted that the dog had the most intelligent-looking eyes I had ever seen on an animal. Almost human. I had a hunch. I unfocused my eyes and used my Sight to look the animal over. Its aura was blue and green, human and animal mixed. Reaching slowly into my cargo pocket, I pulled out the sub sandwich. After unwrapping it, I tossed it up. Half the bread and most of the lettuce fell off it in mid flight, but the meat (ham, I think) and cheese and bottom roll landed right in front of the dog, who sniffed once and gulped twice. Almost immediately, I could see the wounds finish closing.

A yell behind me caused me to turn and look, but it was far away, back at the field. I turned back to the boy and dog, only to find the dog gone and a naked woman in its place. My hunch had been correct. Not that big a stretch, really. Tatiana had told me that werewolves were real. I just didn't expect them to be soccer moms.

"Ma'am, you all right?" I asked.

She nodded, her reddish brown hair plastered to her head with rain. I thought for a moment, then rummaged in my shoulder-slung patrol bag. I tossed her a bottle of water, two granola bars, a cheap one-dollar rain poncho, and a fifteen-dollar Trac fone that I keep as a spare—and an untraceable way to call Gramps if I need to. Her hand shot out and snatched each item from the air like a pro ball player.

"You have someone you can call, ma'am?" I asked.

This time she spoke, slightly louder than a whisper. "Yes, Officer."

"You all right if I leave you, then?" I asked, not wanting to be gone too long. I wasn't part of the triple S group yet, so I didn't think I needed to tell them about the werewolf momma who had killed three of the attackers while protecting her son.

"We'll be fine. Thank you Officer...?"

"Gordon, Ma'am."

"Officer, you smell like vampires."

"Yes Ma'am," I answered and left, heading back to the field.

My absence, of about eight minutes, hadn't been noticed. Instead, everyone's attention was on the capture of the last assailant, who had apparently been hiding in the plastic tunnels that were part of the little playground, north of the ball fields. Listening in, I found that the big field was known as the North Meadow and the entrance we had come through was known as the Girl's Gate.

The last of the six had been flushed from hiding and then tasered when he proved too difficult to manhandle. Arms cuffed behind his back, he was being led to a squad car by two large cops, struggling the whole way. About my height, slender, long, lank hair plastered to his face, eyes wild and mouth snarling, he looked less than human. Again, my gut told me to use my Sight, and I scanned his aura. Blue, but with flashes of white across his personal biofield. And just a trace of greasy black. Human, with twitches of vampire white and demon black. Concerned, I moved up close behind him, not liking the way his bound arms were straining at the cuffs. As they neared the squad car, a female cop opened the rear door and everything went to hell in a hurry.

The cop on his right arm slipped in the muddy grass, and the wilder chose that moment to exert all of his berserk strength against his cuffs, snapping the metal links. Time started to slow as he spun to his left, slamming his fist against the other cop's temple, dropping that one like a wet sack. He then leaped for the lady cop at the squad car.

I was moving as soon as the cop slipped, my fight brain taking over. My right hand snatched a handful of his greasy hair just as he began his leap. Everyone around us seemed frozen, and even the perp was moving a little slower than I. Yanking back hard, I pulled him completely off his feet, slamming him to the wet ground. Scary quick, he bounced to his feet, spinning and slashing his hooked left fingers at my face. I leaned back a little, letting his fingers slide by with a mere half inch to spare. He surged forward a step, swiping at me again, this time with his right hand. My body moved forward on its own, ducking the swing, and my right arm shoved his past me, spinning his back to me. Again, I grabbed his hair in my left hand, but this time, I snaked my right arm around his throat and under his chin, which he obligingly lifted as I pulled on his hair. Keeping my left hand at the back of his head, I stepped in close, grabbed my left bicep with my right hand and squeezed both arms hard, while I bent him over backward.

He flailed for a moment, but off balance and back arched, he was helpless as the pressure of my arms on his carotid arteries shut off all blood flow to his brain. Ten long seconds later, his consciousness shut down. I spun as I dropped backward so that I landed on his back, just as a ton of cops piled on both of us. Spitting out a mouthful of mud, I relaxed my hold enough to keep the creepy kid under me from checking out completely. Swift, efficient hands re-secured Junior's arms, this time with multiple plastic wrist cuffs, and a whole bunch of hands pulled me upright.

"Good job, buddy."

"Atta boy, nice moves."

A couple more pats on the back, and I was able to move aside and straighten my disheveled self.

"Hey Gordon, where the hell did you come from?"

I looked up to see Sommers staring at me.

"Ah... I was over in the woods, following a blood trail, and when I came out, I was just in time to join that little fiasco."

"Roma wants to see us. Nice takedown, by the way. Fast."

"Thanks."

We trudged over to where Roma was holding court under the sheltering branches of a huge maple. There were a few new faces I hadn't met yet, and he made the intros as they all stared at my mud-covered uniform.

"Chris Gordon, meet Fran DeMarco, Brian Takata, and Chet Aikens."

DeMarco was a tough-looking fifty-ish white woman with short dirty blonde hair. Takata was Asian, about five eight, blocky, and had the same military demeanor as the six-foot Sommers. Aikens was a skinny, six-foot-plus black kid with geek glasses.

Roma continued, "Fran is our Medium. Brian comes out of a SWAT background and is our close combat expert. And Chet is our historian and all-round technical wizard," he explained. "Gordon, here, turns out to be the mythical demon hammer we've been hearing about, although it appears he has other talents. Quick thinking, Chris."

I just nodded, keeping my mouth shut. I'm a firm believer in letting them wonder if you're an idiot rather than speaking too quickly and removing all doubt. The Inspector looked around the group and then said, "Well, what have we got? Fran? Why don't you lead off."

She nodded, took a breath and began. "I was able to find the ghost of one of the dead assailants, but he was almost incoherent. He last remembered hanging at a drug party, probably last night, and suddenly found himself here. He's already moved on. I was just talking to the dead woman over there." She waved her hand at the blanket-covered body with the foot sticking out. "She said they came out of nowhere and one of them just lit into her. I couldn't get anything else, 'cause something spooked her, and every other spirit around here, just before the last living perp went nuts and got Gordon all dirty."

I was most likely the thing that scared off the woman's spirit. Ghosts were afraid of me, for some reason. Peter's group wouldn't let me go ghost hunting because nothing showed up when I was around.

"Let me guess, it was a Hance party?" Roma asked.

Fran nodded.

"Gina?" Roma moved to her next.

"The wounded mentioned that the bulk of the attackers targeted a woman and little boy. Someone's guard dog chewed up several of the perps, but no one remembers seeing the kid, the woman, or the dog after. It was, by all accounts, mass confusion."

"Steve?"

"A pair of Central Park Precinct guys were close by and heard the screams. They shot and killed one perp on arrival. We all saw the second-to-last get his button punched just after we got here, and the last one is Gordon's little playmate in the squad car," the big officer reported. "All the living perps responded like they were on Angel Dust, but worse. Buncha officers got slammed around by some skinny, undernourished drug heads."

Takata was nodding agreement with that information.

"Chet?"

"EMTs and Crime Scene types are taking blood samples, but initial guesses indicate N'Hance as the most likely culprit, although they must have all had massive doses. We'll know more in a couple of hours."

Roma nodded and turned to me. "What about you, Gordon? Anything to add?"

I normally hang back a bit, but decided what the hell. "Sir, I tracked six individuals entering the park from the Girl's Gate. Tire tracks and deep footprints look like they came out of a van or other similar vehicle. The six traveled straight west across the main part of the field, till two broke off, one north and one south, each attacking an individual, both of whom were women. One of the women was killed." I waved at the same blanket-covered corpse that Fran had interviewed. "Four of the attackers concentrated on what appears to be a woman and child. Almost immediately, one attacker died of a broken neck. The woman's tracks disappear, and a large dog next takes out two of the attackers. The fourth attacker runs away to the northeast. The boy and the dog headed northwest into the woods, with one of them bleeding, most likely the dog. I tracked them to a big rock arch with a stream and trail running under it. They appeared to have held up in a little crevice, then left. That's all I could come up with, Sir." I didn't add the fact that the dog turned into a naked woman. All six of them were just staring at me.

"You a tracker, Chris?" Roma asked.

"Yes sir, since I was a kid. Worked with Search and Rescue in the Adirondacks back home," I answered.

"Can you take us to the arch?" he asked.

I did one better and walked them through the tracks right back up to the crevice in the arch, which was vacant. I showed them the few remaining blood spots, as the rain had washed away most. Chet, the technical guy, swabbed a sample, which was probably not a good thing, but there was nothing I could do about it. I spied a granola bar wrapper in the little stream that one of the team calls the Loch. The wrapper was ignored, as was the other litter floating down the waterway. The arch was apparently called Huddlestone.

Chapter 10

After walking back to the vehicles, the team broke apart, everyone headed out on separate tasks. Roma sent me back to my home precinct, but told me to meet him at the 68th in the morning. After that, Sommers dropped me at the nearest subway entrance, and I headed home. I boarded a southbound line, ignoring the other passengers' sidelong glances at my muddy uniform. A five-person street crew took up one end of the subway car, their music loud but bearable. One of them stared at me, which I ignored. Finally, I locked eyes with him, expecting a confrontation with the well-muscled young street dancer. Instead, he grinned and snapped his fingers. "I know you. You the dude on the news. Took down that crazy Hancer in the Park."

"It made the news?" I asked.

"Yeah man. Here, let me show ya." He held up his cell phone, and his buddies crowded around as we watched the news clip he'd downloaded.

"Damn man, you fast for a white dude," one the crew commented.

"Thanks." I fumbled my own cell out, thinking I should text Tanya before she saw it. Too late. My cell vibrated with an incoming text.

T: Where are u?

C: Manhattan subway—headed home.

T: Why?

C: long story. Interviewed with a special squad and ended up on a call with them.

T: Is that why you were on the news?

C: yeah. Strange day. Met a WW.

T: What?

C: what we talked about last night. Lions and tigers and bears, Oh my.

T: WHAT? Are you hurt? Bit?

C: no no. I'm fine. I helped WW and young WW.

T: Lydia asks u to describe.

C: Early 30's, reddish brown hair, tall. Kid about 8 or 9, dark brown hair.

T: When will you get home?

C: 30 minutes?

T: see u there.

Twenty minutes later, I got off the subway and headed up to the street where my car was. I had happened to park near a corner diner and as the food smells hit, my stomach protested my lack of attention to it. There wasn't much to eat at my apartment, so I went in and found a booth. The place had a well-used feel to it, and I was risking heart disease just smelling the food. A beefy, middle-aged guy was at the counter, eating his way through something that looked like meatloaf, and he eyed my muddy uniform as I made my way to the back of the restaurant. The waitress was young and punky, with multicolored hair and heavy kohl eyeliner. Her bored eyes perked up slightly as she perused my dirt-encrusted self, her mouth chewing a wad of gum. "Been mud wrestling?" she said with a smirk.

"Yeah, pretty much. How's the meatloaf?" I asked.

"A lot like my feet, worn and tired. 'Cept my feet smell better. Coffee?"

I nodded and started to peruse the menu she handed me. The short, dark cook yelled something at her and she waved him off while still studying me. I looked from him to her, and she gave me a snarky little smile, like she was enjoying irritating everyone. Obviously, she was not leaving without my order and I couldn't decide between a club sandwich and a burger, so I asked for both. She just raised both eyebrows, wrote it down, and left with a snap of her gum and a swish of her hips.

I thought about heading to the men's room and attempting to clean up my uniform. Looking down at myself, I decided it wasn't worth the effort, so I just sat and drank my coffee. The booths each had one of those mini-jukeboxes mounted on the wall above the table. None of them looked like they had worked in years.

A group of teens came in and grabbed a booth. Two girls and a guy. Just normal kids. Four sips of coffee later, two cops came in. They eyed me for a moment, nodded, and headed to the counter.

The waitress brought me the club sandwich.

"The burger will be a few minutes more. Figured you could start in on this one. Wouldn't want you to starve to death waiting."

"Thanks. I am pretty hungry."

"No shit, Sherlock. The way your clothes hang on you, it looks like you haven't seen the inside of a donut shop in weeks." She smiled and sauntered off to wait on the teens. A twenty-something couple came in, dressed casual, laughing at something. They took the booth next to mine, and when I looked up, I found the woman staring at me. The teen girls had been staring, too, and I almost regreted not heading right home to clean up, except the sandwich and fries tasted too damn good to care. Screw 'em if they've never seen a muddy cop before.

The punky waitress brought me the cheeseburger.

"Here ya go, Hero."

I squinted at her. "Huh?'

She pointed to the old television mounted in the ceiling corner behind the counter. The screen was filled with some tan guy with gleaming white teeth, running through the evening news.

"You were just on. And here I thought you were just a dirty cop."

She winked and moved to wait on the couple. The woman was staring at me again, so I put my head down and started on the burger while finishing the fries from the club sandwich. Man, I was hungry all the time now.

I got a funny little, hunchy kind of feeling about five seconds before the door opened. When the room went quiet and I finally looked up, I wasn't at all surprised to see her standing there. Everyone in the room was staring at her, and I couldn't blame them. She was more than stare-worthy. Wearing a fitted black North Face soft shell jacket and painted-on jeans, she looked like the cause of a twenty-car traffic accident.

Her electric blue eyes locked on mine as soon as I looked up. She immediately headed my way, moving with that inhuman grace, and the realization hit me that I had never witnessed her out in public before. If you've ever seen a beautiful woman enter a room and turn every head, then you'll understand a little, a very little about her effect on the diner's inhabitants. Deer in headlights—stunned—dazzled. But whereas most beautiful women would have been acutely aware and enjoying the attention, she was indifferent. Very much aware of everything around her but not interested in anything in that diner—except me. The moment I realized that, the enormity of my situation struck me. I got dizzy for a moment, a maelstrom of emotions overwhelming me. That I, who had always been forced to be alone, should now have a girlfriend because of the Hellbourne, was almost too ironic to stand. Not just any girl. I shook myself and smiled at Tatiana, who was already at the booth and looking concerned for my sanity. "Hi, I got too hungry. I'm sorry I kept you waiting. My healthy diet has gone out the window," I said as I stood up to greet her.

She looked at my empty plate and almost-consumed burger, then nodded. "Your metabolism has been increased way beyond normal. You're going to need several times more calories than you ever did before. My fault."

We both sat down, and the activity resumed in the diner, like a DVD player taken off pause, although everyone in the place was still watching Tatiana.

"Why is it your fault?" I asked quietly.

Her grin was sly. "You're eating for two, so to speak."

I laughed, and she laughed too, a soft throaty laugh that I could feel in my chest.

"Well that's fine, 'cause I really like to eat," I said.

"What a coincidence, so do I," she said with a smile that sent my pulse racing.

The punky waitress appeared, although she appeared to be somewhat intimidated.

"Can I get you anything?" she asked Tatiana.

"A glass of water and a big piece of chocolate cake, if you have any."

The waitress turned away, but I could hear her say under her breath, "Figures, and she probably won't gain an ounce."

I glanced at Tatiana. "Cake?"

"It's for you. You need more calories and you like chocolate cake. You told me so."

Chapter 11

My Xterra fascinated Tatiana, not that it's anything special. She rifled through all the CDs, looked through the glove compartment and center console, and even crawled into the backseat to see what the ride was like from back there, all the while asking questions. Is it good in the snow? Do I drive it off road? Do I like being high off the road?

We were at my apartment in no time, and she danced ahead of me as I trudged into the elevator. Lydia was pacing around my tiny place, talking on her cell, the locks on my door apparently not vampire proof. She was wearing a dark blue dress over black tights and looked like a college kid as she waved hello to us while continuing her conversation. I headed to the shower immediately after dropping my gun belt and vest at the closet. After toweling off, I pulled on a pair of jeans and a halfway clean tee from the bathroom floor and joined the girls, carrying the laundry basket of muddy cop uniform.

Tatiana motioned to Lydia, who was just finishing another call.

"Chris, take off your shirt. I want Lydia to see."

"Hey now, this ain't no strip club!" I joked.

They rolled their eyes in unison.

I pulled my tee off, and Lydia's eyes widened. "Damn, Northern! We gotta feed you more."

I must have looked puzzled because she asked where I had a mirror. I pointed to the closet door, which had a full-length one attached inside.

She opened the closet door wide enough so I could see myself, and I realized what they were talking about. I looked different. I'm five ten, usually one hundred and ninety pounds. Despite my Scottish heritage, I tan easily. Only now, my tan had turned sorta dusky. My cheekbones were really pronounced and my stupid eyes even more freakishly violet than before, highlighted by my dark skin and brown hair. My torso didn't have a scrape of fat under the skin.

I don't look at myself in mirrors except to make sure my uniform is straight. I don't like mirrors because they always show me my odd eyes, the same eyes that caused me so much trouble during my school years. But the image now would have made a bodybuilder jealous, because I was ripped. I never carry much body fat, but I had to be less than two percent now, which was probably dangerous, and that was point the girls were trying to convey. "Wow, I look like even more of a freak."

"No, Northern, freak is not what we were thinking."

Lydia was tapping her bottom lip in thought. "Most humans react to vampire blood with a speeded-up metabolism, but this seems extreme. I think we should take you to the doctor."

"Doctor? You're kidding, right? What doctor would understand vampire stuff?" I asked

"A vampire doctor. He's got about ten medical degrees, so he knows his stuff. Better than a human doctor would. He's been Tanya's doctor all her life."

Lydia's car was a BMW Five series, silver, with lots of power, and she drove it with skill. We raced through the Brooklyn streets, and I should have been nervous about her driving, but Tatiana, who had decided to sit in back, distracted me. She was busy studying me, and I got nervous.

131

Finally, I had enough.

"What?"

She smiled. "I like watching you."

"Well, I like looking at you, too, but you've got that look again."

"What look is that?" she asked.

"It's a cross between a Cheshire Cat grin and a kid with a new toy."

Lydia snorted from up front. "That describes it to a T, Northern."

Tatiana frowned. "You're not a toy. But you are mine. Right?" she asked, seeking reassurance.

"Yes, I am yours—at least till you come to your senses."

Lydia sighed up front and a warm hand gripped my chin, turning my head to meet a pair of sparking blue eyes. Annoyed eyes.

"I have senses you don't even know about, and all of them agree. You are mine, Christian Gordon. You always will be." The hard glint softened and she kissed me, then shook my chin as she let go. "And I'll stare at you if I want. I like to stare at you." She huffed like any girl might. I decided to stare back, getting trapped in her cerulean gaze.

Dr. Singh had been a doctor long before he was Turned. His unassuming house in lower Brooklyn also held his office, which was in the refinished basement and had its own entrance. Refined and possessed of the trademark vampire grace, the doctor greeted Lydia and

Tatiana warmly, while his assistant led me to the exam room, which looked white and institutional like every other exam room I had ever been in. The biggest difference was the lack of pharmaceutical company posters and trade-name drug marketing paraphernalia. Instead, the walls had charts showing the moon phases and sunrise and sunset tables and something called a Druidic Calendar.

Dr. Singh's assistant made me nervous. Tall, maybe five seven, with brown hair and Eurasian features, she was professional and businesslike as she took my vitals. No small talk and very little direct eye contact, which was unusual based on all the vampires I had met so far. But despite her direct, no-nonsense manner, I kept catching her taking little sniffs near me and casting furtive sidelong glances at me. She drew blood, which had me on edge, as she spent an inordinate amount of time settling the vials in their little carrier tray, and I swear she was sniffing their caps. I was greatly relieved when she handed me the obligatory paper gown and told me to strip to down to my underwear. Then she fussed around cleaning up for a long time before finally leaving. I skipped the gown, figuring my boxer briefs would be modest enough for a vampire doctor.

In a radical departure from official physician code, the good doctor came right in with hardly any delay. Unlike his creepy assistant, Dr. Singh was personable and had a soothing bedside manner. He proceeded to give me a thorough exam, including eyesight and hearing, asking me health questions all the while. We started with early childhood illnesses and worked our way finally to recent events. Tatiana and Lydia had told him I had been the recipient of Tatiana's blood.

"Mr. Gordon, it may seem like a waste of time to go back over your history, as I'm sure you feel that your current condition is the result of imbibing Tatiana's rather potent blood, but I like to be thorough," he said., "It is very common for a human who is both fed on and receives blood from his or her vampire, to have an increased metabolic rate and experience heightened senses and greater vitality. These changes occur gradually over time and are beneficial to the donor. It may be an evolved trait of the virus that causes vampirism, helping its host by keeping a healthy donor alive longer. But the degree and speed of your responses are... well... staggering. I'll have to double check, but I'm fairly certain that our records don't reflect any similar case, ever."

"Could it be that Tatiana's blood would do this to anyone?" I asked.

He shook his head.

"I've been studying Tatiana's blood since she was born. I delivered her, you know. And I'm the only one, other than you, to have handled her blood. Tatiana's is very similar to the blood of the Elder vampires, the council that rules us. These individuals are all over a thousand years old, while Tatiana is your age. Your exact age, in fact. Hmmm." He paused in thought for a moment, then continued. "Potent blood like that would convey much greater benefits than younger vampires, but nothing like what you are exhibiting. Your hearing is beyond human normal at both the low and high ranges, your eyesight is twenty/five, your reflexes are just about on par with a newly Turned vampire. And your metabolic rate is about four times higher than that of an average human male your age. I'm hoping that slows down a bit, as it usually does with normal donor cases. Currently, you haven't begun to cannibalize your muscle tissue, but that point can't be far off, and you absolutely must keep some fat tissue for healthy nerve function. You're just at about two percent, based on the near-infrared measurement that my assistant took."

"Was that the thing she aimed at my bicep?" I asked.

"Yes. But we really need to stop you from losing any more. I want you to stop working out. Your fitness levels will continue to improve without effort, and that is one way to slow your fat loss. I also want you to eat as much high-fat, high-calorie food as you can, like these." He handed me a high-calorie protein bar and waited for me to nod my acknowledgement of his instructions, then changed subjects. "Mr. Gordon, can I assume that the ladies have conveyed to you the need to keep our world secret from the general human population?"

I nodded.

"Then you must be careful to not display your new differences to your fellow humans, although I'm not sure you are still human at all."

That statement alarmed me. "What?"

"Well, I won't know till I complete a DNA analysis and review the blood workups, but I don't believe these changes are temporary. I think that you've been changed as much by Tatiana as she has been by you. And by the way, I can't begin to tell you how thrilled I am with her reawakening." He beamed at me, then patted my shoulder. "From what I understand, you've always been different from other humans, eh?"

"Well yeah, between my freaky violet eyes and screwy aura, but nothing like this. Is it fatal? Is it turning me into a vampire?" I asked, beginning to get really worried.

"Fatal? Oh no! In fact, it will most likely extend your life indefinitely. And no, I don't believe it is Turning you. That process is much different. Plus, you show no signs of being drawn to blood or sensitive to the sun, right? There, you see? Nothing to worry about. However, there appears to be one other aspect we should discuss. Lydia mentioned that you were drawing an unusual amount of attention from vampires in the club last Friday."

I just looked at him blankly, and he laughed.

"You probably didn't notice it, but she did. Some humans are naturally more attractive to vampires than others. Your AB blood type is part of the reason. Very rare. Only four percent of the population is AB, and many vampires love it. So you smell good. But there are other factors, like being exceptionally fit and maybe your unusual aura that can attract our attention. Whatever the case, that attractiveness has also been amplified by whatever changes you are going through. So you need to be aware and careful. I don't think most vampires would chance... ah, sampling you and incurring Tatiana's wrath. Especially now that she is aware and becoming more formidable by the day. But newer, less disciplined vampires might lose control. You will need to be on guard."

"You're saying I'm vampire bait."

"Hmmm, I suppose that's as good a name for it as any."

It was one thing to hang out with Tatiana and Lydia, who I trusted, although I had known them both less than a week. But to know that I was going to be attracting every fanged being in the Big Apple was downright scary.

There was a quick knock on the door and Tatiana entered with Lydia on her heels before the doctor could answer.

"Is everything all right? Chris, why are you upset?" Tatiana asked.

"Well, I was just telling him about his... attractiveness to our kind. Tatiana, did you sense his discomfort from outside?" Dr. Singh asked.

"Yes. I can usually tell what Chris is feeling and where he is."

"Yeah Doc. She can locate our boy here from several miles away," Lydia supplied.

"Fascinating. There is usually some form of donor/donee bond, but it takes time to form." He looked thoughtful as he mulled this new piece of information.

"So, the Doc told you about being vamp candy huh?" Lydia asked.

Tatiana's expression was rather stark as I answered, "Yeah, it's a little... unnerving."

"Well, the first thing we're going to do is put an off-limits sign on you to keep away the rifraff," Lydia said.

"An off-limits sign huh?"

"Yeah, we'll mark you with Tanya's sign, and that should keep the smart ones away."

"Sounds like a cattle brand to me," I replied, still out of sorts with the situation. Tatiana froze in place at these words, but Lydia shrugged them right off. "Think of it as a stallion brand if it makes you feel better. It's just a little tattoo, see?" She turned her head and pulled her shirt away from her neck, revealing a small tattoo of three letters: TAD.

"What is that? Some sorta vampire word or something?" I asked.

The girls looked at each other, then back to me.

"No, it's her initials. T. A. D." Lydia shrugged.

"What's the 'A' stand for?" I asked.

Tatiana answered. "Antonovna."

"So that would mean your father's name is Anton?" I guessed.

"Very good, Chris." Tatiana was impressed.

"Well, the Internet knows all, ya know."

We thanked the doctor and climbed back into the BMW. Lydia changed topics as soon as the car was in motion. "So, Chris what was this about werewolves today?" she asked.

So I spent the rest of the car ride explaining the Special Situations Squad job interview, the attack in Central Park, and the redhead werewolf mother and son.

"And you didn't tell them about the woman being a were, or about us?" Tatiana asked.

"No way. I don't know anything about this Special Situation group. I don't know if they know about you guys or about weres, and I'm supposed to serve and protect, so that's what I did."

It seemed pretty clear-cut to me. I didn't struggle with the ethics of it for a moment. Spending your life fighting Hellbourne tends to simplify your moral code a bit.

"You know, Chris, you seem to draw monsters like flies to honey. Do you have any idea who she was?" Lydia asked.

"Er... no," I answered.

"Her name is Afina. She's the mate of the Alpha of the City. And you saved her."

"I didn't save her. She saved herself and her son. I just gave her some food, water, and a cell phone.

I guessed that she would have a Pack or something to help her."

"Well, I spoke to my contact in the Pack, and she and her mate, Brock, are grateful to you. Things have been a little strained between our Coven and the Pack, and today's events could have been a disaster. She smelled the vampire scent on you and she witnessed your wrestling match with the addict in the park. You may have just patched up a pretty good rift between us."

"Dumb luck, really," I answered.

"You seem to have an inordinate amount of that, then," Lydia replied with a grin.

"Dumb or luck?" I questioned, not sure if I had just received a shot.

"Yes," was her reply. Yup, definitely a shot.

Tatiana asked me a question before I could fire anything back at Lydia. "Christian, are you going to work for Inspector Roma in the Special Squad?"

"I don't know if they even want me yet. I'm supposed to meet him tomorrow morning, so I suspect he may have made up his mind by then."

"You know, he's been trying to meet with Galina for years now, but she blows him off every time. I think he suspects what we are. You need to be ready if he asks you to introduce him," Lydia said.

"Well, that's an easy one. I just tell him the truth. Galina hates me. That should take care of it."

"Mother does not hate you, Christian. And I have told her that you will be part of my life unless you choose not to be. I have warned her I will leave if she tries to scare you away."

Lydia chuckled. "Yeah, and since Doctor Singh reports his medical findings about Tat directly to Elder Senka, I'm doubly sure that the Elders will want to meet you Wednesday night."

"What's Wednesday night?" I asked.

"Oh, we hadn't gotten around to that yet. The Elders arrive to see Tanya tomorrow night. Wednesday is a formal reception party, and you are a guest of honor."

"Me? At a vampire party? Is that a good idea? Aren't I sorta bait? Why do they want to see me?" This party sounded like a really bad idea. I liked hanging around with my two vampires—it just seemed natural— but a whole party of unknown and unfriendly vampires didn't sound like my cup of tea.

"Well, they are insisting on meeting the human who saved our girl here, woke her up so to speak, and is the object of her affection. You really need to be there."

"Well, what do I wear? I don't have party clothes, just uniforms and casual clothes. I can't go without a suit or something. There isn't really time to get anything either."

"Jeesh, Northern. Have some faith. We're already on it. You'll not only have the right clothes, but you'll look gooood!"

Without any other excuses, I settled back to silence, thinking that this party would be a fiasco.

Chapter 12

Tuesday was the day that I died. Or maybe the day I should have died. Either way, it felt like I died.

It started off normally enough. I got up and made myself a ten-egg omelet with cheese and ham. Okay, so maybe that's not so normal. That still left my egg supply almost untouched. When the girls took me home from the doctor's the previous night, Tatiana had apparently been placing some calls on the way. A pair of young vampires—I was beginning to get a feel for vampire age—met us at my apartment with a truckload of groceries. My fridge was now stocked with cases of eggs, cheeses, cold cuts, milk, and veggies. My freezer was loaded with Stouffers frozen dinners and half gallons of Häagen-Dazs ice cream. Every flat surface in the galley kitchen held cases of protein bars, canisters of nuts, and six-packs of protein shakes. If that wasn't enough, the front of the fridge had gift cards to a half dozen take-out restaurants, held in place by magnets. I felt like I was being fattened for Christmas dinner, but realistically, I would most likely burn through it in a couple of weeks.

So, I skipped my regular workout and spent the time eating and doing some Internet research on jewelry. The girls had informed me that my presence was also mandatory at the combined Plasma–

Halloween-and-Tatiana-birthday-party on Friday. I would not have to wear a costume, but a gift seemed in order. The last girl I had bought a gift for had been my grandmother, who had died eight years ago. I had never bought a gift for a girlfriend-type person. Seeing how this might be my only chance to do so—who knew if I would make it through another year—and seeing how the income from my trust fund had bulked up my savings account, I decided jewelry was in order.

What do you get a vampire princess who would be called on by some of the oldest and richest beings on the planet over the next few days? The only thing I could think of was a comment that Lydia had made about Tatiana being hard on bracelets because of her sparring. Apparently, she used real blades in practice, and her bracelets were always getting chopped and slashed because she didn't get them off in time. Blocking a blade with her arm was standard practice, as she healed almost instantly from anything but a cut made by silver. Healing gold or platinum wasn't so easy. I found a shop here in Brooklyn that produced the very specialized pieces that I wanted and drove over to finalize my order in person. I paid extra to ensure it would be ready by Friday, and then headed home.

After dressing in one of my few clean uniforms, I went to meet Inspector Roma. That didn't go so well, or maybe it went fine depending on perspective. For our meeting, he had chosen a Bruegger's bagel shop not far from the Sixty-Eighth Precinct house. He was already seated with a large frappuccino and a bagel sandwich, so after loading my own tray with stuff, I sat down across from him. He eyed my tray with a touch of amazement, but cut right to the chase after I started to dig in.

"Chris, I have to tell you that the entire team and I were very impressed yesterday with both your swift and timely actions and your insight into the crime scene. You have a lot of potential in police work. However, most of the team felt you were less than completely forthright with us. They all felt as if you were holding back.

"Chris, you have to understand that we have to be able to trust each other with our lives, which is why the whole team gets to have a say in potential team members. The group just didn't feel like that was there with you." He finished, then waited expectantly for me to answer. I had been chewing a big bite of turkey with provolone on an Everything bagel and had to wipe the excess mayo off my face before I could answer.

"That's cool, Inspector. I understand completely," I said. "I felt the same way about each of them, Sir. Nothing bad, just like everybody was holding back some important stuff. Frankly, I've always worked on my own, so it would be hard to trust them, as well."

"Well Chris, we couldn't bring you fully into the loop until we were more fully certain of you, now could we," he responded, just a touch defensively.

"Absolutely, Sir. I couldn't agree more. But I have to wonder, Sir, just how you build that level of trust so quickly among such a diverse group. I mean, it must be really tough to find someone with such a rare gift or skill set AND have them be instantly trustworthy, so to speak."

He frowned a little at my words.

I continued. "I'm not at all surprised at the outcome, Sir. People have always been a little leery of me. Might be my freaky eye color or just something about my talents that they sense on an unconscious level. I have to tell you, though, that I'm surprised Detective Velasquez even bothered to bring me to your attention in the first place. I don't think she has much use for me personally. Sir."

"Well, your people-reading skills seem to be less acute than your other... skills... which you never really explained. But you should know that Detective Velasquez was your biggest advocate."

He was annoyed by my answers. I was annoyed with his. I never asked to be in his little band of spook hunters anyway. I got the feeling that he had expected a different outcome to this meeting, but as annoyed as I was by yet another rejection by my own kind, it was best for me to stay off the team. I didn't think the vampires and weres of the City would be excited about my sharing their existence with the authorities.

Inspector Roma watched me with a level gaze, and my enhanced vision let me see the color that had flooded his olive-toned face. I finally responded.

"Inspector Roma, thank you for the opportunity to meet your team and witness you all in action. I fully understand the Team's reluctance regarding myself."

No use making an enemy if I could avoid it. He gave me a curt nod, then felt obliged to threaten me.

"Officer Gordon, I trust you understand that any and all information that you have become privy to including the nature of my Squad is absolutely restricted. If I discover that you have divulged anything, you will wish you had never met me."

Not much to say to that, so I simply shook his hand, and he left. I stayed to finish my lunch. Job interviews make me hungry.

I checked in to the Sixty-Eighth's Muster room, and Sarge assigned me to prisoner detail, which is mostly a pain in the ass. All shift, I felt like people were watching me and, in fact, I did pick up on a bunch of glances in my direction, mostly from women, but some males as well. It left me edgy, as I am used to staying under the radar and not drawing much attention. Finally, the shift was over and I headed out into the cold October night. My Xterra was parked quite a ways away, as parking around the Precinct had been tight.

I was three blocks from the Sixty-eighth and a little less than one from my truck when I heard the scream. I was just crossing the opening of an alley between a bookshop and an auto parts place when it ripped through the night. Female, terrified, and in pain. I grabbed my flashlight and raced into the alley, my right hand triggering the mic hooked to my left shirt pocket. The belt radio attached to it gave a blast of static and nothing more just as a second scream sounded up ahead. Feet slapping on the pavement, I raced toward the sound.

A pale figure appeared in my light's beam, instantly recognizable as a woman, the left side of her face dripping blood. Tall, Olive Oyl thin, with sharp, pointed features and large black eyes, she was sobbing hysterically and pointing back the way she came. I put myself between her and the back of the alley, illuminating everything with my light, my right hand now on my Glock. I couldn't see anything, so I turned to ask the woman, and a horse kicked me into the next county. I blacked out for a second, the impact hard enough to jar my brain where I stood. When my lights came back on, I found myself lying against the alley wall, daggers of pain lancing through my chest with every breath. The woman was squatting athletically in front of me, a feral gleam in her black eyes as she licked her lips. Her features seemed to flicker, like her face was struggling with something else's face, a furry one. Her voice was a hissing whisper when she spoke.

"So easy to fool. So easy to kill."

She apparently wasn't much for monologuing because she stood up and pulled a long, slick blade from somewhere under her dress. Wicked fast, the silver edge slashed at my throat, but my left arm magically put itself in the knife's path. I felt a tug across my forearm, but nothing else. She stepped back, a look of disbelief flitting across her ferret features. Nodding to herself, she shot forward, feinting then slashing with the blade, but this time both arms jumped up and received the cuts aimed for my throat. My lungs were hissing, and it occurred to me that her kick had done the job her knife wasn't able to. One of my ribs was broken, despite my vest, and the bone must have punctured a lung. Breathing was fire and life, but the fire was winning.

She paused again, then made a second blade appear in her left hand. Jabbing at me with the left, she pulled her right back for the kill stroke. I couldn't keep my arms up and darkness was crowding the edges of my vision. I was certain I was dying, because I saw a vision of Tatiana's face appear over the weasel-woman's right shoulder. The vision seemed odd, because Tatiana's eyes were jet black, which is not how I would want to remember her as I died. My vision continued to crumble, but it seemed like a big silver object was flashing toward the weasel's head, and then I couldn't see anymore. A wicked growl filled my ears, followed by wet ripping noises and soft thuds, then nothing.

Death seemed to be warm and satiny. And dark. Very dark. Then I realized that I could open my eyes, or, at least, try to open them. Emergency Services Jaws of Life would have been handy, but despite my lack of heavy duty, hydraulically powered rescue gear, I was finally able to get them partially open.

Death was apparently illuminated by a combination of candles and vintage lava lamps. The bed I found myself in was the better part of a half-acre in size, with white satin sheets and a purple satin comforter. Purple?

"Hey, monster bait, you awake?" came a soft greeting from the door of the bedroom.

Lydia moved into the room, and Tatiana appeared immediately behind her. "How are you feeling?" Lydia asked.

"Hmm? Oh, I feel all right... I guess," I answered, my attention still on Tatiana. A much-changed Tatiana. I had never seen her like this before. She was wearing a black, tightly fitted jumpsuit of some leather-like material. Twin sword hilts poked up over her shoulders, and a long-bladed knife was strapped to the outside of each forearm. Her feet were encased in soft, flexible boots that buckled up the front and rose to her calves. But the biggest change was her face. It was cold and remote, her blue eyes frosty.

"What happened?" I finally asked, still watching this alien Tatiana.

"You got suckered in by a were weasel. They are the primary assassins of the were world, and this one was getting ready to punch your ticket. We," Lydia pointed to Tatiana and herself, "were on our way to see you, and suddenly she leaped out of the car and ran off. I followed her, and by the time I caught up, she was finishing off the were. With my car door, which she took with her when she jumped from my car. It was kinda messy. Weasel paste. We got some of her magical blood into you and you healed right up. Like a

vampire would. Freaky. But you feel okay now?" she
asked.

I tore my gaze from Tatiana and gave myself a
quick once over. I felt great, although I seemed to be
naked under the sheets. "Ah, yeah, I guess. Ah, Tanya.
What's up? What's the matter?" I asked, puzzled and
very worried by her appearance.

"Hello, Christian. I'm glad you are well." She
didn't seem glad.

"And now that you're awake, I need to say some
things to you," she continued.

"Jeez, Tanya. What are ya doin'? Not like this!
Not this moment!" Lydia objected.

Tatiana's head snapped to look at the little
vampire, who she addressed after a moment.

"Yes, Lydia. Now. Before a moment longer." I
didn't know what was happening, but the dread I felt in
the pit of my stomach was making me queasy.

"Chris" she began. Not Christian—this was bad.

"I have decided that my Mother was right. I am
grateful to you for saving my life last Friday. And I'm
grateful to you for snapping me out of my... catharsis.
But I'm awake now. And I think we are even at this
point. I find myself growing rapidly, catching up for lost
time. I'm afraid my infatuation with you was, well,
simply a girlish crush."

A microburst of shame flashed across her face as
she said this.

"So, if I misled you, then you have my apologies.
But I'm afraid that the simple truth is that I've outgrown

that stage. I've outgrown you. It would be best for you to leave me alone." She spun on her heel and slipped from the room like a wraith.

My heart had stopped beating as soon as she had said her mother was right. And I couldn't seem to make my diaphragm work. The weasel had kicked like a mule, but this hit me ten times harder. My vision started to darken from the outside in, spiraling down until I couldn't see, some primitive response to my body's inability to decide to fight or flee.

"Chris... Chris, breathe!" Lydia's voice was competing with a train sound that filled my ears.

Reflex kicked in and my lungs filled with a sudden, almost painful *whoosh* of air. After what seemed like thirty or forty years, my vision came back to find Lydia hovering in front of me worriedly.

"What the hell was that? What just happened?"

"Chris, listen to me. You can't believe that she meant that. It's... it's complicated."

I was scrambling out of bed, ignoring my nakedness and moving toward a pile of clothes.

"Complicated? That wasn't fucking complicated!" I yelled. I pulled on a pair of leather pants and a black tee shirt from the pile of folded clothes. "That was exactly what Galina said would happen."

Stunned disbelief was giving over swiftly to red, red rage. Rage at Tatiana, rage at Galina, rage at Lydia for telling me it had been real, and mostly, rage at myself. The pain was unbelievable, worse than any physical feeling I had ever had. I could feel it in every cell of my body, and I needed out. The fight-or-flight decision had been made, and it was flight time. I almost missed it in my hurry to be gone, but a big duffel bag with part of my cop gear sticking out of an open zipper caught my eye just enough for me to grab it.

"Chris, wait! Let me explain!"

" SAVE IT! I'VE GOT ALL THE EXPLANATION I NEED! NOW HOW THE HOLY HELL DO I GET OUTTA HERE?" I was screaming at this point. A human would have flinched, but she just pointed sadly at the doorway and said, "Down the hall to the stairs, down two flights, and out the front door."

Barefoot, I practically flew down the stairs and ended up on the ground floor of Galina's brownstone. The big oak front doors were directly ahead, and the front room and foyer were filled with vampires dressed in expensive clothes, mingling with goblets of thick red blood in hand. I could smell the blood, and I was instantly the center of their curious attention, but I ignored it and headed for the door. A young vampire dressed in a white shirt and black pants, with a tray of goblets, moved to intercept me, his free hand out, palm facing me in an obvious order to halt. I pooled my rage into my right hand and punched my aura in his direction. He was four feet away from my outstretched hand, but he flew back through the air and smashed into the wall seven feet up. Didn't know I could do that. I ignored him and focused on the front door, which was locked and wouldn't open. With no obvious way to unlock it, I looked around and found a vase sitting on a thick marble column.

I grabbed the vase and threw it to the closest vampire, not watching to see if he would snatch it from the air. Instead I grabbed the column, which had to heft a good two hundred pounds, and began to advance on the door, only to find Lydia there ahead of me. She manipulated the lock somehow and opened the door, standing aside. I dropped the column and a moment later made it into the predawn darkness.

Chapter 13

I found myself at home, later, just as the sun was coming up. I was numb, inside and out and standing outside my apartment, pushing at the locked door and not really sure how to get in. If I had applied some thought, I would have looked for my key ring in the dusty duffel that I'd dragged around town, or found my hidden key in the hallway. But thinking was bad, it only led in painful directions, and so I refused to start. The apartment door behind me opened, and I felt someone step out and stop. The scent of peaches and kiwi told me it was Paige, the soft scuffle of her running shoes told me she was headed out for her morning jog.

"Chris? Are you all right?" she asked.

I shook my head and stared at the door, twisting the knob without result. I knew I could force it open, but that didn't seem to be the answer. Paige stepped up beside me, looking at me with a worried expression.

"Did you lock yourself out?"

I nodded.

"What about your spare key?" She reached up, on tiptoe, and brushed the top of my jamb. I don't keep my key there, but her motion triggered a memory, and I moved to the building Super's closet at the end of the hall, between our apartments. The spare was above that jamb. Wow, real clever. I fumbled it at the lock till Paige gently took it from my hand and unlocked the door. Later, I would look back and wonder at how I must have looked—barefoot, torn black tee, leather pants, unkempt—but at that moment, I simply nodded thanks and slid into my apartment dragging my bag behind me.

"Okay, well... I guess I'll just head out on my run. Do you need anything?" she asked.

I shook my head, sat on the edge of my futon, and listened to her gently shut the door. She stood outside my door for a moment, perhaps deciding if she needed to do anything else, then padded down the hall for her morning run. I won't bore you with the details of my morning, but just a comment on the daily grind. As mundane as our regular lives can be, sometimes, when we've had a great shock, that steady regular routine can be a Godsend. It certainly was for me. In fact, it may have been the only merciful thing that God had ever sent me.

Much later in the day, I arrived at work, more or less on time, dressed more or less respectably and essentially functional. Ignoring the steady stream of stares that I seemed to get nowadays, I settled into the Muster room, waiting for the briefing. The room was buzzing with excitement, and after a time, it penetrated my haze. Something big was up. Twenty minutes behind schedule, the Lieutenant took the podium and called us to attention.

"Listen up. We have a big operation going down tonight, here in the Sixty-Eighth. The short and long of it is we've got info on the location of the Hance lab and we're hitting it in about forty-five minutes. Special Ops will run the show, we're providing backup, security, and support. Captain Ortez will brief us on the op order."

Ortez was my height and built like a salt-and-pepper-haired bull. He spent the next twenty minutes detailing the operation, and then we broke out by squad to head to the lab location.

Our squad was specifically tasked to follow the main entry teams into the warehouse where the labs were supposed to be located, an order that puzzled all of us. When I spotted Roma and his Triple S team conferring with Ortez, I understood. Roma was arraigning some special backup if something unusual popped up. The fact that he was using me and putting my unsuspecting squad in harm's way at the same time only added to the pit of rage doing a slow burn in my belly.

The Special Ops teams formed up, the snipers got in position, security fanned out around the property, and the command van was up and running. We hung back, at the very rear of the entry formation, Roma's team just ahead of us. Sommers and the Asian guy were suited up SWAT style, but the rest were dressed normal, with the addition of heavy body armor. Although I did notice the Triple S folks inserting forearm-length thirty-three-round magazines of nine millimeter ammo into their Glocks. Velasquez looked my way a couple of times, but Roma ignored me. Most of the Sixty-Eighth guys were geared normal, but my squad rated assault weight vests and shotguns for Sarge and Henderson. We all had earpieces for our radios. With everyone in position, we hunkered down and waited.

Finally, the word came down and, almost anticlimactically, the operation was underway. Sometimes a raid will be noisy and full of flash, but on a big building like this, with multiple levels and potential booby traps, discretion is a better choice. The doors were breached with a modicum of fanfare, and the teams entered fast but carefully. Bomb squad guys were with each of the entry teams, looking for trip wires and beams of light. It turns out Silly String is great for finding trip wires without setting them off. There were gobs of bright blue and green chemical string smeared into the concrete floor of the warehouse as we moved into the darkness. Sarge and Henderson were following the rest of us, as the squad's ostensible purpose was rear security and they had the firepower. I moved myself up to the front, as I was aware that I was the firepower if things got hincky in a demonic way.

Some of the troops ahead had spread out to clear the first floor, but most headed into stairwells that only went down. As we started down the industrial metal stairs, I noticed that it was the lanky tech guy Aikens who was just ahead of me. More cops split off to cover the first underground level and a second, but we kept going down and were just reaching the third when the shooting started. The sound of full auto fire ripped through the stairwell from below, with a secondary echo coming through the earpiece. Unnaturally calm voices that could have been talking ball scores detailed the action to the rest of us. Groups of crazies like the ones in the park, some apparently armed with guns, were slowing our advance. The well-trained Ops guys were taking them apart with professional ease.

We reached the third level and broke out into a vast underground room, entering at the top level. For some reason, it reminded me of Plasma, with the dance floor being below ground-level entry. Flashes of M4 assault rifle fire lit the dark and handheld lights were probing the darkness in every direction below us. Suddenly, the chatter on the radio became panicked at the same moment an unholy roar filled the room. Magnesium flares burst into light, and the action below was revealed. Teams of Ops guys were bunched up, back to back, firing in every direction. As I watched, horrified, one team was suddenly swept away like bowling pins, but I couldn't see anything hit them.

I unfocused my eyes and looked with my Sight. Something big was moving at incredible speed around the room, ignoring gunfire and swatting men around like toys, roaring as it tore through the heavily armed cops. I couldn't see its shape clearly, but it had four legs and its aura was green, red, and PURPLE. A greasy black strand hung from its neck, stretching back into the inky darkness at the other end of the huge room. A man-sized blot of deeper black moved about in that gloom, and I instantly knew that a Hellbourne held the reins of the monstrous thing crunching up our guys. Without thinking about what I was doing, I hit the stairs that clung to the wall and raced down to the floor below. As I ran, I tried to watch the hell beast with my Sight, but moving while using Sight is like running with three-D glasses on. Not good. After reverting to regular vision, I discovered that the thing gave off sparks as it ravaged the cops in its path. Not a lot, but enough that I could track its otherwise invisible position with some accuracy. "Hey Sparky, over here!" I yelled at it, and two glowing red eyes suddenly swung in my direction. Uh oh! That worked a little too well. It charged me instantly, but things slowed down and it didn't seem quite so fast anymore. I jumped to my right as it ripped through the space I had been occupying and also through the steel railing of the stairway I had just jumped from. I struck at it with my pooled aura, and I know I touched it, because the giant beast grunted, but didn't slow.

>Do you like my pet, Gordon?<

I looked for the source of the voice, but it had come from everywhere and nowhere.

>I brought him here just for you<

Hellbourne had never spoken to me this way before, but the vile quality the words carried with them could only belong to demonkind. I spoke normally, knowing it would hear me as I readied for another charge.

"Yeah, he's frisky all right. Whadda ya call something like that?"

It laughed a greasy laugh, and chills ran down my spine.

>Why, it's a DamnedThing, of course. They take forever to create and train, but I rather enjoy the process, even if they don't.

>I've been saving it for a special occasion and this seems... right<

Sparky charged me again, and again, I was able to jump away while slashing with my aura-infused right hand. This time, the Damnedthing spun and swiped at me. I was very close to it and the center of its taloned paw hit me in the chest and sent me flying, landing hard on the concrete floor. Had I been a half a foot further away when it clocked me, the dimly visible sickle-like claws would have about sliced me in half. It moved unhurriedly toward me and I struggled to get away, but my legs had gone on strike. I couldn't even stand up to face my death head on. It stood over me, and I could see its faint outline. Bear-like, but the size of a Volkswagen Beetle.

>Well, that didn't take long. We'll take good care of your little vampire. Goodbye, Gordon<

The beast lowered its keg-sized head to sniff me, and I saw the nebulous black collar that held its throat like a hell-forged choke chain, the oily black tendrils running into the creature's back and neck. With nothing left to lose, I reached with my left hand and, grabbing the slick blackness, yanked with everything I had. The thick, inky strand squirmed in my hand like an eel, then abruptly parted with the sound of rotten flesh tearing. The black leash let go, releasing the monster from its Hellbourne master. The Damnedthing stood still for a moment, its huge jaws hanging over my torso, dripping gooey saliva onto my chest, then I saw a light of awareness flare in its glowing ember eyes. It reared up on its hind feet like a Kodiak bear and roared at its new freedom, shaking dust from the girders above. Suddenly, it whirled and lunged after the Hellbourne that had recently held its leash. Its roar shook the building, and an enormous crash of metal joined the mix. The sounds receded into the distance, echoing strangely, and were almost immediately replaced by the moans of the wounded and shaken cops calling to each other and trying to restore order. I lay back for a moment, my head pounding from a collision with the concrete floor that I hadn't noticed in the excitement of imminent death.

My squad found me a few minutes later, and Sarge called for a medic. I waved him off, indicating he should help someone seriously injured. The last thing I needed was for a medically trained individual to document my rapidly healing wounds.

The efficient machine that is the NYPD soon had generators, lights, and organization. The Special Situation Squad was running things and pretty quick, Velasquez and Roma had pulled me into a quiet corner to debrief me while DeMarco and Aikens looked over the sophisticated drug lab that had been found in one corner of the vast room. Sommers and Takata moved to the dark part of the room, their weapon lights illuminating the wreckage of double industrial doors leading into a tunnel. Joined by one of the few intact Entry teams, they followed the carnage into the tunnels beyond.

Roma and Velasquez both listened carefully as I ran through my part in the altercation with the Damnedthing and Hellbourne. The Inspector paused me for a moment and called Aikens back over, then had me restart my narrative from the beginning.

"Chet, you ever come across a mention of a Damnedthing before?" Roma asked the skinny technician. Aikens thought about it, then answered, "I don't remember any details, Inspector, but there is something vaguely familiar about it. I'll need to delve into the archives and make some calls."

"Do that now. I'm going to need more information about it before I can even attempt to explain it to the Commissioner," Roma said. I learned a lot from that sentence. Roma had more juice than I thought if he reported directly to the NYPD Commissioner.

Aikens left to get his research underway and I continued with my play-by-play. When I got to the odd conversation between myself and the Hellbourne, Gina interrupted with a question.

"Have the demons ever talked to you before?" she asked.

"Well, the free-floating or geographic kind, the ones you guys rate on your scale-ten system, almost always talk to me. Taunting, insulting, threatening, it's all part of their own brand of psych-ops. But the mobile Hellbourne have never addressed me before. Hellbourne don't linger or hesitate when I show up, they just react really quickly. I think it's because they can't track me. I'm cloaked from them like they're cloaked from everybody else. Pisses them off."

"But this one knew you?"

"Well, they all know of me. They always know stuff about me. That's why I don't have friends or, particularly, girlfriends. They would know immediately and use that person against me," I explained.

They both looked at me blankly for a moment, then Gina's mouth dropped open as she thought about what I had just said.

"Explain that again," Roma said.

So I detailed the results of my one and only date in high school. This time, their expressions reflected a much worse emotion: pity.

"But wait, didn't that Hellbourne say they would take care of your girlfriend?" Gina asked.

I had changed that part of my narrative. I didn't mention the vampire part, just the girlfriend part.

"It was referring to a girl that they have already targeted. I've been actively protecting her, and they aren't happy about it," I said.

"Who is the girl?" Roma asked. I hesitated, not ready to divulge her name, and he frowned at my silence. He started to speak, probably an order, but Velasquez interrupted.

"It was the girl you helped at Plasma last Friday. It was Tatiana Demidova, wasn't it?" she guessed.

My face gave me away, and Roma rocked back on his heels in shock. After a pause, he spoke.

"When we spoke yesterday, Chris, I had no idea that you knew the Demidovas. Gina discovered that little fact when she did some follow-up calls to your Precinct Commander. I've been interested in the Demidovas for years. And I think you know why, don't you?"

I still kept quiet, unwilling to worsen the situation.

"Listen up, Gordon. You WILL tell me what you know. Do you understand me?"

Gina spoke up again, her eyes watching me thoughtfully. "Actually, I don't think he will, Sir."

Roma looked at her in surprise.

"Think about it, Sir. He is protecting this... girl, with his life, from demons. And she is already on the demons' radar, so to speak. On top of that, she's a drop-dead knockout. It's obvious, Sir. He likes her or maybe even loves her."

She was too perceptive. I looked down at a point on the floor between them and focused hard on a chip in the concrete there. Roma pondered Gina's revelation and then finally spoke.

"You like her in spite of what she is? You do know what she is, don't you?" he asked. "I'll take your silence as answer. Boy, I gotta tell you, I didn't see this one coming. How can you reconcile your fight against demons with your... your relationship with her?"

That pissed me off.

"Do you know them? Sir? Or are you judging all of them on stereotypes?"

He stepped back at the tone in my voice, which could have been a lot worse. She might not want anything to do with me, but I would be damned if I would get lectured by someone who had never met her.

"Regardless of what you know or think you know, the Hellbourne want her dead, and that should be reason enough to protect her," I finished.

"I've seen the results of their handiwork, Gordon, and if you think she is all warm and fuzzy, you're kidding yourself."

"Sir, when I was seventeen, I participated in a Search and Rescue in Yellowstone with my grandfather.

We eventually found the missing hiker, or what was left of him. We also found both grizzly and cougar sign. Both had fed on him, and there wasn't enough left for the coroner to decide which had killed him. But while it taught me to respect the hell out of bears and cats, it didn't teach me to hate them all."

Roma was white-faced by this point and started to lean forward for his rebuttal, but Velasquez gently touched his arm and he stopped himself with what appeared to be a tremendous effort. With a foul oath, he turned and stormed away.

Velasquez looked after him for a moment, then turned back to me. "You should know that one of them killed his wife three days after they returned from their honeymoon. He is not... a fan of theirs."

"Well, Gina, I'm sorry for his loss. I really am, but that doesn't mean they're all worthy of his hate. Some are honorable and find alternative ways to survive."

"She must be pretty special, your girlfriend, that is."

"Well, she's not my girlfriend. She doesn't feel that way toward me."

"Hmm, then she's pretty stupid," she said and left before I could think to say anything else.

I got back to the Precinct a couple of hours later, catching a ride with a returning squad car. Roma had finally calmed down and ordered me to report to him at Police Plaza at one p.m. the next day.

The final statistics of the raid had been interesting. There had been four five-man entry teams in that pitch-black basement. One man was dead and four more seriously wounded and in critical condition. The rest had wounds of varying severity, but no one else had died. It was bad, but it should have been worse. The only reason the Damnedthing hadn't killed everyone in the room was because it hadn't chosen to. The Hellbourne wouldn't show mercy, so I had to believe that the monster had avoided inflicting its full fury on those of us in its path, probably paying a price for its defiance.

Roma had briefed the Commissioner, who showed up with an entourage of high-ranking brass and, despite my attempts at avoiding attention, I had been forced to meet the big man himself. He was actually pretty decent, just nodding at me and shaking my hand. That the whole thing had been a trap for me by the Hellbourne was only obvious to Roma, Gina, and myself.

So I found myself walking to my car from the Sixty-Eighth when a small figure appeared silently across the street from me. I stopped and groaned at the sight of the spiky-haired little vampire. "Hey Chris, how ya doin?" Lydia asked quietly.

"Lydia, what the hell do you want? Can't I go a whole day without a vampire toying with me?"

"Look, I just need to make sure that you're all right. Tatiana really needs to be reassured, all right?"

I snorted in disgust. "Yeah, sure. Of course she does. Riiight! Why would I be all right?"

"Please Chris, it's been a really bad night all the way around and I just gotta make sure. She's been... doing poorly and when you went down in that pit, well, let's just say that we all had a bad time of it." I was closer now, and I could see that she was looking tired and her clothes were torn in places. I stared at her for a few minutes, not feeling sorry for her in the slightest.

"Chris, you gotta know she was lying last night, right? I mean, you couldn't believe that? She's the worst liar ever. She was trying to drive you away... to protect you. It was a really stupid idea, one that was not her own, even. It was Galina's."

"Lydia, I saw how ashamed she was for having an *infatuation* with a human. And ya know what? I think she's right. Life was bad enough before, but to think I might have had some friends for a few days and then find out it was all a *mistake*? Well, it turns out I was wrong last Friday when I said the worst you could do was kill me. Nope, giving me hope that I could have someone was worse, way worse. And you all had a bad night? Give me a friggin' break! You were having a party! How bad could it be? Someone picked the wrong appetizer? Should have gone with Italians instead of the Swedes, maybe?"

"You're a real friggin' asshole," she answered. "Our party? Our party consisted of Tatiana trying to get to you, and it took the whole damn Coven to stop her! She threw her father through a wall and if all three Elders hadn't been there, she would have gotten out and gone into that pit after you!" She was yelling now.

167

I was just about to respond in kind when the growling started. Not a vampire-type growl, or even a were. This growl shook the very air around us. Lydia pinpointed its source first, turning her head like a radar till she was staring at an alley opening behind us. I already had a pretty good idea what was doing the growling 'cause I had heard a lot of it a few hours ago, and I quickly put myself between it and Lydia.

Two red eyes appeared about six and a half feet off the ground, but there was nothing else around them. Lydia started to move around me.

"Dammit Lydia! Stay behind me. There is nothing you can do to this thing!"

The eyes moved out of the alley but in a circling motion, like the Damnedthing was trying to get behind me. Why didn't it just charge me? I took a chance and scanned it with my Sight. Same red, green, and purple aura, same grizzly bear outline. But the first time I had seen it, its aura had been streaked and faded in places. Now it looked better, the color more solid, particularly the purple. Great! Sparky was even stronger now.

"What the hell is that thing?" Lydia asked in a shaky voice, clutching my arm in a death grip.

"That's the Damnedthing I was dancing with in the basement. Ah, Lydia, I'm gonna need that arm, and you're just about to break it."

She eased up instantly and I concentrated on the huge monster in front of me.

"It's scared of you?" she asked as it continued to circle and I continued to turn, my arm keeping Lydia behind me.

I snorted.

"Are you kidding? I can't even slow this thing down. Bullets don't touch it. Hell, I doubt a tank would win against this thing."

It was huffing as it circled, and I was struck by how really bear-like its actions were. I put both hands up in front of me and formed a shield of purple aura, not at all certain it would help. The giant Damnedthing immediately leaned up against my shield, the impact about knocking me to my knees. Then it rubbed its neck on the shield.

"What's it doing?" Lydia asked

"Well, I'm not a hundred-percent certain, but I think it's scratching its neck on the strongest shield I can make," I answered.

"Chris, what are we gonna do?"

The big red eyes swiveled to look at us, and I had the strangest mental picture flash through my head. It was like a video of myself and Lydia a few moments earlier, shouting at each other in anger. And suddenly I had the oddest feeling that Sparky was trying to get at Lydia. My brain spun for a moment and it occurred to me that he hadn't started growling till Lydia and I had started yelling at each other.

I spoke quietly.

"Yo, Sparky! You can't have her. She's my friend."

I had the same mental flash as before, with the yelling and everything, and somehow I understood that was his view and he was sending me that picture.

"Yeah, we were pissed at each other. Friends can do that. Doesn't mean I want anything bad to happen to her."

The circling stopped and the eyes moved up to about seven feet off the ground. If I put my hands out with my thumbs pointed at each other and touching, then my little fingers would represent the distance between this thing's eyes. It was huge. The growling stopped and a moment later, the red eyes disappeared. Papers and debris on the street, where the beast had been standing, swirled up into the air like they were caught in a minivan-sized dust devil, and then it was gone.

"Okay Northern. What the hell just happened?"

I had to tell her the story of the Hellbourne and the pit as I walked her to her car.

"So you released this thing and now it's following you around?" she asked.

"Yeah, I guess. Hey, if he follows me home, can I keep him?"

"Asshole," she said without any trace of anger.

"Pretty much," I agreed. "I, um, well, I think when I attacked it with my super purple power, well, I think I healed it. And it was rubbing its neck on the shield, 'cause that's where its collar had been."

She looked at me with wide eyes. "So how do you stop it?"

I shrugged. "I'm pretty sure that I can't. That's why the demon brought it here. But it was a slave and now it's free. I think it will just leave on its own."

She shook her head, green eyes glinting in the streetlights. "I think it will be like every other monster in this city and follow you around like a pet."

"Hmm, I'll need a really big litter box."

"Isn't that what your apartment is?"

"Bitch," I replied.

"Pretty much," she agreed, getting into her car. She rolled down her window and grabbed my hand with hers. "Christian Gordon, you do have friends. I'm one, and you know deep down that Tatiana is as well."

Then she let go with one of her freaky fast moves and drove off before I could respond.

I drove home, thinking about what she had said, ate four massive turkey-and-ham sandwiches, undressed, and collapsed into bed.

Chapter 14

My appointment with Roma was set for one, so that left my morning to myself. While I ate my dozen eggs and sausage (the good news was the scales reported that my weight was stabilizing), I caught up on my backlog of emails. Peter had sent me an apologetic one, but I wasn't ready to forgive him yet. There were three from Gramps, each slightly more alarmed than the previous, so I composed a response.

Gramps,

Sorry I haven't responded. Busy doesn't cover it. I've been recruited to a unit of the NYPD that I didn't know existed. Kind of like the FBI unit in your favorite movie about the red guy [gramps loved the movie Hellboy and would totally get my clue]. *My special skills have been noted so I guess it's for the best. The girl that the Hlbrn are after is much like Beckinsale in my favorite movie* [Okay, so I am a fan of Underworld]. *But don't worry. I'll bring you up to speed at turkey time.*

Love, Chris

Somehow, I knew that wouldn't satisfy him fully, but it would have to do for now. I dressed in khakis and a polo shirt, as Roma had indicated that I would dress plainclothes from now on. My holstered Glock, handcuff case, and badge all went on my belt, and I pulled a leather bomber from the closet to cover everything up, then headed out. My goals for the day were simple: 1) go to one of the local parks and veg out, 2) avoid any vampires, and 3) avoid having my chest and ribs smashed again. I felt pretty good, the knot on my head was gone, my ribs just slightly sore, and my right knee almost better after its painful run-in with the concrete floor in the pit.

I drove to the park, found an open spot curbside, and locked up the Xterra. There was a small bakery near the entrance to the park, and the warm odor of baked goods and hot coffee pulled me in. The girl at the counter gave me a big smile and, with unusual enthusiasm, took my order for a large black coffee and a bear claw (seemed appropriate). I don't usually get that. The whole violet eye thing makes people uneasy. I stepped out of the bakery still puzzled, but my attention was immediately drawn to a woman sitting at one of the outdoor tables. She was blonde, beautiful, dressed in a cream-colored suit with matching hat, gloves, red purse, and red open-toe shoes that cost more than my sidearm. She was staring straight at me with interest—and she was a vampire. I stopped dead in my tracks, looked at my watch—9:27 a.m.—and looked up at the sun. A couple of things clicked in my brain— one of which was that goal number two was already shot—and I walked over and sat down at her table.

Her eyebrows raised in amusement till I spoke. "Elder Senka," I greeted her. Her eyes widened ever so slightly. Tatiana and Lydia had briefed me on the Elders back when it had been assumed that I would be attending the vampire party.

"Mr. Gordon," she greeted me, her accent English.

"I thought my capacity for surprise had been beaten out of me this past week, but you've managed it nonetheless," I said.

"In that case, I will endeavor not to strain your overwrought sense of wonder." Her accent was the heavily educated Oxford kind rather than the rougher Cockney type.

Perfect for delivering biting sarcasm.

I sipped my coffee and waited, watching her over the rim of my cup. Oddly, no one else seemed to notice us. She watched me with dark chocolate eyes and finally spoke after a few seconds' pause. "I was going to offer you some tea, but I see you have sufficient libation for the moment."

Suddenly, a rather dazed young waiter was at her side with a cup, saucer, hot water carafe, and an assortment of teas. He set them down without comment and left. I took a moment to watch the people around us while she selected a packet of Earl Grey. There seemed to be a bubble of avoidance around us, and people came and went without looking at us directly.

Meanwhile, I was hurriedly trying to remember everything that the girls had told me about the Elders. Lydia had stressed that they were very old, extremely powerful, and not as easygoing as the younger vampires. Since I couldn't recall any easygoing vampires other than the girls, I was trying very hard to control my natural wiseassitude.

The ladies had never mentioned that the Elders went about in daylight. Senka was Galina's mother, making her a grandmother of sorts to both Tatiana and Lydia. Elder Fedor was the sire of Anton, Tatiana's father. He generally hung out in Europe. The third was Tzao, an ancient female who mostly stayed in Asia.

"Six nights ago, I get a telephone call from my daughter," she said. "It seems my Tatiana has awoken from her walking coma. A rather dramatic tale followed about demons, silver bolts, and a fascinating young police officer with a penchant for demon slaying."

I fought my urge to correct her use of the word slaying. Banish would be better, but she didn't seem the sort to appreciate a lot of correction or interruption.

"Then, wonder of wonders, Tatiana herself is speaking to me on the phone, as she has every day since. And do you know what her favorite topic is?" Her eyebrows raised in question.

I shook my head.

"Really? No guesses?"

I shrugged.

"Why, it is the very same police officer that saved her. I'm fairly certain that you could not have imagined the joy that her awakening has brought me. And, of course, fate would have it that I was delayed in arriving, being the last, rather than the first." She paused to sip her tea. I decided to remain silent, trying to keep up the illusion of intelligence.

"It never ceases to amaze me, no matter how many centuries I have seen, that timing continues to be everything, as they say." She had locked my gaze and I realized that I couldn't look away if I wanted to. "So here I arrive last night, only to find my beloved Tatiana, essentially insane with worry and anguish, wreaking destruction on her mother's home and flinging all manner of older vampires in every direction. Do you know that the first thing I had to do on my arrival was to help my fellow Elders restrain my granddaughter? And

I'll even tell you that the only real reason that we, the three oldest and most powerful vampires on the planet, could do it at all was because you finally finished your fight in that pit. Lydia then got her settled by handing her, of all things, a certain gray pullover. What a bloody mess."

She took another sip while I processed that bit of information.

"Once Lydia had calmed her down and promised to check on the cause of her worry, I was able to learn the whole rather sad tale," she continued. "Fairly tragic, some might call it. Personally, I find it to be idiocy of a monumental level. It seems that some persons of influence prevailed upon Tatiana that the best method of protecting her beloved police officer would be to drive him away. Make him believe she had fallen out of love with him. Preposterous, really. Only someone completely ignorant of vampire psychology would fall for that. I have since expressed my displeasure, rather forcibly, to both Galina and Anton at this extremely inopportune action on their parts. But then Lydia comes home, reassures Tatiana, and tells us of an encounter with something unheard of. Perhaps you could tell me its name, just in case I heard it wrong from Lydia?" she asked.

I cleared my throat and said, "The Hellbourne called it a Damnedthing."

"And Hellbourne is your rather quaint term for one of the walking demons?" she asked.

I frowned at her sardonic attitude, ready to speak, possibly my last words, but she waved her hand languidly and laughed.

"Oh, please do not think I am amusing myself at your expense, Mr. Gordon. I have nothing but admiration for you. I would have found you admirable for nothing other than your actions in Plasma last Friday. But you continue again and again to put yourself in harm's way for Tatiana and Lydia. And then there are all the other fascinating details, like your improbable time and date of birth. And even the way the tragic death of your family corresponds to Tatiana's own pivotal past. One might almost think you two were linked by fate. Your physiological response to vampire blood, at least Tatiana's, is almost without precedent."

She looked down at her tea, releasing me from her gaze, and I glanced around us to see if we were still going unnoticed. I almost missed it, but a short, rather rotund fellow who was walking by turned slightly toward the street and I spotted a wyrm riding his shoulders.

Glancing back at Senka showed me that she had still not looked up, so I took a quick chance and flicked my right hand in the wyrm's direction. I have developed a technique I think of as the Aura whip. Imagining my aura to be tapered and coiled like a bull whip, I snap it at a demon or, in this case, a wyrm. It worked perfectly, neatly snapping the foul thing in half and instantly freeing the round guy from its grip. He began to straighten up from his hunched posture almost immediately.

I turned back to Senka, only to find myself busted. Her eyes were bright with amazement and I had the uncomfortable feeling that she had seen everything.

"Wonderful. Exactly the kind of thing the girls have been going on and on about. To see your very special abilities in action. Extraordinary," she said.

"Er, I have a sort of personal vow not to let any of them get away. Did you... were you able to actually see that?" I asked.

"Oh yes, Christian. Do you mind if I call you Christian? I feel as if I know you already. The girls have done a remarkable job of describing you. But anyway, the answer is yes. I can see your aura and I could see the thing on the man's shoulder. What do you call that one?" she asked.

"Ah... I call those things wyrms... with a Y," I answered.

She nodded then continued, "You know, I was so excited when Tatiana woke up. As you see, one of my abilities is to foresee people's potential. And I've always known that Tatiana would achieve great things. But then Lydia told me that you were Tatiana's match in potential. I could scarcely believe such a thing despite the enormous value I place on Lydia's opinion. But that girl was right again. Ah Lydia. I consider her one of the best I've ever created. If I could clone that girl, I would make one of her for every day of the week!"

I shuddered as I thought of dealing with seven more Lydias. She laughed at my response. "That is a rather intimidating thought, is it not?"

"Well, Ma'am, it's been all I could do to handle just the one."

"Oh yes, and you have been very put out with Lydia, have you not?" she asked.

I frowned as I thought of how far I had gone in believing in Tatiana's interest in me.

"But wait, I thought Galina Turned Lydia?" I asked as my brain caught up with part of her comments.

"Oh, she did... at my insistence, and I gave Lydia a little dose of my blood at the end of the process, as a boost. Galina doesn't know that detail though."

"So you saw potential in Lydia and assured it came to fruition?" I asked.

"Something like that. And now I have to agree with Lydia. You and Tatiana are a matched set. Complementary, but not identical. You balance each other, bring out the best traits in each other. This changes the dynamic completely."

"Er... what dynamic?"

"Have you wondered why all the vampires treat Tatiana so differently? Even us Elders. It's because of what we believe she will grow into. At twenty-three, she is the equal of vampires that are seven or even eight hundred years old. She's changing and growing so rapidly that we can't begin to predict her powers and abilities. But everyone has always based that on just her. Everyone is jockeying to have influence over her.

Now you're in the picture. Her mirror, the Yang to her Yin. And your influence over her is greatest of all. Can you see why Galina and Anton tried such a stupid attempt to get her to leave you? Like that would have worked! Not to mention the attempt on your life. Tatiana's first true kill was to protect you. That little detail has been noticed.

"Your own abilities and potential are great and equally hard to predict. And that is just starting to be noticed. That vampire you threw across the room last night? Without touching? He hasn't been a vampire since you did that. Reverted to human. Dr. Singh believes it to be only temporary, and I agree, but still. To completely remove a vampire's powers with a flick of your hand. He was one of mine, by the way, and none of the other vampires other than Tatiana and Lydia and the Doctor know that detail. We're keeping it our little secret."

She studied me. "And I notice a tiny little micro flinch whenever I mention Tatiana's name. There it was again."

I continued to frown, very uncomfortable with her ability to read me.

"And you continue to believe that Tatiana has, how was it phrased? Grown beyond you?" She watched my response and nodded. "Yes, I can see you do. What can I do to convince you?"

"I suspect you can make me think anything you want with that little Jedi mind trick you have going on," I said, waving at the people passing us blindly.

Her eyes widened again and she smiled, revealing just a little bit of fang.

"Oh, you are perceptive! Lydia was right again! Except about how you view yourself and Tatiana. Hmm." She tapped her bottom lip thoughtfully.

"Well, Christian, I need to be going. Things to do, people to correct. But it has been my very great pleasure to meet you, and I will daresay that I hope to see you tomorrow night at Tatiana's and your birthday party." She again read my expression. "Oh please, you really must come. Tatiana will be crushed if you don't. Ah yes, I know you don't believe me, but what if the demon that escaped last night shows up? Who will protect her? My power doesn't pierce demon cloaks."

I sighed in resignation. "I'll be there."

"Excellent! Now I must be going."

A huge black BMW limo pulled up to the curb as if summoned by telepathy.

"Ah, Ma'm? Have you ever heard of a Damnedthing before?" I asked before she left.

"Yes Christian, I have. From what little I know, they are elemental animal spirits tortured into obedience by demonkind. They are enormously powerful and quite insane. Can you describe it?" She stood up as she answered me.

"Well, kind of like a cross between a very long-legged Kodiak brown bear with a smushed-in face and the Devil's own Rottweiler. About a ton or so when solid, and fifteen or sixteen feet tall on his back legs. His aura is red, green, and purple. And I think he projects his thoughts in pictures."

She was staring at me in outright astonishment. "Well, Christian, you have succeeded in surprising me today! Several times! How delightful. Your Damnedthing sounds like its base spirit is that of a short-faced bear. They were the largest of the bears to walk our planet, and they died out over ten thousand years ago. So he's a very old being, as well. How such a creature landed in the hands of the demons is a troubling question, and now it is freely roaming about. Be careful, Christian. I would be very put out if you let anything happen to yourself. Goodbye." And she slipped away through the tables and people like a wraith. A wraith with a really great tush.

Chapter 15

Determined to accomplish at least one of my goals, I headed into the park and found a table in the warm October sun, near the little kids' playground, which was busy. I sat, drank my coffee, and ate my bear claw while staring off into the autumn-dressed maple and elm trees that edged the playground. A group of nannies and au pairs were glancing in my direction, maybe nervous to have a potentially dangerous man near their charges. I took off my jacket so that my badge, cuff case, and gun showed, figuring it would reassure them, then resumed my thoughts.

Senka was very convincing, but then, so had Lydia been. I took a bite of bear claw and chewed while thinking the whole thing through. Why would they lie? What reason would they have to want me near Tatiana? I was just working through this line of inquiry when something tugged at my attention. A burst of wind had blown up a swirling column of colorful leaves among the trees.

Then I realized that there was no wind, at least near me or anywhere else that I could see. I looked closer and noticed that the leaves on the trees were all pushed away from each other, like a large object, about the size of a draft horse, was in the middle of them.

An image flashed through my mind, of a small child running toward a man sitting at a picnic table with his back to the child. The child was chasing a ball, and the man was wearing the same clothes as I was. I whipped around and found a sturdy little toddler running in my general direction, his feet inadvertently kicking the ball every time he went to pick it up. He was in danger of heading into the trees where the strange wind had been blowing. I was over to him and stopping the ball before I could think, and the young au pair chasing him came to a sudden stop at my motion. Too quick. I gotta work on keeping to a slower speed around people, but I couldn't chance him heading into the wooded area and encountering what I suspected lurked there.

The girl came up to me to retrieve her charge, her face lighting up in a big smile. She was really quite pretty and as she bent over to collect the young boy, her shirt billowed open in a way that invited my eyes to follow. When she looked up and kept smiling, I realized the view had not been an accident. Uh oh! I was wearing sunglasses, so I took the next step to scare her off, by removing them.

Taking off your sunglasses to show your eyes is a friendly gesture, unless you are possessed of violet eyes. Then, it has been my experience, people beat a hasty retreat. She didn't. In fact, her face flushed and she gulped and smiled even more, if possible. What the hell! When I need to scare someone away to safety, of course, it somehow backfires.

I took the direct approach.

"Ah Miss, there is a dangerous felon loose around here. You and your friends might want to move to a different part of the park, at least until we catch him," I lied.

Her eyes rounded with astonishment. "Oh, then I am very glad that you are here to protect us." Her accent was Slavic. She wasn't acting very alarmed, even though she clutched my arm. Gently, I disengaged her grip and tried again. "Well, I'll keep my eye on all of you, but I really need you to go back over with the others."

"As long as you keep an eye on me, then okay." Reluctantly, she headed back to the group of caretakers, all of whom were watching our byplay avidly. I settled back at the table, only to get another vision. This one was of two bears doing the wild thing.

I spoke softly to the space in the woods.

"Ah Sparky, what was that about?" This time, I got a vision of the girl clutching my arm and then the horny bears in the woods again.

"Ah, no, she's not my mate," I guessed. This time, all I got was a sense of puzzlement.

"Well she is technically a potential mate, and it does appear that for some reason, she is interested, but I can't." Another puzzled thought.

"Well, the demons would kill her if I... er... took her as my, ah, mate." I pictured several of the Hellbourne I had banished. An angry woof sounded, and the trees suddenly shook two stories up.

"Whoa there, Sparky. They're not around now, but they would kill her if I went near her."

It didn't take a UN interpreter to realize that he carried a really big grudge against the Hellbourne. Another flash of thought came, this time of two rocks striking each other and sparking, combined with a negative feeling. That one took a second to figure out.

"Oh, you don't like me calling you Sparky?"

Agreement.

"Well, what do I call you?"

Puzzlement this time.

I thought of the Mohawk word for bear, which made up about one quarter of my entire Mohawk vocabulary.

"How about Okwari?" I asked.

After a moment, a feeling of agreement came.

"Okay, Okwari it is."

Pronounced correctly, it sounds like *oh-kwah-lee*.

A flash of me and Lydia arguing, and then a quick flash of me protecting her from danger.

"Ah, that's Lydia. She's my friend. Sometimes we argue, but we will always protect each other. It's what friends do."

I got an image of myself tearing off Okwari's hell collar. Then he woofed again, but softer, and the leaves swirled up and up, and then the wind was gone. I watched the floating leaves return to earth. All feeling of his presence had disappeared.

I spent the rest of the morning soaking up the sun, which felt amazing after all the night hours I had been logging. I grabbed lunch at a pizza joint, then drove to One Police Plaza.

Roma's squad was housed in a sublevel under the Special Operations Headquarters. There were no signs indicating Special Situations, just a block of offices behind a door numbered 2L117. A young blonde receptionist looked up when I came through after following the directions I had been given by the Desk sergeant upstairs. She gave me her full attention and asked, "May I help you?"

"Ah, I'm looking for Inspector Roma?"

"And you are?"

"Chris Gordon. I have an appointment."

She nodded and finally smiled. "Yes, we've been expecting you, Officer Gordon. You can hang your jacket on the coat rack, and I'll just tell the Inspector that you're here. I'm Olivia, by the way."

"Ah, nice to meet you, Olivia. Please call me Chris." I hung up my jacket and turned back to find a seat in the tiny waiting area. Olivia was speaking into the phone while continuing to watch me. She smiled again as she hung up. "He'll be with you shortly. Can I get you some coffee?"

"Ah, coffee would be great."

"How do you take it?"

"Black, please"

She got up and moved to another door. Early twenties, dark-rimmed librarian glasses, hair pulled back, black skirt, and a blue blouse. Pretty, in a businesslike kind of way. She filled a cup from the machine in the little nook behind the door.

"Here you go, Chris." Another big smile as she handed me the cup, making eye contact the whole time. "Thanks." I was a little flustered by the friendly reception. I hadn't been sure what kind of greeting I would get when I met with Roma again, but so far, so good. Olivia moved back to the center of her kingdom and proceeded to work at her computer.

I settled back and looked around. Pretty bland decorations. The furniture was corporate and functional, the walls had some framed posters of Special Ops units and were painted an off-white color. From time to time, my peripheral vision showed Olivia checking on me. The coffee was good, as most cop coffee is.

The outer door opened and Aikens, Sommers, and Velasquez came in and headed toward the inner door next to Olivia's desk. Gina looked over and noticed me. "Hi Chris, how ya doing?"

"Hi Gina, hi Steve, Chet. I'm fine," I answered.

She nodded and said, "We'll each be seeing you later, but right now, we have to follow up on some stuff."

"Hey, Olivia? How come Gordon gets coffee? I never get coffee." Aikens complained after he spotted the mug in my hand.

"That's because he's polite, unlike you. You pretty much kissed any chance of coffee goodbye when you made the comment the other day," she answered primly.

"Yo, I was just complimenting you, that's all, baby. You know I didn't mean anything nasty or nothing."

She just glared at him while Sommers laughed. Then all three went out the door, Aikens arguing with Sommers, while Velasquez glanced back once.

"More coffee, Chris?"

"Ah, no thanks. Is there a place I can wash this mug?" I asked

"Oh, I'll take it."

I walked it over to her and she smiled as she replaced it in the coffee nook.

After five more minutes, the inner door opened and Roma beckoned me to him.

He led me through the inner door and I stepped into the center of the Special Situations domain. We had walked into a conference room with a long black table, four chairs per side, and one at its head. A very large flat-screen monitor dominated the end of the room nearest me, and one of the seats at the table was equipped with a wireless keyboard and mouse. The walls on either side were glass and looked into individual offices. The first office on the right side was actually about two offices in size and looked more laboratory and workshop than office. Chet Aikens was ensconced in the middle of a battery of monitors, computers, keyboards, an electronics workbench at one end of the space. A tall bookshelf against the far wall of his space was stuffed with books, some looking newly published and others like they were hand drawn by monks in the Dark Ages. Steve Sommers was seated at his desk in the small amount of remaining space, with a gunsmith's workbench and cartridge reloading machine against his wall. A high-grade gun safe took up the corner.

Next to that space had to be Brian Takata's office/dojo. Wrestling mats took up most of the floor space, along with a realistically molded punching dummy. Martial arts weapons and blades of all types covered the walls, and his only concession to standard office décor was a small computer workstation tucked in the corner. Brian wasn't in residence at the moment.

On the left side, the first office looked relatively normal, with a desk, computer, bookshelves, and several plaques on the walls. Gina Velasquez was at the desk, typing away at her workstation. The next office also looked normal and, by process of elimination, was most likely Fran DeMarco's, although like Brian, she wasn't currently there. Last on the left side was an office sized the same as the other two, but holding a copier and shelves of office supplies. Three fireproof, heavy-duty security filing cabinets lined up against the wall, and opposite them was a folding table with a coffee pot, microwave, and small standing fridge. The far wall of the conference room was solid and opaque, with a single door in it and the name plate on the door that read *Inspector Roma* in large black letters. The Inspector led me through this door into his inner sanctum, which was the largest office yet. Decorated like a scholar's den, it was furnished with a large cherry desk and matching bookshelves and credenza. Four comfortable arm chairs surrounded a circular glass coffee table. One wall was the *I love me* wall that many professional cops, firefighters, and military officers seem to feel is obligatory. It was filled with framed citations and photos of Roma with various dignitaries, high-ranking cops, and political figures and certificates of law enforcement training schools. His desk was conspicuously neat, just a phone, pen, legal pad, and a small framed photograph that was turned toward his chair, its back to me.

"Have a seat, Chris." He indicated the sitting area.

I grabbed a chair that put my back to the door and farthest from his desk. After noting my choice, he took the seat across from me.

"Well, here we are. I'll spare you the chitchat and get right down to the heart of the matter. Any misgivings the team may have had about your trustworthiness were wiped away last night. Once again, your actions saved lives, at grave risk to your own. Unfortunately, because of the unnatural nature of the perpetrators, we can't give you official recognition. The casualties are being blamed on the drugged Hancers that attacked us. As none of them survived to dispute us and none of the Special Operations officers had a clue what they were really facing, this explanation will stand.

"And as for you, effective immediately, you have been reassigned to the Special Situations group. Frankly, it's the only place for you now. None of your fellow officers knows what you did, but they all know you did something. And they all know that something saved lives. Questions?" he asked.

"Er. Sir, how much does the brass know?"

"Chris, the knowledge that unnatural things live among us is a carefully guarded secret. The Commissioner, Deputy Commissioner, myself, and the team are it for the NYPD. Each time a Commissioner is appointed, he or she receives a special briefing from the Department of Homeland Security. "

"The Feddies know, Sir?"

"Of course. They have a department much like this one, but tasked with covering the whole country. In addition, each of the major metropolitan cities has a department like this, although only LAPD's is similar in size and ability. Or I should say, used to be similar in ability. They don't have you, now do they?" he said.

"Ah, me? Sir?" I asked.

"Chris, I feel comfortable in saying that I don't believe there is anyone with your abilities, anywhere. Also, it appears you are a defacto liaison with the vampire and possibly the were communities, which again is something that no other department, including the Feds, have. We know the supernaturals exist, but they refuse to communicate with us. I was hoping you might facilitate that."

"Sir, I got the impression that you hate vampires."

He frowned. "Well, I won't kid you. I have no use for them. But they do seem to police themselves, and we really aren't sure how we would go about it if we had to. They're rather formidable, as I believe you know."

"Yes Sir, that would be an understatement." I paused to think about what he was requesting. "Ah Sir, you should know that I've only been... involved... in their world for the better part of a week. I'm not qualified to be your expert."

"Granted, you're new to the role, but you appear to be in favor with the Demidovas and as far as I know, they rule the New York roost."

"Actually, Sir, Galina Demidova hates me. My relationship has been with her daughter, Tatiana, and I'm not at all certain where that stands at the moment. As far as the weres go, I am only slightly acquainted with the local Pack. I don't know the other species at all." I left out the wereweasel altercation.

"Other species?" he asked.

"Er. Yeah. Weretigers, werebears, and all that."

He looked at me blankly for a moment, then shook himself.

"Chris, our hope would be to expand your knowledge and contacts because whatever little you have is way more than we've ever had before."

"Well sir, seeing as your people already know, I guess I can help with that. But you need to know that I can't betray certain confidences, pretty much on pain of death, or if it would endanger certain of my... er... contacts."

"Well, that seems reasonable." I was glad he didn't try to BS me with any crap about protecting me from the wrath of the supernatural world. Because none of them, including the feds, would be able to stop weres or vamps from hunting me down if I betrayed their secrets.

"Great! Now, I thought we would have you attend our afternoon briefing and then spend some time with each of the team members. Tomorrow, we'll get started at nine a.m., and the whole team will be going as a group to the funeral of the officer who died last night, then we'll see what the afternoon brings us. How's that?"

"Ah, Sir, I should tell you that I have a function to attend tomorrow night at Plasma. It's a vampire type of event and my invitation was delivered face to face by someone who ranks over Galina, so I don't feel it would be a good idea for me to miss it."

"By all means. Any meeting or event of that nature that will help you liaise with that... world is now part of your job."

That would actually make life a lot easier. Not having to juggle the job with the vamps was a huge load off my plate.

We headed back into the conference room, and he quickly called the troops together. Brian and Fran had come in while we were in Roma's office, so the gang was all present.

Roma took the head of the table, and I found a seat between him and Gina. Everyone greeted me or nodded, and then Roma opened it up.

"All right, Chet, it's your show."

Aikens was sitting at the computer keyboard, and he fired up the giant wall monitor as he began.

"Preliminary analysis indicates that lab was the source of all the Hance we have come across so far. Details of the molecule are the same as what we already knew."

"Could you explain what we already know again? Let's bring Chris up to speed."

Aikens nodded and the monitor displayed a complex molecule, the image rotating to show it three dimensionally.

"Chris, the molecule before you is the Hance protein. It appears to be an incomplete copy of what we believe to be a naturally occurring protein. However, we haven't figured out where it originates. The protein travels the bloodstream, attaching itself to the red blood cells. As it moves throughout the body, it has wide-ranging effects on the sensory nerve bundles, skeletal muscles, and the central nervous system. It actually does speed up reflexes and improves eyesight, hearing, smell, and tactile senses."

"Can I get a copy of that image? I may have a lead on its origin."

They all looked at me in surprise. Aikens glanced at Roma, who after a moment nodded his agreement. Chet typed a command, and a printer in his office whirred in response.

"Did you uncover anything in your archives about the ... Damnedthing?" Roma asked.

"A little. There is mention of a subclass of elementals that carry that name," Chet said.

"Excuse me, what's an Elemental?" Fran asked.

"Elementals are multidimensional entities that can phase between our plane of existence and others. They can take solid shape or an energetic state that allows them to travel wherever they wish. They seem to range from fairly powerful to demigod class. The Damnedthings are elementals that have been twisted and warped by demonic influence and are held in bondage by a demon handler."

Silence greeted that statement. After a moment, Roma spoke.

"So, you're telling me that we have a deranged demigod roaming the city?"

"I'm telling you that Gordon released some form of elemental from servitude and that it could still be around if it chose to. And it appears to be an exceptionally powerful one. Maybe demigod class."

"Gordon, any thoughts?" Roma asked.

"Well, I think it is most dangerous to the demons, Sir. It really seems to hate them. Other than that, I don't think it'll hang around." I didn't think they needed to know about my conversations with Okwari.

"Okay, thanks, Chris. Chet, good job. Anyone have anything to add?" he asked.

"Inspector, my regular set of sources indicates that a rather large buildup of vampires has been occurring over the past few days. They're in quite a tizzy over it. Oddly, though, none of the ghosts are around right now," Fran said.

I cleared my throat. "That would be my fault. The missing ghosts, that is."

Again, they all looked at me in amazement.

"Ghosts don't like me. They all disappear whenever I'm around. Peter's group won't let me near any of their haunting locations because the spirits will vacate and not come back for weeks," I shrugged.

"So you're saying that if I'm anywhere near you, all the ghosts will stay away?" Fran asked.

"Yeah, pretty much. Sorry," I said.

"Sorry? Are you kidding me? Inspector, can Chris have the office next to mine? Hell, he can share mine if it'll give me a moment of peace from all the spooks that are constantly hounding me. Chris, can you move into my apartment? No rent, no utilities, free groceries. Whatta ya say?"

We all laughed, although I was pretty certain she was half-serious. Of course, she couldn't know what my average grocery bill was or she wouldn't have offered.

"Fran's solitude aside, any thoughts about the traffic in vampires?"

I took my time answering him, thinking through what I could and couldn't say.

"Yes Sir. Basically, it's my fault," I said. Roma raised his eyebrows.

"I intervened on Tatiana Demidova's behalf last Friday, and I sort of jolted her from a state of... mental withdrawal. The visitors are here to see her."

"Chet, do you have those photos I asked you to get?" Roma asked.

"Yes sir, the feds finally ponied them up, but I had to really jump through hoops to get them." Chet said.

A picture of Galina appeared on the monitor. It was a surveillance photo taken at dusk as she exited her limo. Sommers wolf-whistled in appreciation.

Roma explained. "For those of you who don't know who we speak of, this is the elusive Galina Demidova, real estate tycoon and business wonder. She has only been photographed once recently, this being the photo. Prior to this, her last photo was from a decade ago."

A second older, and much poorer quality, photo of Galina appeared next to the newer one. Despite the difference in quality, it was obvious that she hadn't changed a bit from one photo to the other.

"Galina is the head of the New York Coven, and seems to carry some weight with the other covens, as well. She refuses to meet with myself or any of the feds, and her army of attorneys has been effective in blocking all attempts to get at her. Surveillance is almost impossible, as they always seem able to anticipate us."

A certain blonde mind reader might have something to do with that. But that information seemed to come under the sensitive category, so I kept it to myself.

"Chet, next photo, please," Roma said.

"This one is probably worth a cool million, million and a half to the media," Chet said as he typed a command.

Tatiana suddenly filled the screen, and my heart stopped beating. I hadn't seen her in a few days, and I'd never seen a photograph of her. I wasn't prepared for the shock, and it took me a couple of moments to handle the flood of emotions that swarmed through me. Others had their own reactions.

"Holy mother of God!" Sommers said. Takata just sort of let out a grunt, like someone had hit him in the stomach. Gina was wide-eyed as she turned from the picture to look my way. Fran's mouth was hanging open, and Roma looked shocked. It wasn't even her best look. Taken outside of Plasma, at night, the picture showed what I believed was a preawakened Tatiana, with Lydia following her out of the club's door. Tatiana was dressed in designer jeans and a form-fitted shirt, with calf-high leather boots. Lydia was dressed in a black denim skirt and an artfully tattered white Plasma shirt.

Despite her awesome physical beauty, Tatiana seemed sad and withdrawn.

After a moment, Roma finally spoke. "This is Tatiana Demidova, reputed to be Galina's daughter, although that claim has never been explained satisfactorily. To the best of our knowledge, vampires are only made, not born. Yet Miss Demidova resembles her mother to a very high degree. Chris, what detail can you share?"

I opened my mouth to answer, but my cell phone buzzed with an incoming text. I looked up apologetically.

"Sorry, I don't understand how I could be receiving a signal down here."

Chet spoke up. "Easy. The building has been wired for secure wireless, even down here."

I glanced at the name of the text sender on my cell, then spoke. "Ah Sir, I really need to answer this."

Gina spoke first. "It's her, isn't it? It's Tatiana!"

Detective Velasquez was proving to be uncomfortably perceptive.

"That seems rather coincidental. Go ahead, Chris." Roma said.

I opened the text.

T: Are U all right?

C: yes, why?

T: U just had some kind of shock? It woke me up.

"Shouldn't she be asleep or whatever they do during daylight?" Takata asked.

"Yeah, she was." I said.

"What woke her up?" Fran asked.

"I think I did," I said, then answered Tat's last line.

C: Yeah, I did, but not bad or anything. I'm fine. You should go back to sleep.

T: What was the shock?

"Explain," Roma ordered.

"I seem to have a kind of link with her. She knows where I am and can sense strong emotion," I said.

C: Just a picture.

T: Of what?

C: You.

"If she is at her mother's residence," he looked at me for confirmation and I nodded, "then she is about two miles away. And you woke her from a sound sleep?"

"Well, I haven't seen her in a few days and we've been having some... issues. The photo caught me off guard," I replied.

My phone buzzed again.

T: I really need to talk to you. I didn't mean any of what I said. Please tell me I can see you tonight? Please?

C: We should talk. Come by later. I have to go now, I'm in a meeting. Go back to sleep. Bye.

T: Bye, till later. I love U.

I put the phone away and looked up into six pairs of questioning eyes.

"What would have happened if you hadn't answered her?" Roma asked.

"Most likely nothing. My shock went by fairly quickly and she would know I was basically okay."

"What if you had displayed fear or excessive anger?" he asked.

"That might have been a problem. She's sorta protective."

Gina snorted. "You're understating it by a lot, judging from your expression."

"Wait a minute. It's the middle of the afternoon, broad daylight, and we're in the sublevel of friggin' Police Plaza. Are you saying she would try to come here if you were in danger? That tiny little fox?" Chet said.

Roma spoke before I could answer. "Don't any of you get fooled for a second into thinking they aren't more dangerous than you can truly imagine. And Chris, don't try to sell us that she's not a killer!"

"Actually, I was going to say that tiny little fox is one of the most dangerous people on the planet. It took the entire Coven of New York City to keep her away from the Hance lab takedown last night. If she decided to come here, middle of the day or not, she would already be here."

"And she sucks blood and all that?" Chet asked.

"Yup, but it is bagged blood from the blood bank that they own. They're killers by nature, but killing is a bad move, and they know it," I said.

"You're not telling us everything. There's more than just bagged blood," Gina said.

"You are a pain in the ass," I said, starting to get annoyed. "But yes, she does drink from a donor, but only one, and the donor is willing."

"You! You're the donor," Gina said.

I sighed. It was unbelievable how easily she could read me. "Yes, I am the only human she will drink from directly. There. Happy?" I said to Gina.

Now they were all looking at me with differing expressions. Roma looked mildly disgusted, Chet was admiring, Sommers and Takata looked intrigued, DeMarco was flat-out shocked, and Gina was frowning slightly. Great way to start a new job.

After the meeting, Chet pulled me into his workspace and started my orientation.

"Okay, this is my hub, my web. The place from which all good information flows," he said, gesturing at the multiple monitors, keyboards, computers, and a lot of things I couldn't identify..

"From here, I monitor all the news feeds, as well as the NYPD and federal crime reporting systems. I also, have programs to monitor various occult-based forums and chat rooms for key phrases. I run all that data through filters to drill down on the most likely stories and crimes that we need to look into, as well as information that we might be interested in."

"Like, Damnedthings?" I asked.

"Yup. Did you know there's a very old short story by a man named Ambrose Bierce called "The Damned Thing"? Popped up during my search."

"Er, no. Never heard of it. Anything to do with our Damnedthing?"

"Well, it has a number of similar details. Invisible monster, animal-based, violent, and, of course, the name of the creature itself. "

"So you're saying the author might have been exposed to the real deal?" I asked.

"Possible, but anyway, let's talk about the one we're interested in. You said it was originally a short-faced bear?" he asked as his fingers flew over one of the keyboards. Pictures and descriptions popped up on several different monitors. Chet read from the Wikipedia listing.

"*Arctodus simus*, short-faced bear, died out twelve thousand, five hundred years ago. Largest bear, six to seven feet at the shoulder, over eleven feet standing upright, and approximately two thousand pounds. That sound like your monster?"

"Those are averages, right? 'Cause my bear is a bit bigger than that," I said.

"Well, of course, there is always variation along the bell curve in any species, some bigger, some smaller. The thing that interests me is that the species died out over twelve millenia ago. If your Damnedthing originated from one of those, then it is very, very old."

"What does that mean?" I asked.

"Well, generally speaking, we seem to find that among the paranormal, older is stronger."

I thought about the vampires that I knew. Chet's theory fit in pretty well there.

"So you're saying this one could be strong?" I asked.

"Based on what we witnessed in the lab, and based on what you tell me, plus the physical size of this thing when it's solid, then, hell yeah, I think it's powerful!"

"So what's the whole demigod thing?" I asked.

"Well, demigods are by definition, half god, half human. Think Hercules, son of Zeus and a human mother. We, the fed team and the other Special Situation squads around the country, have agreed on a standardized language to describe and compare the things we run into. Demigods are at the upper end of what we might run into."

I looked at him for a moment, letting all the information just sort of gel.

"See, I woulda thought a dude like you would have an easier time believing all this shit, but you look like you're trippin'," Chet said.

"Well, I think I'm more bugged by the idea that the federal government and the largest police departments in the country have teams to deal with this."

He laughed and then started to hand me books to read.

"There are a few more, but you'll have to read them here. I don't let anyone take them outta my library, if ya know what I mean."

Next, I was scheduled to sit with Gina. She was on the phone when she waved me into her office, so I took a moment to look over the plaques on the wall. She had a Masters in psychology from Columbia, as well as certificates of completion from various profiling courses at the FBI Academy at Quantico. She also had a certificate of completion in Facial Action Coding System signed by a Dr. Paul Ekman.

Next to that was a framed diploma from The Princeton Engineering Anomalies Research group. As I finished the last title, she hung up the phone and looked at me for a moment. Then she spoke.

"So, by now you'll have figured out that I am a psychologist as well the group's parapsychologist. I'm also the profiler for our little squad."

"That's a lot of hats you wear," I said.

She smiled. "Yes, but we all wear many hats here. Fran is our medium, but she is also our Case Manager. Steve is our weapons expert but assists Chet with technology while acting as one half of our own little spec ops team. Brian is the other half of that team and our close combat trainer. Fighting with stronger, faster opponents takes skill, you know."

Oh, how very well I knew that lesson.

"Brian also has Crime Scene Technician training, as does Chet. Inspector Roma is our leader, but he is also the team Medic, although I am backup medic. And even Olivia is more than she seems, acting as our logistics coordinator, and dispatcher. So that brings us to you. What hats do you see yourself wearing?"

"Well, despite living in the Big Apple, my favorite hat is a Red Sox ball cap, followed closely by a Springfield Armory hat."

She didn't laugh. "Your humor tells me a lot about you, you know."

She was under my skin, just that quick.

"Tell me, by all means, about myself," I said.

So she did, in a calm, even voice. "You are angry and lonely, but you cover it with humor. You feel set upon by God, perhaps cursed by Him."

"Anything else?" I said through clenched teeth.

"Just one more thing. You feel that you are a coward at heart."

I exploded to my feet, my chair flying back, clattering to the floor. In my peripheral vision, I could see Brian and Steve moving into the central conference room, but Gina's face remained calm and un-alarmed, and she spoke again before I could start yelling at her.

"And despite all those feelings, you still put your life in danger daily to protect others. Why is that?"

Her statement and question deflated the rawest part of my anger.

"What the hell do you mean?"

"Why do you continue to help others? After all that God has done to you? Why haven't you just walked away? Why did you help that little girl?"

"What kind of questions are those? Are you saying I shouldn't help people?"

"It's a very reasonable question. If God has cursed you and taken from you, why should you do His Will?"

"I don't! I do what I do because I choose to! My will, not His. And how could I not help people? How could I stand by and let others go through what I had to? To lose what I lost?"

"But isn't it easier and safer to just avoid the demons?"

My anger had bled away, replaced now by cold calm and a stubborn resolve to keep from responding to her ploy. I hadn't been prepared, hadn't been ready for her button pushing. A tiny part of me was admiring her skill while the lion's share resented her manipulation. I righted my chair and sat, before answering. "Sure, you're right. That would be easier," I agreed.

"Then why not take that route?" she persisted.

"Maybe I will, at some point. Hell, maybe I'll join them," I said.

She surprised me by smiling. My cell buzzed.

T: ?

C: I'm fine. Mind games with a shrink.

T: O.K. See u later?

C: Yes.

T: Can u come here? They are fussy.

C: Sure.

I really didn't want to go to Galina's house, but after meeting Senka, and hearing about last night's trouble, I understood why they didn't want Tatiana traveling about.

"That the girl who isn't your girlfriend?" Gina asked.

I refused to get caught in her games again, so I just nodded coldly.

She looked at me levelly for a moment, then continued in a different direction.

"Chris, has anyone ever told you what it's like when you exorcise a demon?"

Damn, she was confusing. "What? No one is ever with me when I exorcise demons."

"I'm talking about the people outside, the ones waiting," she said.

"Detective Velasquez , I don't have the foggiest idea what you're talking about."

"When you exorcised that little girl's home, everyone outside felt it. We all knew that you had banished it. Didn't you know that people could sense what you do?"

I shook my head. No one had ever mentioned it before.

"Well, let me tell you about it. Every time I had been to that house right up till you went in, it felt wrong. Evil. It made my skin crawl. Then you walked in and after a minute, I felt a... vibration. Like the thrum of a guitar or a note on a harp. Crystal-clear, pure. It wasn't a sound, but a feeling. Then a sharp snap or a pop. Like pressure released. And the wrongness was gone. I looked around and I could tell that everyone else held felt it. I could read it in their faces. But no one said a thing, reluctant to speak, like we were not supposed to talk about it. Like we shouldn't. It wasn't something you could put into words and even now, I haven't done a good job of it. But I'll tell you this, every one of us felt instantly better. I, for one, felt like God was nearby and watching over us," she said.

For once, I had nothing to say, dumbfounded at this revelation.

"Now, I have a lot of work to do, so if you'll excuse me, I believe you are scheduled to meet next with Brian."

And just like that, she ushered me out of her office and shut the door.

My time with Brian was much more straightforward. He didn't say a word about my outburst in Gina's office, but took me into his little dojo and asked me about my martial arts background.

So I gave him my background, but he surprised me by asking for details, instructor's names, years of study, belt rank, dojo names. I had never thought about my training in that manner, and it made me defensive. I hadn't studied for belt rank, but for survival.

Next he had me change into sweatpants and a tee shirt, and he began to test my knowledge by sparring. I held my speed and strength back for a couple of reasons. First, the team was just starting to accept me a little. Being more of a freak than I already was wouldn't help that. The second reason was my promise to Dr. Singh, and third, Brian Takata knew a lot more about practical technique than anyone I had ever met. I figured the best way to learn was to push him enough to make it a challenge and see what he brought to the mat. He didn't disappoint. I learned more in twenty minutes than I had in the last year. I also learned that had I exerted my full strength and speed, I could have beaten him. He showed me a flying arm bar I hadn't come across before, a version that was purely functional, stripped of all glitz. Arm bars are basic joint locks that work by exerting leverage on frail human joints. A flying arm bar uses the body weight of the person employing it to bring down the person who is the recipient of this less-than-gentle treatment. Had I chosen, I was certain I could have held his full body weight and flexed my arm through the lock. While that gave me confidence, it also told me that many of these techniques would be worthless against vampires, weres, and other supernaturally strong critters.

After an hour with Brian, Steve Sommers, who had watched much of the sparring, laid claim to me, and we were off to the range. Located in the same vast building but seemingly half a county away, the range was mostly empty and we had one end all to ourselves.

"First, let's see how you handle your issue sidearm," he said.

So I drew my Glock 19 and worked through a couple of qualification targets. It had been awhile since I had been to a range, but my enhanced vision and reflexes handed me perfect scores.

"Excellent shooting! Let me guess, you've been shooting long before the academy?"

"Actually, since I was twelve." I filled him in on my teenage training years.

He just looked at me for a moment, then grinned. "We're gonna skip all the basic crap and get right to the good stuff!" he said with enthusiasm. He pulled out a molded plastic handgun case and opened it up. Inside was another Glock, this one looking almost identical to a Glock 17, the larger service model of my 19. But this gun had a small circular switch on the left side of the rear slide, and that one difference told me all I needed.

"That's a Glock 18!" I said, as excited as he was. He nodded and pulled a loaded thirty-three-round magazine from another bag. Locking the extended mag into the gun's grip, he racked a round into the chamber and handed it to me. "The selector is on full auto. Show me what you can do," he said.

The Glock 18 is a select fire, full automatic pistol originally developed for Austrian counter-terrorist forces. In semi auto mode, it fires just like the model 17, but in full auto mode, it will fire at rates of up to twelve hundred rounds per minute. A two second pull of the trigger will empty a thirty-three-round magazine. I'm pretty sure that's what Steve expected me to do. But my childhood instructors had given me a good grounding in full auto technique. Instead of spraying the mag empty, I tapped the trigger for a series of five- and ten-round bursts, keeping all the rounds on target. The gun was ridiculously easy to control and I had a huge grin on my face when the slide locked back on an empty chamber. Seeing the results of my first attempt, Sommers took the gun back, placed it back in its case, packed up his stuff, and said simply, "Come on!" He led me through a short series of doors till we came to another range, this one open, without shooting lanes. A control panel sat on a desk at the back and as he powered up the range systems, he instructed me to retrieve the Glock and several mags of ammo. Shooting glasses and earmuffs on, and I was on the firing line. What followed was a full hour of action shooting on automated popup targets. It was the most fun I'd had at work since I started with the NYPD. When we finished, I cleaned the 18 to his satisfaction, packed it away, and we headed back to the squad's offices.

Roma greeted us as we entered. "How'd he do?" he asked.

"He cleared the first four simulations almost perfectly. We ran outta time for the other two, but I'm ready to issue him the 18 right now!" Sommers answered.

"Really? Well, by all means, proceed. Chris, when you're done I'd like to see you."

"Sure thing, Inspector."

Sommers had a small forest's worth of papers for me to sign, formally issuing the Glock 18 to me. He pulled out a kydex holster, double mag carrier, three twenty-round mags, and three thirty-three-round mags. Then he went to a closet door next to his gun safe, unlocked it, and pulled out a metal GI ammo can. Popping it open, he showed me the contents, six fifty-round blocks of nine millimeter ammunition. He plucked a round out of its individual slot and offered it to me for inspection. Viewed from the side, it looked like a standard hollowpoint round. A look at the business end revealed that the hollow cavity was filled with silver. "Silver itself is hard enough to make a decent bullet, but casting them is a bitch. The melting point is ridiculously high, and the metal cools so fast that there are almost always serious flaws with the finished bullet. So, we've opted to fill standard copper jackets with silver instead. They fly true and are quite effective on impact. They behave more like a flatnose solid, with little expansion, but penetrating heavy muscle is usually of more concern than anything else," he said.

"So silver really is effective against weres?" I asked.

"Yes, as well as on vamps and most other supernaturals. Something about the metal is poisonous to them."

I knew from personal experience that silver worked on vampires—my introduction to Tatiana had demonstrated that. I was also aware that silver killed most viruses and bacteria on contact, as well.

"Conventional rounds will eventually kill weres and vamps, too. Just takes a ton of them on target to get the job done. Not likely with the speed they both can move at. As it is, we have to shoot the crap out of them with the silver. They're friggin' tough!"

"How many have you shot?" I asked.

"I shot one vamp in Dallas. I used to be a feddie, but Roma recruited me. But shootings happen very rarely. Mostly, they take care of their own problems for us. We just sometimes have to show them that we're aware of an issue," he said. "Tomorrow, we'll run the other two scenarios. Both are run at a much faster speed than the four you did today. I'll be interested to see how you handle them. You pretty much cleaned house today!"

I thanked Steve, grabbed the gun bag he had given me, and headed out to find Roma.

The Inspector was in his office with the door open when I knocked.

"Come in, Chris," he said.

He pushed a small, tidy stack of files across his desktop to me as I took a chair.

"It occurred to me that we come from very different backgrounds and experiences in the supernatural world. Gina helped me understand that you deal with the worst of the worst—the demons. As such, it's natural for you to view the others as more... benign, maybe?"

Not sure where he was going, I just nodded.

"Right, well, as you indicated last night, they're not all the same. Some might be relatively okay—" He frowned as he spoke. "And others are very, very malignant, indeed."

I opened the first file and found a table listing missing person statistics for the United States over the past decade. A second table showed unsolved murder statistics in the U.S. for the same time frame. The files that followed were all homicide cases that a quick glance showed to be horrifically violent.

Roma continued when I looked back up at him, "Each year, well over one hundred thousand people go missing without being found. Each year, there are thousands of murder cases that go unsolved. Those are just the reported cases. It is fairly safe to assume that thousands of other missing person cases go unreported. That first file works through the numbers, and you'll see a close correspondence with the kill ratios that scientists have observed in natural predator-prey relationships. Some are the work of humans, but, as you'll see from the rest of the files, some are the work of supernatural predators, vampires, and weres." He rubbed his temples for a moment before continuing.

"Chris, I want you to read through these files tonight with an open mind. My goal is to make sure you have the proper... respect for these predators. We run various shifts as needed here, but why don't you come in tomorrow at nine? That way, you can make it to that important party tomorrow night. Good night," he said, in obvious dismissal.

Chapter 16

When I got home, I threw a frozen macaroni and cheese dinner into the microwave, then sat down to load pistol mags with silver-filled rounds. I was hungry, but not as bad as the last few days. Maybe Dr. Singh was right and my metabolism would slow from its current crazy pace. Thinking of the doctor reminded me of the Hance protein image that I had folded in my jacket pocket. It only took a moment or two to scan it into my laptop and then fire off an email to the doctor, requesting his opinion of the molecule. That done, I cracked a cold beer and started my homework.

The homicide files were enlightening. Roma had a point, as the amount and kind of damage the victims exhibited would have been very difficult for a standard human maniac to achieve. Some had been torn apart with obviously superhuman strength. Some had bite and tear wounds that were strongly indicative of large wild carnivores, in geographic locations that had no native examples of said carnivores. Tracks disappeared into thin air, doors and other human obstacles were breached with hands, not force, and at least one attack occurred high up in an apartment building where the murderer came through a fourteenth-floor window to rip out the victims' throat and a large portion of the blood supply was gone.

Taken together with the missing person and homicide statistics, the overall picture was fairly alarming. The human race had its own predators, just as folklore and mythology had faithfully reported all along. Only, today's enlightened world ignored the fact that we weren't at the top of the food chain.

I had a lot to think about as I ate the entire family-sized mac and cheese. I really only had regular contact with Tanya and Lydia. My experience with other vampires had been meager. I kept Roma's lesson in mind as I got ready to visit the Demidova residence. My new Glock went on my hip, a twenty-round mag in place and one round chambered. Two more twenty-rounders went in the mag holder on my belt, and after a moment's hesitation, I slipped a thirty-three-rounder into the inside document pocket of my leather jacket. Wearing jeans and a long-sleeve black tee, I hopped into the Xterra and headed out.

The night was cold and windy, the moon overhead almost full, as I trudged up the sidewalk to Galina's front door. The dead, dry leaves swirled around the street, each gust causing me to bring my Sight to bear, looking for a green, red, and purple image. I rang the bell and waited, wondering at the truly strange nature of my life as I waited to see the vampire girl I was still infatuated with. After a minute, the door opened to reveal the blonde Nika. Not saying a word, she slid back out of the doorway, her expression blank. She was wearing a rather formal gown of soft yellow. I tried to keep my thoughts bland as I entered the brightly lit mansion. Classical music played on hidden speakers, and the air was scented heavily by the numerous floral arrangements spread throughout the front foyer and formal living room. A dozen or so formally attired vampires were present, standing in eerie stillness, staring at me. There was nothing remotely human or friendly on those pale, frozen faces, and I felt like a bug looking up as the giant shoe descends. A small, spiky-haired form in a black lace-trimmed top and matching black tights blurred down the stairs and right up to me.

"Chris, come on. I'll take you to her," Lydia said in a quiet voice. But as we turned to the stairs, a tall, lean form floated into our path, effectively blocking the route. Movie star handsome, in a pale, severe sort of way, he was wearing a charcoal gray suit of expensive cut. The word dapper popped into my head as I watched him approach, a cold smile on his face.

"Lydia, introduce me to your friend," he commanded. "I have so wanted to meet Tanya's human pet."

"Quickly then, Anton. She really needs to see him now," Lydia replied.

"Oh, we wouldn't want to hold up my darling daughter, now would we?" he said, his pale blue eyes never leaving mine.

"Christian, this is Anton, Tanya's father," Lydia said.

Of course, my life being what it is, my first time meeting a girlfriend's father and he had to be a two-hundred-and-seventy-five-year-old vampire.

"Sir," I said. He said nothing but continued to stare directly into my eyes. I sensed small flutters of movement around us, as the others moved a little closer. Finally, he spoke.

"So much emotion over so little of value," he said.

A redheaded female, gowned in white, moved closer, speaking as she came, her voice sultry and teasing. "Oh, I don't know, Anton. He looks and smells rather delicious. Quite a treat, don't you think?"

He laughed. "And what would be the trick, my dear?"

"Why, getting up the stairs, my Lord," she said.

"So, no trick at all then, huh Akilina?" said a cold, familiar voice from the top of the stairs.

Wearing torn jeans and my gray sweatshirt, looking tired and worn, with dark, bruised circles under her eyes, she still outshone every vampire present. The redhead, Akilina, looked scared. Anton smoothly covered his own small start, which I had only seen because our eyes had remained locked throughout the whole discussion. "Ah, my darling daughter, you have decided to honor us with your presence."

"Actually, Anton, I am honoring you by letting you stand so close to my *sputnik jizni*. And, of course, only my sister, Lydia, is allowed to touch him." Her voice carried the chill of death.

The creeping vampires that had frozen at her first words were suddenly as far from me as possible, and Akilina fled in a swirl of white ruffles, leaving only Anton standing very still.

"Chris, would you please come up?" she asked in much warmer tones. I didn't need a second invitation.

Once upstairs, we traveled back down the hall I had run through two nights previously, giving me a chance to notice detail. A series of portraits lined the hall, each of Galina clothed in the fashions of a different period of time. Several had a Russian feel to them, and the last four were more American. The final portrait was of Senka, Galina, and a young Tatiana. I paused a moment to study it, my companions stopping instantly as well. "What is a *sputnik jizni*?" I asked as I looked at the detail of the painting. Lydia answered. "It translates as *satellite life* and would mean something like the western concept of Soul Mate, although it is more serious, especially among vampires."

"Oh." It was all I could think to say. We continued to the door to Tatiana's suite, and Lydia turned off to a separate room with a parting comment: "Play nice, you two."

Tatiana led me to her room and stood with her back to me while I closed the large double doors. She turned slowly, clenching both hands together, her posture much less certain than the girl who had just dominated a room full of deadly, older vampires.

"Christian... I have made a grave mistake. When... when I spoke to you here the other night, I was telling you falsehoods. My mother and Anton convinced me that you were better off without me around you, telling me that the assassin that attacked you was sent by the weres of the city. Our coven has not always had a smooth relationship with the weres." She paused, her eyes bright with tears. "I believed them, and so I told you those things; things I never, ever meant. Things I could never mean. I know you believed me then and I don't expect you to forgive me, but I had to tell you, face to face, here where it... happened." Tears were streaming down her face and a small part of me was startled that she could cry real tears. The rest of me was a real mess. On the drive to her house, I had given myself a stern pep talk. I would be solid, I would not cave. What a load of crap! Faced with her tears, I was helpless. I took two fast steps forward and wrapped her in my arms, not able to speak. She went rigid for a moment, then relaxed into my chest. After a moment, I found my voice.

"Tanya, when was the last time you ate?" She shrugged and looked down at the floor. I lifted her chin till her brilliant blues were looking me in the eye. "We need to feed you. Like right now, my love." She had started to shake her head, but froze when I called her *my love*. Taking her by the hand, I led her over to an ornate dressing-table chair. I sat down and pulled her onto my lap, making her straddle me. Then I leaned my head back and turned it, exposing my jugular.

"Are you certain?" she asked in a very small voice.

"Yes Tanya, I'm certain."

When she bit down, the feeling that overwhelmed me was many times more powerful than any of the previous feedings. My body's reaction was even stronger than before and, given her seating arrangement, there was no way to hide it from her. Not that I cared. I was too caught up in the waves of pleasure to notice anything else. But her reaction was anything but offended. She moaned around a mouthful of my blood and her hands, which were knotted into my tee shirt, flexed briefly and I was shirtless. Not long after that, we were both naked. The amount of blood she took was small and didn't require much time, but the rest of our responses took much, much longer. Our first time was amazing, but over too fast. Our second was longer and slower, building to a spectacular finish. This was what I had been missing my entire adult life? No wonder Scott Henderson was such a sex addict. Near instant healing and supernatural endurance, mixed with youth and an almost insane mutual attraction combined to make our first night together a true marathon.

It took my stomach growling to finally stop us. Tanya laughed as we lay entangled in her sheets, her left hand pressed on my chest, feeling my heart's rhythm.

A soft knock came at the door and Tanya called out, "Come in, Lydia." The door snicked open and a pair of emerald green eyes peeked at us through the opening. I should have been embarrassed or bothered but couldn't seem to work up to either emotion as the little vampire spun into the room.

"About time!" she said.

"Hey, we've got a lot of lost time to make up for," I said.

"No, you moron, it's about time you two had sex. I thought I'd have to dose you both with Spanish Fly and lock you in a bank vault!"

Tanya slipped out of bed and stretched lithely, still gloriously naked. She padded to her closet, emerging after a moment in light blue short shorts and a tight, stretchy tee that left her midriff bare.

The bruises under her eyes were gone and her alabaster skin glowed against her shiny, raven-black hair. Her blue eyes sparking, she tossed my jeans onto the bed and said, "Come on lover. Let's find you a shirt and get you something to eat before you starve away to nothing."

As I pulled on my pants, I commented, "I could just go shirtless, or will I offend the other vampires?"

Tanya growled instantly. "No! I won't have them seeing you shirtless. They don't need any more reason to want you!"

Lydia smirked as she tossed me the NYPD hoodie that Tanya had flung across the room. "Remember, North boy, my girl here is very territorial, even for a Darkkin."

"A what?" I asked.

"Darkkin is a name we use for ourselves. Vampire is way overused," Lydia said.

The mansion's kitchen was a surprise. I had zero expectations of finding food there, but the walk-in fridge was packed with all manner of goodies, both prepared and raw. Tanya saw my puzzled expression and laughed. "Did you forget that Mr. Deckert and his men are all human?"

"And big!" Lydia threw in.

"Actually, I did. I've been meaning to ask how it is that a whole group of humans knows that you're vampires?" I asked.

Tanya answered, "We have always employed humans as daytime guardians and agents of business. We hire ex-military with high clearance levels so that we know they can keep a secret. We pay them extremely well, with excellent benefits. That's why we have a stocked kitchen and a vampire who was a chef in his human life. Keep the troops happy." She smiled and then added, "And, of course, we explain in great detail what will happen if they betray us."

I shuddered a little at the blithe manner in which she mentioned a death threat. Occasionally, I seemed to forget that my two favorite vampires were by nature highly efficient killers.

The monstrous fridge yielded cold chicken sandwiches, with German potato salad and a huge glass of ice-cold milk. Lydia looked slightly disgusted, but intrigued as she watched me eat. "Human food is so smelly and bulky," she commented.

"But oh so flavorful, my little Pita," I said.

Tanya whirled around from her curious examination of the kitchen's massive commercial range.

"What did you call her?" Her voice carried a slight tone of jealousy.

"Pita, P.I.T.A." I smiled at her. "It stands for Pain In the Ass."

They both burst out laughing.

I ended up spending the night, as Tanya was unwilling to let me leave, and I was easily convinced. I did end up getting a few hours of sleep, then drove home as the sun came up, after kissing my sleepy Darkkin good day. Halloween had dawned crisp and clear and the weatherman said it would last through the evening, perfect trick-or-treat weather for all the young monsters eagerly awaiting the evening's candy storm. Tanya had made me swear to show up at Plasma for the club's major night of the year. Because of her awakening, an enormous birthday bash was scheduled, and the club would almost have more vampires in attendance than humans. But the only thing she wanted for her birthday was me. Although, when I had told her I was picking up her gift after breakfast, she freaked.

"You got me a gift? Really? What is it? Tell me!" she demanded, but I just laughed and refused to be bullied into revealing the surprise. I honestly didn't know if she would even like them, but it was too late now. She threatened to call Nika, but I still refused. "You just have to wait. You might not even like my gift, plus you have some of the richest people in the world bringing you gifts. Mine will be modest by comparison."

She tried a new weapon on me... she pouted. It was devastatingly powerful, but I still managed to keep my secret and when I picked her gift up from the specialty jeweler, my expectations were exceeded. Whether or not she would agree, I didn't have a clue.

The funeral for the slain officer was scheduled for ten a.m., and I shined my shoes before putting on my dress uniform. My plainclothes went into a small duffel for after the somber morning.

Smiling stupidly, I headed into work.

Chapter 17

I arrived at the Special Situations offices a few minutes after nine, all of my extra time being eaten up by the drive and parking. I was gonna have to figure out the best subway schedule, but I wanted my own ride to get to Plasma after work. I didn't know what you wore to a Halloween/Vampire Princess birthday bash, but Lydia had told me she would have something appropriate sent to my office.

My tardiness was ignored, as everyone was busy getting ready for the funeral. We drove to the church in two big Chevy Suburbans that the squad regularly appropriated. It was a full Mass funeral, and open casket, to boot. Officer Sanchez had bled out from a claw slash that severed the femoral artery in his right thigh. It had been his only wound, and it was pure bad luck that his artery had been nicked. All of which convinced me that the Damnedthing had not been interested in killing humans. Not that he cared one way or the other about humans, but I got the sense that Okwari had been a very difficult and rebellious slave. As I sat through the Mass, I wondered at the Damnedthing's nature and his place in the metaphysical scheme of things. Religion and theology are not my usual cup of tea, but it's hard to avoid those thoughts when you're at a funeral for a fallen comrade. It was a long sad ceremony; Sanchez had left behind a young wife and ten-month-old baby.

When it was over, Inspector Roma decided we should all go to lunch at his expense, picking a family-owned Italian restaurant where he was known. The pretty hostess greeted him by name, calling out behind her, "Papa, it's Inspector Roma! He brought the whole police force!"

This statement pretty much cleared the kitchen, as the whole family bustled out to greet the squad. From the familiarity they displayed toward the rest of the Special Situations group, this was not the first time the squad had been to Tony's Place. My guess was confirmed when Roma introduced me to Tony, his wife Carlotta, his daughter—the hostess—Adriana , and his son, Benito. Also Benito's wife, Jacobella, who looked very pregnant. They all looked at me a little strangely, probably due to the dark sunglasses I had worn into the restaurant.

Gina elbowed me. "Take off the glasses, Chris, it's rude," she said, as we were led to the big table in the back.

"I don't want to freak them out," I said.

"Oh, get over it! Just take em off."

So I folded my shades and tucked them into my uniform pocket. Poor Adriana turned to point us at the table and froze in her tracks at the sight of my eyes. I just pretended not to notice and parked myself at the back end of the table, burying my head in a menu. She took our drink orders, getting flustered when she got to me, but again, I ignored her reaction as I asked for a diet Pepsi. The restaurant was tiny, but the smells from the kitchen were amazing and the basket of rolls Carlotta brought to the table was fresh baked and still hot.

Sommers, who was sitting on my left, batted at my hand as I reached for a roll. "Senior team members first, Gordon," he said.

But my hand dodged his swat and snagged it right out from under him.

"Damn, you're a fast little son of perdition!" he said with a laugh.

"Just really hungry," I replied.

"So are you ready to order…" Carlotta's voice trailed off as I looked up and met her gaze. She lost her words for just a second, but then started to take orders.

Adriana came back at that moment with a tray of glasses and, ignoring me completely, started to hand out drinks. Her mother had started with Gina at the other end of the table, taking our requests in a clockwise fashion. I had been conscious of Gina's eyes on me, measuring my reactions, studying me, and I looked up and met her gaze. She surprised me by smiling slightly and nodding assurance, as if my appearance was nothing out of the ordinary. Last time I take off my sunglasses in front of strangers, I decided. Adriana continued to serve our drinks and even put her hand on my shoulder, ostensibly to steady herself as she leaned around me to place Steve's 7-UP in front of him. No back down in that girl. When Carlotta came to me, I kept my eyes down as I ordered a pepperoni-and-sausage calzone.

"Gordon, why the hell do you get diet soda when you order fifteen-hundred-calorie meals?" Fran asked.

"Cause I'm watching my girlish figure," I replied, and everyone laughed.

"Why, you are too skinny, Officer Gordon, not enough meat on your bones. But don't you worry, we will feed you right!" Carlotta said. "You like Italian food?"

"Actually, he likes Russian!" Chet Aikens said from down the table.

The squad laughed, Carlotta looked bewildered, and I threw a roll at Chet as I said, "Yes ma'am, I love Italian food."

Mother and daughter headed back toward the kitchen, and as they did, the front door opened and a couple of werewolves walked in. I can't tell you how I knew, I just did. Maybe something about their aggressive stance, the feral gleam in their eyes, or the animal grace of their movements, whatever, it was plain as day to me. One was tall, about six feet, with sand-colored hair; the other was five eight or nine and stocky, with dark brown hair. Adriana met them at the door and led them to a small table in the front by the big window. They both turned and made a point of looking me square in the eye. Adriana took their drink requests and left to get them, glancing at our table as she did. The werewolves were still looking at me, and the tall one gave me a deliberate, slow nod.

I excused myself to go to the men's room, which was near the front. As I came back from the restroom, they both caught my eye, and I headed to their table.

"Officer, our... Leader sends his regards and asks that you accept these replacements in lieu of your originals."

He handed me a plastic shopping bag as he said this and a quick glance inside showed me two Trac Fones, still in their packages, as well as a couple of Powerbars, a pair of folded ponchos and a plastic water bottle with the logo for Lupine Sporting Goods. I looked back at the two weres and nodded.

"These are great. Please thank Brock for me."

Their eyes widened and then narrowed at hearing their Alpha's name out loud. Brock's message was sophisticated on many levels. By having his men drop off this stuff, he was telling me he knew who I was, where I worked, and where I was. The cheap phones and other stuff weren't important, although he was telling me he was aware of my small contribution to his mate and child. I, for my part, was telling him that I knew who I had helped. The tall one nodded and dropped a fifty on the table, then they both left with one parting comment. "Brock is aware that his debt to you remains unpaid. He looks forward to paying it in full."

I turned to head back to the table and my cell phone lit up with a text from Dr. Singh. I had included my cell number in the email I sent him.

DOC S: Chris, the picture you sent is of a protein from the blood of my people. Although it is not an accurate copy. Twisted slightly. I'm not certain, but I think it could have bad side effects if taken by your people.

I typed a thank you and as I put my phone away, a very pregnant Jacobella came out of the kitchen carrying a big tray of salads. She was straining under the weight, listing heavily to her left side, and I saw her foot catch a chair leg. I reacted without thinking, dropping my new bag of stuff while sliding my left hand under the tray as my right arm wrapped around her waist and under her right arm, stopping her from falling. I lifted her upright and made sure she was on her feet, then carried the tray to our table. The others were watching me with varying degrees of disbelief, and no one said anything for a moment. I was glad for the excuse to go back and get the bag with the Trac Fones. I slipped into my seat and took a sip of soda, acting casual.

Velasquez and Roma exchanged looks before looking back my way. "Receiving deliveries?" He nodded at the bag. My mind had been racing in overdrive over how to explain the bag, let alone Dr. Singh's info. With Gina watching, there wasn't much I could do but give them most of the truth. I glanced around to be sure no civilians were in earshot.

"They were werewolves, confirming that the woman attacked at the park was a Were protecting her child. The bag is some stuff my were contact owed me."

"And she was targeted by the Hancers. Why?" Roma asked.

"The text I just received from another contact indicates that the Hance protein is a twisted version of a protein found in vampire blood," I added.

Silence greeted that revelation. "So people drugged with a vampire protein attacked a werewolf female. It sounds like someone is trying to create trouble between the weres and the vampires." Gina said. "Who?"

"When I scanned the Hancers' auras, they had flecks of white, which would be explained by the vampire protein," I said.

"White?" Takata asked.

So I explained. "Humans are blue, weres are blue and green, vampires are white, and demons are black, which I also saw flecks of in the Hancers' auras."

"Demons? Is that what twisted the protein?" Chet asked.

They all looked at me like I was some kind of expert or something.

"Look, demons thrive on chaos, despair, anguish, and other negative emotions. Spreading a street drug that causes its users to freak out in the most violent ways possible makes a lot of sense if you're a demon."

It was quiet for a few minutes as everyone started in on their salads and pondered the new information I had provided. No one had mentioned my abnormally adroit intervention with Jacobella's near fall, and I certainly wasn't gonna bring it up, but I knew it hadn't been missed. Maybe they would just chalk it up to the rest of my strange nature. I hoped so, because I didn't want them to suspect that the purest form of the protein Hance was based on was circulating through my veins and arteries. Something must have been said in the kitchen though, because the whole family came out to serve our main entrees and clear our now-empty salad plates. I just tried to keep my head down and concentrate on the huge calzone Adriana deposited in front of me. I thanked her without looking up, hoping she would choose to ignore me. Alas, it was not to be, because as I took my first bite, I became aware that that Tony, Carlotta, and Jacobella were all waiting on my reaction.

"Um, this is excellent!" I said.

Apparently, that was the right response because they stopped staring and went back to their other customers. I looked up to find Chet watching me with a grin.

"Damn, Gordon, I've been here five times and they --" He nodded in the direction of the Russo family, "-- never waited on my opinion. You are one smooth son of a bitch!" he said.

It was just dumb luck on my part that I had helped keep their daughter-in-law from falling, but I didn't want to bring that incident back up, so I just grinned at him, shrugged, and kept eating. The calzone was really good and I was pretty hungry, although not as bad as I had been the last few days.

The rest of lunch was uneventful, although my soda glass was always full and nothing would do for Mama Carlotta but that I eat a full dessert on the house.

We headed back to One Police Plaza. I was riding with Takata, who was driving, Sommers, and Fran, who seemed glued to my side. Apparently, I was providing her first relief from the constant attentions of the dead in years. Sommers got a cell call just before we arrived back at headquarters and turned to Takata.

"Roma wants us to take Gordon straight to the range without going to the office."

"He say why?" Takata asked.

"Olivia called. Duclair and Adler are waiting for Roma," Sommers said. "They're all worked up about the Hance raid and shit. You leave your stuff in the office?" he asked me.

"Yeah, I threw my duffel in the copier room, but I have my Glock with me, of course."

"I'll get it and I'll grab your stuff too, Brian. You take Chris right to the range. Roma doesn't want him anywhere near the Feddies."

The nice thing about a Glock 18 is that it looks just like its semiautomatic parent model, the 17. The only visible difference is the selector on the left side of the slide. When holstered on the right hip, it is indistinguishable from the standard service piece.

As Brian led me through yet another warren of tunnels, I threw a question at him. "Who are Duclair and Adler, and why shouldn't I meet them?"

He didn't answer at first and I thought he was going to ignore me, but after a dozen steps, he finally spoke.

"Briana Duclair is the head of Homeland Security's Directorate of Anomalous Activity, our federal counterparts. Eric Adler is her second in command."

He paused to punch in a key code at a locked door.

"Anyway, she's wicked jealous of the Inspector, always trying to scoop him to prove her importance to her chain of command. They have a huge budget, try to get all the best people and gear. By now, she'll have heard rumors about the Hance raid, the Damnedthing, and seen some of the intell that we scored. She's here to sniff out Roma's ace in the hole."

I thought about that as we trudged along quiet corridors. "What's his ace in the hole, or can't you tell me?" I asked.

He looked at me sidelong without breaking stride. "You don't know?" he asked back.

"Brian, this is like my second day on the job. I don't know crap."

"Well, Chris, you're his ace in the hole."

I hadn't seen that one coming, and it left me speechless.

After a moment, he spoke again. "You know, you could pretty much write your own ticket with the feds. Be a real big pay increase, not to mention perks and really cool stuff," he threw out.

"They are based here in New York?" I asked.

"Yup, but they travel all over the country. They have their own Gulfstream on standby at JFK International. Big league stuff." He was watching me to gauge my reaction.

"Well, that's out then. Me traveling around the country wouldn't sit well with my girl. She might get... anxious," I said.

"You ironed out your differences then?" he asked.

"Yeah, pretty much," I replied. "Besides, their group's letters are D.O.A.A. That's kinda nerdy."

He laughed. "Yeah, we refer to them as 'Dead on Arrival, Always'!"

Sommers joined us at the simulator range, and we changed out of our dress uniforms in favor of tactical khakis. I started running the scenarios, keeping my gun semi auto. I could tell that Steve and Brian were talking about me, but between the gunfire and hearing protection, I couldn't hear them. Steve was relaxed and friendly when we finished the first one though, so Brian must have relayed our conversation. I ran it again to see if I could get a better time. Finishing the shoot, I headed back to the gun table to reload my mags and noticed the Inspector was there, observing and talking with Takata and Sommers.

"Chris, you shaved about three seconds off your time with that run," Sommers informed me.

"How was my accuracy score?"

"Fine," he said without elaborating. "Ready for the last scenario?"

"Sure, bring it!"

The first five scenarios all had human-looking pop-up targets, some stand-alone and some holding hostages. You had to avoid shooting innocent bystanders and correctly take out the thugs while avoiding getting shot by the computer-controlled paintball guns the dummy bad guys carried. The last simulation was designed just for our squad, and the guys would replace many of the pop-ups with vampire and were look-alikes taken from a locked closet. They made me sit out in the hallway while they changed it up. Inspector Roma kept me company. "Chris, Brian told me about your conversation regarding the DOAA folks."

"Well, Inspector, jetting around the country is not an option for me. I need to stay here in the city and work on those lines of communication we talked about. Tatiana would insist on going with me and frankly, I don't want her anywhere near the feds."

"Well, I can't tell you how relieved I am to hear that, although you should know that the Commissioner himself approved a significant pay raise for you."

"Ah, thanks sir." I said. "Brian said that this Agent Duclair was kind of a thorn in our group's side."

"Well, Briana is tough, that's for sure. And a little too Machiavellian in her methods for my tastes, but she does want to protect her country."

Sommers opened the door. "All right, Chris. We're ready."

I entered the darkened room, put on my safety glasses and hearing protection, checked my loaded mags and holstered gun, and pronounced myself ready. Takata gave the order to proceed, and I slowly walked into the shoot zone. This range was one hundred and fifty yards long, with pop-ups all down its length. Designed to look like a typical New York street at night, you simply walked toward the far end and engaged targets as they came. The first pop-up was a glaring vampire, but it didn't rush me, so I held my fire. After a second, it popped back down, out of sight. The next was a fast-rushing werewolf, and I automatically gave it a burst of nine rounds, full automatic. The rest were similar, with rushing vampires and charging weres, monsters holding human victims and even a flying vampire, although I hadn't heard from my vampires that flying was possible.

The simulation ended and the lights came up. I walked back to the control station, and all three officers were staring at me. "How did I do?"

Roma spoke first. "You failed. You froze up on the first target."

"Ah, Inspector, I didn't freeze. It was a non-attacking vampire, so I held my fire."

He looked at me like I was crazy. "Chris, they're all hostile. You have to engage them all. If you had left it behind you, it could have come up and killed you

239

anytime while you were engaged with the rest of them."

"Sir, with all due respect, I can't go around shooting every vampire or were I see, or I'll be declaring war on the supernatural community. And a lot of them snarl from time to time. It would be like shooting a human that yelled or swore."

He started to disagree, then stopped himself and thought about it for a moment. He nodded slowly. "I get your point." The implications of the simulation were sinking in on all three of them. Without really thinking about it, they had created a training program that taught the squad to shoot any and all supernaturals on sight. It made me realize just how little contact the team had with actual vampires and weres. I needed to correct that as soon as I could, or there would be a real bad incident in the future.

"What did you think of the rest of the simulation?" Sommers asked.

"Well, honestly, it's kinda slow. Most weres and vampires move faster than that. Older vampires move a lot faster."

They looked at me, a little stunned. Finally, Roma asked a question. "How was his shooting?"

Takata answered from the control station. "One hundred percent on accuracy. Reaction time... I'm going to have to recheck, because the numbers look... unreal."

What can I say? I got carried away with the simulation.

"Go ahead and recheck them, but I think you'll find that they are real." Roma turned and addressed me. "Chris, your reflexes appear to be outside human normal. Any thoughts?"

I shrugged, not willing to go down that road.

"Hmm, I suppose we should just lump it in with the rest of your unusual quirks," he said.

He seemed a little too willing to ignore my lapse of control, but then, he might not want to upset me into jumping to the federal team, either.

"What do you think fellas? Are you done with him for the day?"

The two tactical operations officers looked at each other and then nodded.

"Okay, I'm gonna take him back to the offices while you guys lock down the range."

I thanked them for the shooting and followed the Inspector back to the squad offices. Olivia smiled at me as we walked through and into the conference room. "Ah sir, I was wondering if it might be a good idea for me to see about introducing the team to a couple of my... ah... friends?"

He didn't answer immediately, but then nodded. "I, for one, would like to meet Galina Demidova if possible."

"She doesn't like me much, but her boss seems to. I'll ask Tatiana what she thinks."

He shook his head in disbelief. "You say that like you're talking about someone you met at church or a cocktail party or something. Wait a minute. Did you say 'her boss'?"

"Yeah, Galina is a little young to be running a coven. She holds her position because of some special circumstances. But like all of the vampires, she answers to an Elder. Her Elder likes me... I think."

"Is one of the special circumstances named Tatiana?" he guessed.

I didn't want to answer, but he read my expression and nodded to himself. "I thought it was something like that. We hear enough to know that your girlfriend holds some special spot in the vampire hierarchy. Care to explain?"

"Not really, sir. I'm not sure I fully understand it all myself. I'll know more after tonight. Big party for Tatiana at club Plasma. Her birthday and Halloween and all that."

"How is it that she has a birthday?" he asked.

"That, Sir, is the best question that you've asked so far."

We were standing in the conference room, and just then, the door opened behind us and Olivia came in with a plate of cupcakes, one of which had a candle in it. Gina, Fran, and Chet all appeared in the doorways of their respective offices and called out, almost in unison, "Happy birthday!"

It was extremely awkward and Roma looked more surprised than I felt, but it had been a long time since anyone other than Gramps had acknowledged my birthday. It was an absurdly pleasant feeling. I blew out the candle before anyone could start singing, and we all grabbed a cupcake. Olivia explained, "I happened to notice your birthdate in your personnel file and mentioned it to Gina. The local bakery only had cupcakes, but they're very cakey."

"Thanks, I, ah, I haven't had a group birthday thing since I was eight."

They all looked at me like that was the most pitiful thing they had ever heard.

"Well, if we had known there was a party, we wouldn't have left," a voice said from the open doorway to Olivia's office. A tall, blonde woman dressed in a dark suit stood in the doorway with a sardonic smile on her face. A really large, dark-haired man loomed behind her. Her eyes looked me over from head to toe in stark appraisal. She was attractive, but she gave off a serious *don't screw with me* attitude.

Roma recovered after a moment, a frown flickering across his face.

"Agent Duclair, I didn't expect to see you again quite so soon." His voice was cold.

"Oh you know how it is, Martin, forgotten questions that you suddenly remember. We were still in the building, so I thought I would pop back in to ask them in person." She hadn't taken her eyes off me the whole time, and there was something smugly triumphant in her expression. "But I see you have a new team member who I haven't had the pleasure of meeting. Hi, I'm Special Agent Briana Duclair, Homeland

Security --" She advanced with her hand out. "-- and you are?"

"Chris Gordon, ma'am." I automatically shook her hand. Her grip was strong and forceful, like a man's would be. The rest of my squad had sour expressions and Olivia looked angry, like her space had been violated, which, in a manner of speaking, it had.

"Shame on you, Martin! You never told me you had a new member of your little squad. And such a handsome one at that." Now she was making fun of the team and me in one shot. I stepped back a pace from her in annoyance. Her right eyebrow raised slightly as she took in my expression and I had the sinking feeling I had another facial coding expert on my hands. Gina Velasquez had a blank look on her face, and I realized she was wearing her poker face. I glanced at the big man who had moved into the doorway when Agent Duclair had stepped forward. He would be Eric Adler, I figured. About six-four or six-five, probably two hundred and thirty pounds, short brown hair, and pale gray eyes that focused like lasers on me. Takata and Sommers entered the outer office behind him, and he swung back to put his back to the wall, watching them like a bodyguard in hostile territory. Both officers went on point like attack dogs, and you could feel the tension ratchet up immediately. Duclair ignored all that and continued to appraise me. "So Officer Gordon, what is your specialty? Psychic? Clairvoyant?" she asked.

I could feel Gina and the Inspector tighten up at the question, but I had an answer ready.

"I'm a tracker, ma'am."

"A tracker?" she said, a frown flashing across her face.

"Yes ma'am. Born and raised in the Adirondacks. Worked with Search and Rescue. My gramps trained me, ma'am." I sounded like a hick. A slow-witted hick. The big guy in the doorway snorted his opinion of my statement. The light of victory in Agent Duclair's eyes dimmed a little as she took in my statement, the truth of which was written on my face.

"A tracker. Martin, why the hell would you put a tracker on the team?" she turned, bewildered, to the Inspector.

"Why Briana, Gordon here already proved his worth at the Park with those Hancers. It's amazing the way he can recreate the crime timeline from tracks," Roma answered, swiftly recovering.

The big guy in the door swiveled his head like a tank turret, his eyes once more locked on me. "You're the one in the Youtube video. You took down the last perp when he broke his cuffs," he stated, his voice deep. Now it was his turn to appraise me, but I recognized the gaze as one fighter evaluating another. Apparently he wasn't impressed because he snorted again and went back to watching Sommers and Takata watch him.

Duclair still looked bewildered by the tracker stuff, and Gina chose that moment to intervene. "Well, if the introductions are out of the way, I need to talk to Chris about his previous evaluations."

She pointed at her door like I was a new and somewhat slow student on the first day of school. I took her cue and slipped into her office. She closed the door behind me and then shuttered the blinds on the window into the conference room. She turned to me, let out a breath of relief, and smiled.

"That was fast thinking, Chris. And you did it without lying."

I shrugged. "I had the creepy feeling that she could read micro expressions like you do."

She nodded. "Briana and I were in the same class. She can pick up a lie in a heartbeat. But I'm afraid you have only bought us some time. She's smart. She'll think about it, do some digging, look at your files, and know you're not just a tracker. But you did throw her for a loop. That's not something that very many people can lay claim to."

"Brian felt that I was the reason she was nosing around here in the first place," I said.

"And did he tell you what she would do if she found you?"

I nodded. "Yeah, offer me a job and a big fat raise."

She looked surprised. "You aren't interested in her job offer?"

"Well, from what I understand, they cover the whole country. That kind of travel would be difficult in my situation."

She smiled. "I hadn't thought of that. Would Tatiana be upset?"

"Well, not if she went with me. But that would stir up the all the vampires. And if she couldn't go with me, she would just follow on her own."

"Well, stirring up all the vampires in the city should be avoided." She smiled again.

"No Gina, I mean, it would stir up ALL the vampires, everywhere. Tatiana is the Prodigal Daughter, so to speak. I haven't yet met a vampire that didn't either want to worship her or want to control her."

Her eyes got wider and wider as I spoke. "That puts you in a tough spot, doesn't it?"

"Well, it makes me unpopular with the ones that want to control her. As if I needed that. I already have problems with vampires as it is."

"What do you mean?" she asked.

"Well, apparently, I'm particularly attractive to most vampires."

"I can understand the females, but males too?"

"Huh? I smell good to all vampires, something about AB blood types. What were you talking about?"

She studied me for a moment, surprised. "You really don't see yourself very well, do you?"

"If you mean, do I know that I'm a freak, then the answer is yes. Most people figure something is wrong with me when they see my eyes."

She smiled again, shaking her head. "No Chris, you're really far off the mark. Most women don't see you as a freak. They see you as hot."

I frowned, not sure what my body temperature had to do with it. Then an alternative meaning to her words hit me. "Ah, no, I think you made a mistake. People have always been weirded out by my eyes."

"Maybe when you were younger that was true, but I can assure you that almost every female that I've observed come in contact with you has found you attractive."

Before I could argue further, there was a knock at the door and Roma popped in, the rest of the team behind him. "All right, I got rid of her, and Olivia's got the door locked," he said. "Quick thinking, Chris!"

"Er, thanks Sir," I replied.

"Gina, what do you think? Will she catch on?" Roma asked.

"Sir, with Briana it's a matter of when, not if. She'll start sniffing around in earnest and the pieces will come together."

"You're right, of course," he admitted. "Hmm, I better talk to the Commissioner and the Mayor." He looked at his watch. "Chris, you should head out soon. We don't want Halloween traffic to make you late for your engagement, now do we?"

I nodded and he was gone, headed to his office to make calls.

Gina looked at me with a hint of amusement. "So, we'll see you on Monday at nine a.m., unless we get called out. Have fun, and be careful."

Chapter 18

I wished her a good weekend and left, saying goodbye to the others as I headed out. As I walked to my car, I started a mental list of things to do. First, I needed to call Gramps. Second, look up any info on Briana Duclair. Third, figure out what in my pitiful wardrobe would be fit to wear tonight, as Lydia's delivery had never made it. Traffic was bad, and it took me forty frigging minutes to get back to my part of Brooklyn. When I got off the elevator, a package was waiting in front of my door. I took it inside and hit the answering machine as I opened it. There were four messages on the machine, all from Gramps, starting from late last night to this afternoon. No real message, just a terse, "Chris, call me."

I tried his number, but got the answering machine at the farm house. Next, I called his cell, but it must have been off, because I got shunted to his voicemail. I left a quick message on both and then looked at the contents of the package.

When I got the box open, I found a note on top of a pile of clothes.

Chris, THIS is what you need to wear tonight. Your black Sketchers will do for shoes. NO JACKET!
L

On top of the stack was a fitted white v-neck long-sleeve tee shirt made from very light cotton and, according to the label, five percent lycra. Bloody red ink drops flowed from the v-neck and became gothic letters spelling *Plasma's best: AB+* with a black stencil underneath *Property of TAD.* Across the back was a drawing of a fanged vampire skull under the words *Suck Off!*

Hmm, subtle. I was pretty sure this was a one-of-a-kind shirt. Under the tee was a pair of soft black leather pants, cut like jeans. I didn't bother to try the clothes on, trusting that Lydia pretty much had my sizes down pat.

Thinking I was in for a long night, I made myself a huge plate of cold chicken, three kinds of cheese, and fruit from the fridge, washed down with a Sam Adams Octoberfest that I found behind a gallon of full fat milk.

Tanya's gift was in a flat, black box, with a fitted lid that would pop right off. I wrapped it in deep red metallic paper that I had picked up before work and tied it with long piece of black ribbon from the same store. Then I just hung out and chilled, listening to my iPod and trying not to think of anything at all. When I couldn't stand waiting around anymore, I looked at the clock: eight fifty-two. Close enough. I called a cab, got dressed in my Lydia-approved clothes, and headed out.

My cabbie asked me if I wanted to be dropped off at the front of the club or back near the end of the line, which I'm sure he figured would save me a two-block walk. I told him the front of the club would be fine. "It is your shoe leather," he shrugged.

The line stretched like a black leather-and-lace snake down the street and around the corner. Every imaginable variation of a vampire costume was on display. Everywhere the eye could see, ruffled white shirts, jagged black skirts, leather corsets, velvet jackets, fishnet stockings, pale, made-up faces, and blood red lips. I was seriously underdressed.

Arkady was manning the door, guarding the velvet rope with a grim expression. I hadn't really realized just how big he was. Had to go six-five, two hundred and sixty pounds of mean vampire. Despite the crowds' intent on getting in, there was a three-foot gap between the rope and the next in line. His yellow eyes swiveled to me like gun emplacements and his expression didn't change. I looked back calmly, but I started to hear the mutters and voices in the crowd.

" -- End of the line, sucker—"

"-- Don't even think about it, dude!—"

"-- Ohhh, me likee—"

"-- Hey Chris!—"

I turned to the last one, locating two female gothic types about fifty people back. It was Paige and Kathy, dressed like Dracula's brides in gauzy white gowns. I walked over to them.

"Hi, Chris. I thought you didn't like this place?" Kathy greeted me while both looked me up and down.

"Well, I don't really, but I like some of the people and I wasn't given much of a choice."

Paige spoke up. "Good luck getting in. You could jump in with us, but I think it would start a fight."

"--Damn right—"

"--I'll kick his ass—" That one came from a tiny little girl in black tights and a shredded white shirt.

Chests puffed up and eyes frowned in menace in my direction, but before I could answer, the line went dead quiet and all eyes looked over my shoulder at something behind me. I turned and looked back, then up. Arkady was about six feet behind me, his glare menacing.

"What the hell are you doing?" he demanded.

A couple of people looked at me like I was gonna get my ass kicked, and they were happy about that.

"Are you hating me, then? Trying to get me in trouble? You need to go in! She will know by now!" he said.

"Arkady, these two are my friends. They need to go in with me."

He instantly moved toward the girls, the crowd parting away from him like the Red Sea.

"What the hell is going on?" an angry female voice said from the front door of the club.

Lydia, dressed in a black micro skirt over white scale-pattern tights and a red blouse, stood just outside the club, her arms crossed and her left foot tapping.

"Northern, get your ass in here! Arkady, what's he doing in line?" she demanded.

By now, Arkady had herded the three of us toward the door like a giant Russian sheepdog, his expression slightly worried.

"Why, Lydia, you look lovely tonight," I said with a smirk.

"Cut the shit, Gordon, and get in here. You do know that all hell broke loose as soon as you got outta that cab, right? Who are these two?" she directed the last at Paige and Kathy, whose eyes were the size of gumballs and just as round.

"These are my friends! Kathy and Paige are my neighbors, and I want assurances that they will be looked after properly." My emphasis on the word friends did not go unnoticed, and the little vampire instantly knew what I was talking about. She turned her head slightly toward the door and spoke in a normal voice. "Trenton."

A lean, six-foot-tall vampire slid around the door frame, looking like a pale Abercrombie model. "Ma'am?"

"These are Mr. Gordon's friends. They are to be seated at a VIP table, and you are responsible for them tonight." She gave him a level look and he nodded acknowledgment after a brief glance in my direction. A brief, nervous glance. What was that about?

"Should I clear out one of the celebrities, then?" he asked.

"Why don't you let the ladies decide which celebrities should sit with them? Use your judgement."

Again, he nodded and led the two awestruck girls away into the club. Lydia, meanwhile, grabbed my hand and pulled me in and down the stairs, past the bar, and into the corridor beyond. I'm pretty sure my feet never hit the ground after the first step. We slowed down outside the same dressing room that Tatiana had cleaned up in a week ago. Lydia glanced down at the red-wrapped package in my left hand.

"It's a damn good thing you remembered that. She's been talking about nothing else all day."

"I'm not sure if she'll like it," I said.

She snorted. "We'll know soon enough."

She reached for the door but it yanked open from the inside, and I was lost. Tatiana was wearing a black spiderweb that somehow managed to barely cover her breasts and seemed to grow out of a skintight sheath that hugged her hips and extended in wispy fabric down to her knees. Both sides of the dress were slit almost to her hips, and my eyes didn't know which portion of exposed creamy white skin to look at first. She looked me over from top to bottom and then turned to Lydia.

"Oh, thank you for my present. Can I unwrap him now?" she said with a sly grin.

Lydia laughed. "Oh you might want to wait until you open his gift before... um... unwrapping mine."

Tatiana's gaze shot down to the pitiful package in my hand. Then she squealed, like a teen girl at a boy band concert. Her liquid blue eyes lit up and she pulled me into the room hard enough to give me whiplash. Figuring that my life depended on it, I surrendered the gift and awaited her disappointment. No way could it live up to this level of expectation. Fingers that could tear steel gently untied the ribbon and carefully pulled the paper open. The flat black box slid onto her waiting palm and, after a quick glance at Lydia and me, she opened it. Two silver bracelets sat in nests of black velvet. Tatiana looked at them in a puzzled manner.

Lydia spoke first. "Silver? You got her silver bracelets, Northern?" She asked in a voice that questioned my sanity.

I shook my head quickly. "No! Not silver. Polished tungsten carbide, inset with sapphires," I said.

They both looked at me quizzically.

I explained, hoping I could salvage some tiny part of the moment. "Tungsten is one of the hardest metals known. It takes something as hard as a diamond to really scratch it. They won't ever need polishing and they won't ever tarnish. And they should turn pretty much any knife or sword strike. That's the theory at least," I finished, a little lamely.

Lydia started to smile and Tatiana touched one gingerly, then with more assurance, pulling it from the velvet.

"I had them sized to fit your forearms, Tanya, figuring you block with that part of your arm."

Her head lifted to meet my gaze, and her smile lit up the room. There was a slight blur and I was wrapped in one hundred and twenty pounds of vampire girl. After kissing me to within an inch of my life, she peeled herself off and slid the bracelet up her arm. Thank heavens it fit. The other bracelet swiftly found its new home on her other arm, and she was bouncing up and down with excitement, which had an interesting effect on her anatomy. Suddenly, she went from mid-bounce to fighting stance, blurring through a series of blocks and strikes. Apparently more than satisfied with the results, she proceeded to kiss the hell out of me again. When she came up for air and stepped back, Lydia reached over and turned each bracelet so that the three sapphires were visible, their blue a close match to Tatiana's eyes.

"Holy Crap, Chris. These are really cool. You really do pay attention when I'm telling you stuff," Lydia said.

"Huh? Did you say something?" I deadpanned, earning a smack on the shoulder.

"If you look on the inside, they have your initials and... well, mine, too," I said.

A split second later, Tanya was looking inside both bracelets to confirm this new feature. She looked up at me.

"You have the same middle initial as I do," she said.

"Actually, my middle name is rather a lot like yours. It's Anthony."

"Anthony is another form of Anton," Lydia said. "That's kinda weird."

"Well, my mom was half Russian and half American. Her father's name was Anthony," I explained.

They both just stared at me.

"How did that happen?" Tanya asked.

"The way it normally does. Russian boy meets American girl."

Lydia gave me a patient look, the sort you reserve for kindly idiots. I decided I better continue. "My grandmother on my mom's side was an army nurse in World War II. She met my grandfather just after the war ended. He had been held in a prison camp somewhere in Germany, and when U.S. troops rescued him, he was taken to the hospital where she was working," I said.

"He was Jewish?" Lydia asked.

Tanya was inspecting at her bracelets carefully.

"No, it wasn't a death camp. Some other kind of prison camp. Mom said that he would never talk about it, but I know he had horrible nightmares about it his entire remaining life."

Lydia was tapping her bottom lip thoughtfully, and Tanya was turning one of the bracelets over in her hands.

"So, Tanya, do you like them?" I asked, just to be sure.

And when she looked up, I suddenly wasn't sure, because she had tears running down her cheeks.

"Whoa, we can take them back if you don't like them," I said.

"You idiot, she's crying because she loves them!" Lydia said.

Tatiana started to speak in Russian, and I couldn't understand anything other than the words *sputnik jezni.* But I could understand that she really, really liked the gift.

The she stopped and her eyes got wide for a moment. "Oh, I almost forgot. I have gift for you." Her accent was stronger when she was excited. I thought it was about the most exotic sound I'd ever heard.

She danced across the room, scooped up a huge, gift-wrapped box, and glided back to me. I took the box , which was much heavier than I had expected, and set it on the floor. Pulling out my ever-present tactical folding knife (it's usually an Emerson CQC), I slit the package open. Tanya's hand beckoned to see the knife, so I deposited it, handle-first, into her grasp. While she examined the blade, I opened the box, then rocked back, stunned.

About fifteen thousand dollars' worth of tactical gear sat inside. Two new Dragonskin vests; one for concealment, the other a full-military-grade class V heavy armor vest. Hatch kevlar patrol gloves, Wiley-X ballistic sunglasses, Bates tactical boots, 5.11 plainclothes pants and jackets, multiple LED flashlights, three different automatic knives, along with batteries and other accessories.

Tanya was watching my reaction closely as I looked back up at her in wonder.

"You have got to be the coolest girl on the planet!" I said. "This stuff is awesome! But you spent a fortune."

She laughed and bounced up and down again, which dropped my I.Q. by about fifty points. She flicked the heavy box with her foot, shooting it across the floor and into the far wall.

"Come on, I want to show off my bracelets!" she said.

"Wait!" I held up my hand and then turned to Lydia.

"What did you get me?" I asked.

She didn't hesitate a moment. "I designed and commissioned Tanya's dress!"

I looked her in the eyes with the most sincere gratitude. "Thank you!"

This being only my second time in Plasma, there was a lot I hadn't noticed the first time through. I had been pretty busy, after all. The building was rectangular, with the narrow walls being the front and back of the structure. The right-hand wall was a common wall shared with the building next door, but the left side contained the door and corridor where I first met Tatiana. This side of the dance floor was private and reserved for vampires only. Of course, it didn't have that printed on signs or anything. Despite being a vampire club, the coven was counting on humanity's disbelief, and essentially the club was a wonderful example of hiding in plain sight. Who would believe the resident vampires of Plasma were real and not just highly trained actors?

Despite the lack of signage, highly visible bouncers kept the area clear of humans. Tonight, the exclusive zone was packed with vampires, all wishing to pay homage to their young princess. Tatiana led me straight into this tangle of dangerous predators with complete disregard. It was a stark reminder that the girl I found myself falling in love with was more deadly than most of the others and would one day be the apex vampire.

Instantly, all attention was on us. I knew some of the pale, cold faces. Blonde Nika was there, Galina watched me with ice in her eyes, Anton held court at a table near the dance floor, Vadim hovered against the back wall, and Senka stood with two other extremely old vampires in the center, a discreet space around them. The fact that I could gauge vampire age as well as tell humans, weres, and vampires apart at a glance was not something I was comfortable with yet, let alone understand.

Tatiana flowed up to the three Elders, her smile capturing their immediate attention. Three pairs of cold eyes looked me over with interest. Senka spoke first.

"Granddaughter, am I to assume that your radiant smile has something to do with the silver-colored bracelets that you are wearing?" she asked.

"Yes, Grandmother. They are gifts from Christian. Elder Fedor and Elder Tzao, may I introduce my *sputnik jizni*, Christian Gordon."

Fedor was just over five feet tall, slim and boyish-looking, dressed in an immaculate black Armani suit. His bronze hair was almost a helmet of tight curls, framing a pair of cold blue eyes. He looked me over, from head to toe, his expression bland.

Tzao was even smaller, well under five feet, and petite. Her jet black hair and upturned jade eyes gave the impression of a kewpie doll. A deadly kewpie doll. Her ruby lips twitched slightly in what might have be a flicker of a smile—or maybe a contemptuous sneer. Neither offered to shake hands, but I was getting used to that quirk of vampire nature. Extremely touchy feely with family, vampires are aloof and disdain physical contact with strangers and acquaintances. Whatever chilly welcome I felt from Fedor and Tzao, Senka countered by giving me a pointed and public hug.

"Tell us about these wonderful bracelets, Granddaughter," she said.

Tatiana explained about tungsten carbide, demonstrating by slashing at her left bracelet with my knife. Senka raised one sculpted eyebrow and looked over to me.

"Beautiful and practical at the same time," she said.

I shrugged. "If they are going to survive Tatiana's hobbies, they better be tough."

"Yes dear. Your comment and mine apply to all of Tanya's recent acquisitions," she said.

Oh, she was including me in that group.

By now, a group of younger vampires were crowding around Tanya, admiring her bracelets. I took advantage of the lack of attention and moved back to observe. Some, like Nika, seemed sincere; others were fawning butt kissers. Anton's redhead, Akilina, was one of the fawners, and I noticed she was discreetly trying to move Tanya's attention and field of view away from where I was standing. It didn't work very well, because Tanya simply reoriented herself, keeping me in the middle of her field of view. Her sapphire eyes touched mine every so often, usually with a smile following on her blood-red lips. While her fans were admiring her jewelry, I was simply admiring her. Lydia had outdone herself with that amazing spiderweb dress. A sudden breath of rose and musk announced the dress designer herself, by my left elbow. I glanced over and met her sparkling emerald eyes. "Go ahead and admit it! I kick designer ass!" she said, handing me a frosty Corona.

"No question that you're my favorite designer. What ya drinking? A negative?" I asked.

She looked down at the goblet of thick red fluid in her hand.

"An unpretentious little B positive," she said, laughing. "So tell me, what was your grandfather's last name?" she asked.

"Volkov." I said. "Well, she seems to like the bracelets. She's having fun showing them off."

Lydia sighed. "Chris, you're a sweet boy, but a bit clueless. Her favorite gift isn't your gift, it's mine."

"What are you talking about? "

"Look where you're standing," she said.

I glanced around. We were almost smack dab in the middle of the vampire space, with a clear six-foot zone around the two of us. I frowned at her.

"She's got you center stage for everyone to admire, but no touchy. Your shirt might seem like a joke, but it is really rather a loud statement. And I got the fit exactly right. Looks like it was spray painted on," she said in a very self-satisfied way.

I had been watching Tanya, but now as I looked around, I noticed that much of the vampire attention was focused on Lydia and I. Suddenly feeling extremely self-conscious, I looked at the rest of the club. The tables across the dance floor were all occupied by a rather amazing group of celebrities. I noticed two NFL football players, a controversial Yankee third baseman and his supermodel date, several rock stars, and more than a few actors. Paige and Kathy were seated at the centermost table, looking dazed as they listened raptly to the handsome actor who had made drunken pirates a favorite with women the world over. Despite the level of star power on that side of the room, most of the club—celebrities included—were watching Tatiana and her court. The lead singer of the band started to walk over to the vampire area and Nika suddenly turned to look at her, then leaned in and whispered in Tanya's ear.

She grinned in excitement, nodded, and beckoned Lydia to her. Nika headed to the railing and met the lead singer, leaning down to give her instructions. Tanya whispered in Lydia's ear and then gave me a broad wink. Nika rejoined her, and the three of them moved gracefully over to the dance floor. The club lights dimmed to almost full black, although I could still see quite well. It had seemed much darker last Friday when Tanya and Nika had danced. The club patrons started going crazy as soon as the first light dimmed, yelling "Tatiana, Tatiana". The music came up slowly, the song different from the previous week but having a similar beat. Heavy bass pushed in regular pulses against my chest and pant legs. This time, I knew what to expect when the spotlight illuminated Tanya, Nika, and Lydia. My attention focused fully on Tanya's midnight gossamer form as she stood motionless for a moment, then spun into motion.

One of my old martial arts instructors used to talk about moving from your center. Difficult to master, moving from your center involves the body's center of gravity and the martial artist's ability to locate and work from it. Vampires seemed to have a natural aptitude for harnessing their centers, but Tanya's was absolute, giving her perfect balance and control. As she spun in supernatural grace, her electric blue eyes sought me out, and her dance became a gift to me and me alone.

It was then that the vision struck.

Tatiana, the dance floor, and the Hellbourne from the Hance lab. Immediately, my body went on alert and I started to scan the crowded railings, looking for the demon that I knew was in the room. From the corner of my eye, I could see that all three dancers knew something was wrong. Tatiana could sense what I felt, Nika could read my damn mind, and Lydia was just Lydia. Perceptive as hell. I found what I was looking for up on the second level, near the middle of the railing, almost directly above Paige and Kathy's table. A blank face leaning over, head tracking the dancers' motions below. I couldn't understand how he was homing in on Tatiana, as the necklace she wore should have blanked her from his sight. Then I saw his eyes following the gazes of the onlookers and realized what he was doing. Virtually everyone in the club was watching the vision-made-flesh that was Tanya dancing. The demon was watching them watch her and triangulating her position accordingly. I could tell the moment he locked her in his sights and as he leapt over the railing, I propelled myself in a forward dive across the dance floor and into a roll. I came to my feet, grabbed my girl and spun, throwing her back to the vampires behind me. My luck held, as Senka had moved fluidly into the position I abandoned, and as Tanya landed lightly on both feet, the Elder wrapped her arms around her granddaughter and held her back. I saw all of that and then a heavy weight smashed into my shoulders and back and a greasy blackness impacted my aura. Landing on my stomach with my arms and hands against the floor, I pushed off in the mother of all push- ups. Instead of coming to just the full extension of my arms, I came back all the way to my feet, just in time to catch a blow on my left arm. But a punch that would have disabled my arm a week ago was now less than a minor annoyance. For the first time in my life, I was fighting a demon on at least equal terms of strength and speed. Then he ruined it by pulling a foot-long knife and stabbing at my gut. I didn't care. Tanya was safe in her grandmother's steel arms and I could give myself over to the rage that was bubbling up from my core. Surrendering control to my fight brain, I let the berserker free.

Paige and Kathy told me days later that it was the most fantastic fight scene they had ever seen performed live. First, there was just my blurring dive and artful Tanya toss. But when the Hellbourne crashed into me, his cloak failed and he suddenly appeared to all the onlookers. What followed after that was a jerky fast, flickering martial arts beatdown that put Jet Li, Jackie Chan, and Bruce Lee to shame.

I remember very little of it, mainly just the incredibly fierce joy of all-out combat with a serious opponent. But I can remember slamming my left palm down on the point of his blade, running it through my hand until I could wrench the knife from his grasp. And the memory is crystal clear of my right hook crushing his ribcage, my left jab breaking his nose, my right palm heel strike cracking his sternum and my left hand knotting his hair, spinning him around and breaking his spine with a side kick. I felt a slight jab in my leg as I pulled the slick oily blackness from its shell and flung it into the waiting claws of the smoky raptor that I don't remember calling. Twelve-foot-wide wings beat once, and Kirby's keening cry filled my ears as he flicked out of our world.

What happened next is a confusing jumble of images. Vadim, suddenly by my side, holding my hand over my head like a victorious prize fighter while the club's patrons thundered their approval of the night's entertainment. The bald giant holding the empty body of the Hellbourne by its neck in an effortless grip, making it look like it was standing on its own feet. A pain in my left leg called my attention to the syringe that was the demon's parting gift to me. And, finally, dimming vision as everything crashed down to silent blackness.

Chapter 19

I awoke abruptly, no gradual rise to consciousness, but more of a jarring slam to full alertness. It was dark, I was face down on cold, wet metal, my nose full of the fishy, salty stench of the New York harbor. My skin felt like it was covered in cobwebs and when I tried to brush my face off, I found my hands were bound behind my back. At least three pairs of handcuffs by the feel of it. I rolled to my back and wrenched myself to an upright sitting position. Taking stock, I found no major wounds or broken bones, the result no doubt of being exposed to Tanya's blood. But the mother of all headaches was living behind my eyes and the cobwebby feeling persisted. Even my vision seemed to be gauzy.

Immediately, additional odors begged for attention, the predominant one being the sour body odor of long-unwashed humans, along with rat piss and diesel fuel. The sound of water lapping at solid surfaces hit my ears as did a whisper of cloth that was coming closer. Sitting up, I found the room wasn't fully dark; a small puddle of light was coming from the open metal door, which suddenly screeched open to admit the hulking form of Vadim. His entrance let in more light, enough for me to see that I was inside a shipping container. Following him was a slender silhouette that resolved into the dapper form of Anton. Cold, icy blue eyes surveyed me with immense satisfaction, a small smirk on his face.

"Ah, see, Vadim. Tanya's human blood cow is awake right on time. Meals taste so much better warm and awake, don't you think?"

The big man said nothing, ignoring me while he crossed to the rear of the container and retrieved a sheathed two-handed sword from a small table in the corner.

Anton chuckled coldly to himself. "Our pragmatic warrior is more interested in being prepared than savoring your admittedly succulent blood, Mr. Blood Cow. Or should I call you 'American Cow boy'," he said, laughing again. I grimaced.

"Handcuffs too tight?" he asked, noting my expression. "Or is it the after-effects of the little cocktail you received?"

"None of the above. It's the pain of your crappy jokes," I said.

Vadim snorted quietly, earning him a glare from Anton before the lean vampire turned back to me.

"Very well, Gordon. But I should think you would want to go to the grave knowing your part in tonight's drama. Your continued interference in preventing our partners from getting their hands on my daughter's blood has forced this rather precipitous action."

"You're telling me that you're in bed with the Hellbourne at the expense of your own daughter?" I asked. I tried to churn up some aura or chi or anything, but all I got was nauseated. Whatever had been in that syringe was blocking my abilities.

"Bah, that ignorant, ungrateful twit should be honored to donate to the cause. Imagine a street drug made from Tatiana's potent blood. A thousand times stronger than the stuff made from Vadim's contribution. And you are the bait to bring her here. After you ruined that last demon, we were forced to grab you and run."

"Well, I gotta say, your secret lair for world domination smells like rat piss and dead fish. Couldn't you afford something a little better?"

"Actually, you might be surprised to find out just how much we paid for it. Our shipping company rents this entire section of the waterfront, and we have free rein to emplace these containers as we choose. The result is a perfect place to trap Tatiana. When she gets a lock on your meager brain, she will come straight here, moving much faster than the rest of the coven. We'll overwhelm her with the last of the Hanced humans, and Vadim will take her down."

When she gets a lock? Didn't he know that she always has a lock and it covers more than two miles? I allowed a tiny amount of hope to sprout inside me.

"Tell me, how did you keep all this from Nika?" I asked.

"Bah, after two hundred years of age, most vampires can block even the best mind reader."

"So, you're providing the demons with vampire blood, they're twisting it with their own vile essence, and then it's going to unsuspecting humans? What in God's name could you gain from that?" I asked.

"Everything, Officer Gordon, everything. The time is long past when vampires, the preeminent lifeform on earth, should hide in the shadows and skulk like rats. Vampires, not pathetic cattle like humans, belong at the top of the food chain, ruling the planet."

"And Hance will help you get there?" I asked.

"Hance was just an experiment. But a new drug, based on Tanya's proteins, will be exponentially more addictive, spreading through the human population like wildfire, causing the confusion and chaos our partners crave and giving us the opportunity to seize the reins of power. Humans are weak, but their science is progressing too rapidly, you see. Their weapons are growing more powerful with each passing month. Man-portable, laser-based weapons will soon be a reality, and that would pose a real threat to our kind."

"And you think you can accomplish this against the will of the Elders?" I asked.

A different voice spoke from the doorway.

"Idiot, of course they have the support of an Elder. As the only Elder fit to rule, it falls to me to bring this about."

Fedor looked tiny next to Vadim's mass, but he exuded menace and power. A gust of wind blew in through the open door, swirling some papers across the floor. I watched the debris float into the darkness while I thought about their plan.

"So what do the demons get from this?" I asked.

Fedor didn't answer, having settled into an eerie stillness. After a moment, Anton spoke up.

"I already told you. Weren't you listening? They get the chaos and anguish they feed on."

I snorted but didn't say anything. Both Anton and Vadim looked at me.

"You think you know different?" Anton asked.

"Demons only crave negative emotions to get stronger. They only get stronger to bring more demons into our world," I said. "Riddle me this, Batman. What happens to Hancers that overdose?" I asked, having a pretty good idea of the answer.

"They go insane," Anton said.

All three vampires were paying attention to me now.

I nodded. "Do you know where most of the empty meat shells come from that demons inhabit?" I asked.

None of them said anything, so I went ahead and answered.

"People that have lost themselves on drugs, alcohol, and depression. Sounds like you're creating meat shells in huge numbers while providing the chaos and fear they need to bring their own kind over. So you will have your reign of power for what? Maybe a day?"

They all went still, then suddenly I was suspended from Fedor's hand, his razor-sharp fingernails buried deep in the muscles of my chest. I never saw him move. The pain was unlike anything I had felt before. Like five red-hot pokers buried an inch deep in my pectorals. His face was inches from mine, his eyes glowing with insane fury, and he smelled, oddly enough, like a leather jacket.

"Thank you for the warning. I have to admit certain... suspicions regarding my partner's intentions. Now I have ample time to prepare and adjust my plan. Maybe a delayed poison mixed with Tatiana's blood?"

He flicked his hand and I smashed into the steel wall of the container, hitting my head and wrenching my bound arms.

"But this changes nothing regarding Tatiana's fate. As if I would ever allow an infant to rule me. Senka grows more addled with every decade that passes."

Now my headache was keeping company with the large knot on the back of my skull, but I suddenly realized that the cobweb feeling was gone. I tried looking with my Sight and was rewarded with a brief flash of their auras before it flicked off like a faulty television.

I also got the feeling that Tanya was near. I needed to stall.

"What makes you think that Vadim can take Tatiana?"

"Because, while Vadim has taught her everything she knows, he hasn't taught her everything he knows. Vadim was fighting Swedes for Prince Nevsky in Russia eight hundred years ago. You really think a twenty-year-old anything can match his experience? And he will have a measure of my much older blood to lend him an extra edge. Not to mention that when I drain you dead, she will most likely go catatonic. "

He pulled up the sleeve of his dress shirt and motioned Vadim to his exposed wrist. Two-handed sword slung over his shoulder, the big vampire dropped gracefully to his knees and reverently brought Fedor's wrist to his mouth. My kernel of hope was collapsing under despair. Anton and Fedor both raised their heads, and a moment later, my slightly less-sensitive ears picked up the sound of something rushing over hollow metal.

"She's here! Much sooner than we expected," Fedor said. He yanked his wrist from Vadim's clutch and pointed to the doorway. "Get out there now!"

Vadim vanished in a rush of air and Fedor turned to me, his eyes expectant. I tried pooling my aura, but the results were weaker than I had hoped for. Still, it was all I had to work with, so I prepared to use it as best I could.

"She's just gonna run over the top of the containers and avoid all your pets," I said.

"These steel shipping boxes are stacked five and six deep, with an unusual cross stack pattern. She has no choice but to approach on our terms," Fedor said.

He turned to Anton and issued orders. "Get out there and control those mutants of yours." The dapper vampire left in blur. The papers that had floated up when Vadim left were still swirling in a mini tornado behind Fedor. It expanded in size, and the kernel of hope flared back.

"Now then, you've had enough time to distract me. Or didn't you think I was aware you were trying to get me talking?" he said.

"It's called monologuing, and of course I was trying to get you to do it. That would give my rescuers a chance to get here in time."

His smile was pure malice. "I'm afraid none of your fans will make it in time, as I'm tired of waiting, and frankly, you smell delicious." He started in my direction.

At that moment, the front of the box suddenly disappeared in a shriek of twisted steel.

"Actually I think one of them is already here," I said.

The container door and much of the surrounding metal was gone, torn away like tissue paper. But nothing was there, just a pile of shredded metal and a broken light pole, the still-shining bulb swinging in the eerie quiet. I never saw Fedor turn around; he was just suddenly facing the empty space outside the container. When nothing happened, he took a slow, predatory step forward. I tried my Sight again and was rewarded with the giant green, red, and purple form of Okwari just as he slammed his two dinner-platter-sized paws together on Fedor's torso. I have no way of telling for sure how much power was involved, but I'm guessing it had to be similar to two thirty-millimeter cannon shells slamming together head on. Fedor did a remarkable impersonation of a caterpillar being crushed under a bike tire. Blood, brains, and gore spattered the ceiling, the floor, and me.

Vampires are reported to be hard to kill, particularly the old ones. However, when the crushed husk that had been Fedor fell over, I had absolutely no doubt he was dead and gone. I would have liked to wipe the gore from my face, but my arms were still secured behind my back.

"Thank you Okwari," I said to the not-so-empty space in front of me. In fact, the air was blurry across most of the opening. A mental image of me pulling his collar off and of me stepping in front of Lydia flashed through my head.

"Yes, we certainly are friends." I responded to the theme of the message. "You don't know anything about handcuffs do you?" I asked, wistfully.

A picture of me turning around to present my secured arms popped into my mind. Doing as told and hoping for the best, I spun in place and held my arms as far from my body as possible. A talon that felt the size of a banana gently moved between my arms and, with an effortless motion, parted the handcuff links.

"Thank you again. Now I have to find my mate and help her," I said, using my Sight to see him.

He woofed in agreement then backed out of the opening and swung his whiskey-barrel-sized head to look in the direction of the fighting noises, which had suddenly started.

The corridors formed by the seemingly haphazard placement of containers were long, dark, and confining. Just as they had been intended to be. I raced down the one leading in the direction of the fight, pausing just long enough to snap the head off a heavy-duty broom I found, giving me a weapon. The ground shook behind me as more than a ton of prehistoric spirit bear followed me. I didn't know if Okwari would fight alongside me or not, but just his massive presence would be a boon. Invisible or not, the acute senses of the vampires would make them aware that something was in their midst.

The sounds of close quarters combat grew louder as I ran through the tunnels and alleys formed by the stacked shipping containers. Rounding a lefthand turn, I found myself at one end of a large corridor, the other end full of screaming Hancers. Vadim and Anton stood with their backs to me, watching a blurry form in black leather spin glittering blades of steel through the closely packed addicts like a weed wacker through crabgrass. Body parts were flying everywhere and, after a brief glance in my direction, Vadim flowed forward to meet Tatiana's arrival.

His giant two-handed sword met her smaller pair of blades in a crash of metal, and the real fight began in earnest. Anton grimaced in shock at the blood-covered sight of me, torn between the urge to attack and the need to flee from whatever had befallen his much more powerful Elder.

I sensed Okwari sliding around the corner behind me, and his impact into the closest shipping container made enough noise to pause the fighting for a microsecond. If the sound wasn't enough, the car-sized dent that magically buckled into the side of the container was more than sufficient to convince Anton that he needed to be elsewhere fast.

The slick vampire darted up the corridor, keeping as far away from Vadim and Tatiana as possible, his finely shod feet dancing over top of the blood-soaked mess that had been twenty or thirty people a few seconds before.

I wasn't sure how best to help Tatiana without distracting her, but before I could come to a decision, she skipped back a few steps to gain room and paused to look in my direction. Her rimless black eyes locked onto my gore-covered form, and I could literally feel the rage that flowed from her. She thought the blood was mine!

My enhanced vision had let me see some of the blows that she and Vadim had traded in the first exchange, but her next attack was too fast to process. Whatever edge that eight centuries of practice and the blood of an Elder had given Vadim in the first round evaporated in the heat of Tatiana's fury. As best I could tell, she met him head on, trading him blow for blow, her enraged strength stopping his much heavier sword dead. To his credit, faced with more than he had envisioned, Vadim fought with everything he had. It wasn't enough.

The finish came so quickly, if I had blinked, I would have missed it. One moment, it was head to head, like steel meeting iron. Then she suddenly folded away from a blow and was past him. He started to turn to face her, but his right leg, from the thigh down, stayed where it was. He fell over, part way around. His left arm shot down, arresting his fall, in a move that would have been incredible except for the fact that Tatiana was suddenly standing back in her starting position and Vadim's big, gleaming, bald head was sliding free from his neck. His body stayed in a grotesque side lean, blood spraying from the stump of neck and leg in opposite arcs. Then it collapsed into the dirt.

My view of his carcass was suddenly eclipsed by a pair of rimless black eyes framed with raven hair as Tatiana stood in front of me, searching for the massive wounds that had covered me in blood. Her nostrils flared, telling her the truth, at the same moment I spoke. "This isn't mine. It's Fedor's." Small blue specks appeared in the center of her eyes, swiftly replacing the coal black. She looked confused.

"How... where-- ?" she struggled to ask, but I interrupted.

"Tatiana Demidova, please meet my friend, Okwari," I said.

Slowly his giant form materialized as he willed himself visible. I hadn't known he could do that. Tatiana took a deep breath but held her ground as a wet black nose the size of my fist slowly gave her a sniff. He was very close in appearance to the paleontologists' images I had seen, but there were some differences. I don't believe the short-faced bears that had roamed the prehistoric world had short black horns emerging from their skulls and flowing back toward their necks.

His eyes were the hot orange-red of lava, and he was even bigger than I had imagined. A mental image of Tatiana and I engaged in sex appeared in my mind. Ignoring the sudden rush of lust I felt from the image, I nodded at him. "Yes, she is most certainly my mate," I said.

Her expression was equal parts wary, disbelief, and happiness at my statement.

"He sends me extremely clear images and understands what I say in response." I explained. "He pretty much made Fedor paste back there, kinda like you made Weasel paste with Lydia's car door."

Okwari lifted his head and looked behind Tatiana at the same time she turned to look over her shoulder. An object about the size of a soccer ball arced through the sky and landed in the dirt by Vadim's body. It rolled to a stop, leaving Anton's still blinking eyes looking right at us. Tatiana spoke. "Senka is here, with the others."

Okwari lifted up to his full fifteen-plus feet and stared in the direction the head had come from.

"It's okay. It's Lydia and other friends, here to help," I explained to him. He fell back to all fours, the ground shaking at his heavy impact. He woofed once, snuffled me hard enough to push me sideways, and disappeared in a swirl of cold air.

"That was your Damnedthing?" Tatiana asked.

"Yeah, but I don't really like that term any more. I don't think he's damned now that his collar is gone," I said.

"Lydia said you might have a new pet," she said, her expression halfway between amusement and awe.

"More like a new friend," I said.

Fast-moving figures appeared at the other end of the corridor, quickly resolving into Senka, Lydia, and a host of scary, serious vampires that I hadn't met before.

"Jeeze, Chris! What did you do? Take a blood shower or something?" Lydia greeted us. Senka had paused at Vadim's body, studying it with a thoughtful expression. Presently, she headed our way, ignoring the dangerous-looking vampires who had flowed past to take up security positions around us, a few moving back the way I had come. I looked them over while Senka looked Tatiana and I over, her expression unreadable.

The security vamps were hard and edgy sorts, dressed in black military and tactical gear. Weapons covered the gamut from state-of-the-art assault weapons to antique swords from a dozen cultures. Black, white, Asian, male and female; no two were alike in appearance, but all had a similar, professional carriage.

The two that had gone behind us came back at a sprint and, being vampires, showed no sign of being winded. One approached Senka and reported, "We found the remains of Elder Fedor in a torn-up container, Lady. Tracks and claw marks in the metal indicated an extremely large predator of some type, possibly a bear, but... well... larger."

He paused and noticed Lydia pointing at the ground by his feet, where a series of dinner-platter-sized tracks dimpled the dirt.

"Ah, yes, the tracks look just like these." He looked around warily, like the track maker was going to sneak up on him. "Also, no scent of any kind to go with the tracks," He finished.

Senka turned to me, her expression sardonic. "Your Damnedthing I presume?" she asked.

"My friend," I corrected with a smile. "Who took exception to Fedor's attitude toward me."

"I just met him," Tanya said with wide eyes. "He's a lot bigger than I expected, but nice."

"Nice?" Lydia asked, incredulous. "He was scary as hell when I met him."

The tiny vampire shuddered.

"Actually, Lydia, I believe he is rather fond of you," I said, thinking of how many times he replayed the image of me stepping in front of Lydia. It seemed to define for him the essence of friendship.

Senka's security detail had gone from ignoring me to suddenly studying me carefully, like something unexpected and possibly threatening. The soldier who had reported was studying my blood-covered form, and I could almost see the light bulb go on over his head as the link between my condition and Fedor's became apparent to him. It wouldn't take CSI:NY to figure out how the giant paw-shaped impressions on the ancient vampire's body came about.

It struck me at that moment that vampire bodies didn't fade to dust or immolate on death as some works of fiction would have it. They just lay around like any other dead body. It raised a whole series of questions for Dr. Singh when next I saw him, which, based on the protective gleam in Tatiana's eyes, would be rather soon.

Senka had been studying me while I was thinking my way through some things, frozen into that spooky stillness that all vampires seemed to favor, and she finally turned to Lydia with a nod. "I find myself agreeing with your theory more and more, young Guardian."

Then she turned away and began to issue orders for the removal of bodies, body parts, blood, and other forensic evidence. More vampires were arriving, bearing a plethora of serious-looking and completely unfamiliar equipment.

I looked at Lydia questionly, and she simply shrugged and grinned at me. "Guardian?" I asked.

Before she could answer, Tatiana spoke up. "Senka's specially trained agents are called Guardians. She assigned her very best Guardian to keep track of me—and apparently you," she said in a matter-of-fact tone.

I struggled with that concept before remembering the rest of Senka's words. "Theory?" I asked.

Lydia laughed. "I can't give away all my secrets. It would ruin my mysterious allure," she said.

I snorted. "Lydia, I couldn't figure you out with a four-hundred-page manual and a telephone help line."

She winked and spun away to intercept a vampire carrying cleaning supplies.

Tatiana had moved very close to me during this exchange, her side almost pressed against mine, while she looked at the wreckage that had been Vadim. He had been her weapons instructor her entire life, and she had been forced to kill him. On top of that, her father and one of the three Elders had wanted to use her, living or dead, to advance their own agendas. I didn't have a clue how that must have felt. Nudging her with my shoulder, I asked, "How are you doing?"

A line of emotions paraded across her face as she thought about my question. Sadness, anger, and fierce resolve were the biggest, mixed with a glimmer of pride and, oddly enough, joy. After a moment's reflection, she spoke in a quiet voice. "I have always... valued Vadim's instruction. He was skilled in a wide variety of disciplines, was patient, and always made my training interesting, which helped with the... life, such as it was, that I had while I waited for you." She looked me in the eye and continued, "You see, I always knew on some level, that something... someone was coming. It's what kept me going."

She leaned forward slowly and gave me a kiss on my blood-covered lips. "But --" Her voice took on a hard tone. "He chose to attack that which is dearest to me. Bad move."

Her voice was cold as arctic ice. Bad move, indeed.

"I'm sorry about your father," I said.

She snorted. "Anton contributed DNA to me, but he was never, in any sense of the word, my father! And Fedor was old, snotty, and condescending. I think Oh-Kwah-lee --" she looked at me to check her pronunciation, which I nodded at, "-- made a most excellent mess of him!"

She looked back at Vadim's remains for a moment and then continued, "I will miss his instruction, though."

I'm not real good with emotional stuff, my family being just Gramps and myself, so I was at a loss of what to say.

Senka saved me by stepping back over to our location and fixing me in her gaze. "I trust, Officer, that you will allow us to handle this mess," she said.

I hadn't thought about the aftermath and my responsibilities as a police officer until she said that.

On the one hand, I was sworn to uphold the laws of the city, the state, and the country. On the other, Roma had made it clear that the leaders of the human society preferred that the supernaturals police themselves to the greatest extent possible. So the dead vampires were a no-brainer.

The Hancers that Tatiana had chopped her way through had been human, though. That was harder to sort out. But then I reasoned that Hance was a supernaturally derived drug and the Hance addicts had become part of the supernatural world. The fact that Anton had controlled them lent this line of reasoning greater support.

At the end of this elegant line of bullshit rationalization was the awareness that human courts and law enforcement were, at present, completely incapable of dealing with the shadowy world of vampires, demons, and weres. To a degree, it was like trying to impose human laws on the natural world. Trying a pack of timber wolves for coyote killing in a human court of law wasn't any more ridiculous than pressing charges on a vampire for killing a werewolf.

In fact, from my limited experience with Special Situations and the D.O.A.A. unit, they were more like monitors than law enforcement. A vampire or were that came to the attention of human authorities for killing humans would be treated like a dangerous wild animal or rabid dog: hunted down and killed. And there most likely existed a federal black ops unit that wanted specimens for weapons research.

My own work hunting demons had no basis in human law. So I looked back up at Senka after the several moments it took me to process this train of thought and gave her a nod. I got the impression that she was curious about my internal resolution of this dilemma, but she just smiled and turned to my girl and said, "You and Lydia need to take Chris to Dr. Singh and make sure whatever was pumped into him is gone. And clean him up. He's a bloody mess," she said in her cultured Oxford accent. Then she was gone, back to organizing a cleanup that I didn't want to know about.

Lydia wouldn't let me in her car, her new car, until I put on one of the cleaning crews' white tyvex coveralls. I sat in the back seat, looking like a lean Michelin Tire man, and examined the links of the handcuffs that Tanya had removed from my wrists. She had simply pulled the hardened steel bracelets apart like taffy until they tore. I was interested in the laser clean cuts that Okwari's claw had made through the steel links.

Bear claws are like meat hooks, with no real inner edge to cut with, yet his claw had sliced the tough metal like a chef's knife would cut a cucumber, better even. I was going to have Chet analyze the cuts. Any information I could get would help in figuring out my giant, invisible friend.

A thought occurred to me, and I voiced the question to the vampire ladies in the front seat. "I'm kinda foggy about how I ended up with Fedor and company. What happened at the club -- " I looked at my watch, "-- three hours ago?"

Tanya turned to look back at me as she answered, her blue eyes glowing from the dark front seat.

"Vadim hustled you and the demon's body off the dance floor and into the back, or so we thought. We think he must have just kept going right out the fire door and then met Anton before going to the shipping yard."

"And Fedor delayed us from heading back to check on you by saying we had to bow out first to keep the club patrons believing it was all an act," Lydia added. " Your fight was a huge hit, by the way. I'll be surprised if it doesn't get mentioned in a half dozen of this morning's newspapers."

I yawned, as it was now past two a.m. and long past my normal bedtime. Tanya was still watching me, concern written across her face. "I'm just tired," I said.

She shook her head. "I've only known you for a week, and I've almost lost you a half dozen times."

I didn't have a good answer so I just shrugged. "I'll try to be more careful."

Lydia laughed, and Tanya smiled a little.

"Honestly, though, I've gotta think with the demise of Fedor and the others, that things will possibly calm down," I said.

"Regardless, you will be more careful, because you will be training with me!" Tatiana said.

I gulped, remembering her brutal treatment of Vadim and the Hancers. As much as I enjoyed bedroom wrestling with her, training at her level promised to be painful.

Lydia's green eyes sparkled with amusement in the rearview mirror as she watched my reaction.

Chapter 20

Lydia parked in front of Dr. Singh's house/office, and we hustled into the entrance to the lower level. The doctor and his creepy assistant met us at the door, alerted to our arrival by Tanya's cell call from the car. The assistant led me to a bathroom with shower, tersely directing me to leave my destroyed clothes in a black garbage bag and leaving me a set of blue hospital scrubs to wear. With one last sidelong glance at me, she left me to get cleaned up.

Dr. Singh's water pressure was excellent, and the steaming hot water sluiced away Fedor's blood and gore. The fact that the shower floor was equipped with an industrial-sized drain that would have been at home in a car wash or slaughter house was a little disturbing. I didn't want to think of the number of other gruesome cleanups this bathroom had seen.

When I emerged twenty minutes later, my skin red from the harsh scrubbing I had put myself through, Assistant spooky was waiting to lead me to the Doctor's exam room. Dr. Singh and the girls were there, discussing the night's events. A plastic zip lock baggie with a used syringe inside was on one of the countertops, an oily black residue remaining in the mostly empty tube.

"So Chris, how are you feeling?"

"A little cleaner."

He smiled briefly. "I was wondering more about your physical well-being."

"Well, I still feel a little woozy from whatever the demon shot me up with and I'm not up to full power, aura-wise. But overall, I feel pretty good. Hungry, though."

Lydia rolled her eyes, Tanya smiled, and the Doctor nodded.

"I've taken the liberty of ordering a pizza from a late-night establishment. I will need to do a complete workup on the contents of the hypodermic, but I feel confident in theorizing that it is demon blood."

"Demon blood?" I questioned.

"Yes, I've had the opportunity to analyze the body of the demon you neutralized at Tatiana's residence the other day. The body's blood was drastically changed by the demon's habitation. I think it would have a pretty nasty effect on your abilities. In fact, I believe demon blood is the other ingredient in the production of the Hance drug."

Dr. Singh had begun an examination of me while he talked, checking my blood pressure, heart rate, temperature, and other basic factors. He made notes on a clipboard and then handed it to the assistant, who typed it into a laptop computer.

"Chris, how's your appetite been lately?"

"Strong, but less than it was. Maybe two thirds of what it was."

He nodded. "I would expect it to slow considerably as your body completes more of the transformation."

"Ah, what transformation?" I asked

"Well, let's back up and start with the process by which vampires are created," he said.

Lydia and Tanya both leaned forward, obviously very interested in the topic.

"When a human is Turned, the process is very specific, if deceptively simple. Over the course of several days, the human is progressively drained of more and more blood, while also drinking more and more of the vampire's own blood. This has the effect of exposing all of the cells in the body to larger amounts of the virus that all vampires carry."

"Virus?" I asked.

"Yes, Chris. Both vampirism and lycanthropy are caused by viruses. The virus carries new bits of DNA that permanently change the host. In both cases, the change actually happens at the mitochondrial level, not the nucleus level. You know what mitochondria are, right?" he asked.

I remembered my high school biology pretty well. "Yeah, the powerhouses of the cell, right?

Production of ATP, which is... wait... adenosine triphosphate!" I said, a little smugly.

"That's what they're best known for. They also perform quite a few other jobs, as well. Steroid and various protein productions, involvement in the aging process, cellular differentiation, and cellular signaling, among others. The mitochondrion has its own DNA, which is inherited from the mother's egg cell. The vampire virus—we call it V-squared—adds new DNA to the mitochondrial DNA. The resulting proteins provide the enhanced sensory, strength, speed, reflexes, and anti-aging benefits. They also allow the body to use blood as its only food source. The last is a major mutation of the ATP cycle."

He paused to see if I was keeping up.

"The Lycanthrope virus, or LV, is similar but more aggressive, which is why only a single bite is needed to fully infect someone. And both viruses have about a sixty to seventy-percent infection rate. With V-squared, the other thirty to forty-percent die. With LV, they just heal up normally and go on being human. Got it so far?"

"Yeah, I guess. So the Hance protein is a bad copy of just one of the V-squared proteins that an infected mitochondrion would produce?" I asked.

"That's correct, Chris. A V-squared mitochondrion kicks out a smorgasbord of proteins that are beneficial to the host."

"And regular humans that imbibe vampire blood, orally, get a mix of proteins, but they are short-lived?" I guessed.

"Yes. But the virus is not as hardy as the LV, and it is destroyed by the body's immune response. That's why a candidate is exposed to ever greater quantities of the virus while their total blood supply is being drained down, which reduces the immune response. By the end of the cycle, the candidate is flooded with virus in a weak body, and the change is initiated. Once V-squared is fully established, the human is now a vampire. As time goes on, the virus continues to spread and strengthen and change its host."

"But what about being undead and all that?" I asked.

"Just human terms to attempt to describe the enormous differences in body function. You see, Chris, vampire hearts do beat, just differently, at different times. As changeover is made, a new vampire's heartbeat will accelerate way past human normal. This has the effect of pressurizing the vampire circulatory system. Our veins and arteries are much stronger and have greater elasticity. Once pumped to high pressure, the heart stops normal functions and starts to operate so slowly that heartbeats don't register as such. Blood is moved one chamber at a time. Because of the complete change in blood metabolism, we don't need fast-moving blood. It's complicated, involves particle physics, and we could discuss it all night, but know this:vampires' hearts do function. Just differently," he said.

I scratched my head, taking it all in.

"But the Weres still eat regular food. How does that work?" I asked.

"LV is a much different virus, and while it also affects the mitochondria, it does so differently. How much do you know about particle physics, Chris?" he asked.

I shook my head. "Not much. You're talking atoms, protons, and neutrons, right?"

"Oh, much, much more. There are far more interesting ones, like quarks, gluons, neutrinos, Higgs Bosun particles, and things like dark matter and dark energy. It's a fascinating science and has direct application to the study of the so-called supernaturals. Trying to explain how vampires can survive, thrive, and exceed human potential on a diet of blood doesn't work until you can bring in other types of matter and energy. Very simply, vampire mitochondria harness additional energy from sources that current science would have difficulty measuring. It also works to explain how a one-hundred-and-seventy-five-pound man can transform into a three-hundred-pound werewolf, which on the face of it defies the Law of Conservation of Mass. However, mass is matter, and matter is made up of particles, and the particles of matter are subject to change." He shook his head in frustration.

"It's okay, Doc. That actually makes sense to me. So you're saying that the changes in the mitochondria allow vamps and weres to utilize particles and energy that normal humans can't."

He nodded, so I continued, "That also helps give me a basis for demons and Damnedthings phasing between dimensions and changing from spirit to solid."

"Yes, exactly. Quantum physics has multiple dimension theories like String theory and others. Which brings us to you, my unique friend," he smiled.

"Okay, let me have it Doc. What makes me such a freak?"

All three of them winced at my casual self-description.

"Chris, when I studied your blood samples, I, knowing what I know about V-squared and LV, focused on your mitochondria. And I found they were different. Changed."

"You mean by Tanya's blood?" I asked.

"Well yes, but they were different to begin with. As if you, or your mother had been exposed to one of the viruses or a similar virus before."

"My mother?" I asked.

"Remember, mitochondria are inherited from the mother. So yours came from her. Before you finished your shower, I was asking the girls what they knew about your mother and they told me about your Russian grandfather and the German camp. What more do you know about him?" he asked.

"Not a great deal. He was a child when he went into the camp and was only nineteen or twenty when he was rescued and met my grandmother. He wouldn't speak about it, and we never asked. They lived in Florida at the time my family was killed. I visited them a few times and they came to New York a couple of times, but other than that, it was letters and phone calls."

"Do you know what the name of the camp was?"

I shook my head and answered, "He never said, but I know it wasn't one of the well-known camps. It was somewhere in the Bavarian Alps, I think. Small and secret."

I shrugged.

He looked thoughtful. "Well, anyway. Your mitochondria were already different. Which may be why you have your unique abilities with demons. When you drank Tanya's blood, the tiny amount of virus, which would normally be wiped out, was somehow able to effect additional changes. Each additional dose of blood just continued the changes. Most of your current mitochondria look almost like they came from a vampire, but with a few of the characteristics of an LV-modified mitochondrion as well. So you are producing your own set of vampire-like proteins, your metabolism is fast like a Were's, your red blood cell production is crazy high, your immune system is all kinds of enhanced. The changes continue to spread, and we will have to monitor the effects. But you seem to be some kind of altogether new supernatural."

We all just looked at him. I couldn't think of anything to say.

Tanya spoke first. "What about his aging process?" she asked.

"That part of his mitochondria seems to be just like a vampire's," he replied.

"So wait, I won't age?" I asked.

"I would say not. Can't tell anything for certain, but that's my best guess. You seem to have many of the benefits that a young vampire would have. Notice I didn't say a new vampire, because you have already progressed beyond that point. Probably due to Tanya's blood being the source of your changes."

"Okay, how does that work?" Lydia asked.

"Well, Tanya also inherited her mitochondria from her mother, Galina. As best we can determine, Tanya was conceived the same night both Galina and Anton were changed. Their reproductive systems hadn't been shut down yet. So the embryonic Tanya was chock full of virus from conception. Her blood carries enormously high quantities of very strong virus. So you were accelerated, so to speak."

"What about Chris's reproductive system?" Lydia asked.

"Hey, why do you want to know about that?" I asked, feeling oddly uncomfortable.

"Hush, Junior, and let the grownups talk," Lydia said.

Dr. Singh smiled at this exchange and then spoke. "That part seems to be more like the LV virus. Weres reproduce normally, in addition to infecting others, although their fertility rates are very, very low. That is somewhat in keeping with other apex predators.

Too many bears, wolves, and tigers means no more prey animals, so they produce few young," he said.

"Lydia, why is that important?" I pressed.

She gave a little shrug. "Just curious."

Yeah right! Like I believe that.

I asked my own question. "Doc, is Tanya like other vampires and won't have kids, or is she different?" I glanced at her, but she was looking mildly curious.

"We aren't certain, Chris. She seems to have viable eggs but doesn't have a human female's menstrual cycle. Of course, she would never be fertile with another vampire – " She hissed in anger and he continued hurriedly, "-- not that she will ever have another mate but you. But whether the two of you could have children is a very large unknown."

Whoa! Kids? Me and Tanya? Now, there was a picture.

Assistant creepy came into the room with a pizza box that she unceremoniously handed to me and left. It gave me a chance to think about the implications of all Dr. Singh had told me while I fed my empty stomach. But before I could get very far, we all heard the outer door to the office stairs open and footsteps head down to our level.

Tanya and Lydia looked at each other after a moment and, in unison, said, "Senka!"

Sure enough, the blonde elder came through the doorway looking like a young, upscale soccer mom in designer jeans and an Oxford sweatshirt, her hair in a ponytail. I straightened up and tried to wipe the pizza grease off my face in an attempt to look a little better, but then I realized I was standing barefoot, wearing just scrub pants, in a doctor's office. It was sorta pointless. She gave us all a quick perusal before concentrating her formidable gaze on me.

"How is our patient, Dr. Singh?" she asked, frowning slightly.

I didn't care to have any more vampire Elders frowning at me tonight. Fedor had been quite enough, thank you.

"He's in good shape, and I think the effects of the demon blood are almost worn off," Dr. Singh said.

"I disagree, at least about the demon blood. His aura is very dark, much darker than the other day."

"I don't feel a hundred percent yet, so maybe a few hours of sleep will help," I suggested, hoping to move her attention away from myself.

She looked at me for a few moments longer, than changed topics. "I've been in touch with Fedor's lieutenants in Europe, informing them of recent events. I'll be leaving in the next few hours to head over and clean house if necessary. Galina will be going with me to help review Fedor's finances and business arrangements. So Tanya, you're in charge of the NY coven for the near future. It'll be good practice for you. Lydia will, of course, be your right arm. You will need a new head of security. Any ideas?"

Tanya looked at Lydia for a moment, then answered, "Arkady would be my first choice. He worked with Vadim for years, and I'm confident of his loyalty."

"Excellent choice. I took the liberty of bringing him along, thinking you might choose him." She looked back at the doorway and raised her voice several levels. "Arkady?"

Immediately, the upper door opened and heavy footsteps pounded down the stairs. The massive Russian vampire appeared in the doorway. "Lady, you called?"

"Congratulations, Arkady. You are Tatiana's new head of security. Any suggestions for her?"

"Thank you," he said, then turned and spoke to Tanya. "Young Queen, I would suggest using Nika to check the entire household for anyone who feels the same as Fedor did."

Lydia was nodding agreement as Tanya responded, "Good idea. Please see to it. Anything else?"

He paused for a moment, seeming a bit unsure, but then went ahead and spoke again. "I think most of the New York coven will fall in line easy enough, but I would suggest having him with you at your first formal gathering." He nodded in my direction, and everyone turned to look in my direction. I froze in place, a slice of pizza mere inches from my open mouth.

Lydia asked the obvious question. "Why?"

"Because rumors were already spreading about what happened to the vampire waiter that tried to stop him the other night. By now, they will have linked him to the Fedor's spectacular death. Having a *sputnik jizni* who is responsible at some level for the absolute destruction of Europe's Elder can only help. They will fear him as much as you. Fear is good."

Senka turned to Tanya. "His points are all solid. Good first decision." She looked at her watch.

"Okay, by now, several shipping containers of remains are sinking to the ocean floor. My jet will be ready shortly, so I will say goodbye for now. Tanya and Lydia, I will expect reports nightly. Christian, I trust I will see you when I return. Doctor, please walk me out. Goodbye."

With that, she left, Dr. Singh following her out. I put on the scrub shirt and polished off the last piece of pizza, while Tanya spoke to Arkady.

"Please have Nika start checking the Darkkin who remain at the house. We will be along after we drop Chris back at his own place, much as I would rather he came home with me," she said.

Chapter 21

As we pulled up in front of my building, I noticed a particular truck outside, and sat up.

"Uh oh!"

Immediately, both vampires were thoroughly alarmed.

"What's wrong?" Tanya asked, looking in all directions for the threat.

I groaned. "That's Gramps' truck! Shit! He didn't like my email responses, and I didn't call him back in time. I don't believe it! He friggin' drove all the way down here!" I said.

"Where is he now?" Lydia asked after exchanging a glance with Tanya.

"Most likely in my apartment. He knows where I hide the spare key."

I sat still for moment, wondering if I could just go back to Tanya's house and avoid the verbal beat down that was in my immediate future. Naw, the old man would probably start calling the Sixty-eighth precinct in another hour or two if I didn't appear.

I sighed in resignation. "All right. I guess I better face the music. I'll call you later, Tanya."

"Do you want us to go with you?" Lydia asked, puzzled by my response to my grandfather's surprise visit.

"No!" I said, thoroughly alarmed at that idea. "No, he might shoot someone. I need to talk to him, prepare him, before he meets the two of you. Maybe later tonight. I'll call. Oh, Happy Birthday, Tanya," I said.

Tanya's frown turned into a smile and she gave me a big kiss before letting me out of the car.

It was still very dark at four-seventeen in the morning that November first. Dark and cold, although I wasn't feeling it even though I was only wearing a thin set of hospital scrubs. Dr. Singh had told me my new body temperature would most likely settle in at around one hundred and two degrees Fahrenheit, about the same as most Weres. Actually, about the same as most canines, period.

I looked at the green Ford F-150 extended cab as I walked past it to the building's front door. That truck, or one much like it, had been part of my life for as long as I could remember. From twelve and a half feet away—I can't tell you how I knew that measurement, but would bet money it was right—I could feel the heat of the engine block on my skin. Gramps hadn't been here too awful long yet. Good.

The television was on in my apartment, the volume low, and I could smell fresh-brewed coffee as I walked down the hallway to my door. Bracing myself mentally, I turned the key in the lock and cautiously pushed the door open.

The man sitting in my leather chair looked a good ten years younger than his seventy-four years, his features clear in the pool of light from my chairside reading light, the comforting aroma of Captain Black pipe tobacco wafting from his position. The rest of the apartment was dark, except for the little light over the stove in the galley. At five-foot-eleven, my grandfather is an inch taller than I am, a fact he loves to remind me about. His weight has stayed a remarkably even one hundred and ninety pounds for most of the last four decades, a result of a naturally sound metabolism and a long life of hard physical labor. Dressed in Carhart pants, Timberland work boots, and a green John Deere sweatshirt, his flint gray eyes studied me carefully from under a thick head of gray hair.   His left hand was wrapped around a mug of coffee (which would be black, no doubt), while his right hand rested on the Smith and Wesson short barreled .44 Magnum that was occupying the armrest. The gun had been my father's, the practical purchase of a thoughtful man who had enjoyed introducing his young family to the Adirondack wilderness. Gramps and I both had the gun registered on our pistol permits, neither of which were valid within the boundaries of New York City. He looked me over from head to toe—the latter he could see, because I was barefoot.

"Musta been some party you been at?" he remarked. My best guess pegged him at equal parts annoyed and concerned.

"Gramps, you have absolutely no idea," I said without a hint of levity in my voice. He frowned, picking up on my lack of humor. Gramps always said he went on full alert whenever I stopped being a wiseass, which is pretty much my normal state of being. He shifted slightly in the chair and asked, "You okay, boy?"

"Yes Sir. But I am glad to see you. I tried to call you back in a timely manner, but events have conspired against me for the whole last week."

"You look leaner... and darker, like you been tannin' or some such?" he remarked.

"Yeah, well that's part of the story. Let me get a mug of that java I smell and I'll fill you in. Take about an hour or more, so if you're tired, we can do it later?" I offered.

"Nope, I'm fine. You look all done in, though," he said.

"I'll survive for a bit more, but I will have some of those Boston crème donuts that you brought."

He frowned again, no doubt because the pastry box wasn't visible from where I was standing and ordinary people wouldn't have smelled them like I had. Moving into the tiny kitchenette, I found the Dunkin' Donuts box on the stovetop and, after filling a mug with black coffee, I took the whole thing back into the room, seating myself on the futon.

"You move different," he accused. "More controlled. Kinda like one of those trained dancers on So You Think You Can Dance. Only not so girly."

That took me by surprise because I hadn't been aware of it. I knew I was more coordinated and much faster, but the grace or control of center he was referring to had escaped my attention.

Not knowing what else to do, I told the story chronologically, the same way I've been telling it in these pages. It took a solid fifty minutes to get through all the particulars. He listened carefully, without asking questions or interrupting, the same way he had always listened to my troubles and adventures. I finished and then went into the kitchen to get more coffee, knowing he would think it through a bit before speaking. Settling back onto my futon, I noted sadly that the donuts were long gone, five for me, one for him. He scratched the stubble on his chin, looked at me with a glint in his eye, and finally spoke. "A girlfriend? You have a girlfriend?"

"Yes Sir. You'll meet her later if you want to. I'll warn you, though, she might be a bit nervous."

He started at that. "You said she was the future queen of the vampires."

I nodded.

"And she'll be nervous about meeting me?" he asked.

"Yeah, pretty much. You're my only family, and she has heard all about you. Your opinion of her counts pretty heavy."

"Will I meet this Lydia, too?" he asked.

I laughed, my first since I got in. "Yeah, that's pretty much a given. And she most likely won't be nervous. She's a piece of work. You'll probably like her, although she seems to find great joy in making me nuts."

He grunted as he thought about meeting a pair of real vampire girls.

"You don't seem very surprised," I noted.

"I always told you these things... er... beings were real. I saw enough of the world during my time with the Marines to know the truth of that. Saw a vampire in Korea, once. From a distance. Never wanted to see one again. Scary looking thing. Your girl is she... well... does she look normal?"

I laughed again. "Not even close to normal. You know those Victoria Secret catalogs that occasionally show up in the mail and never seem to get thrown out?"

He nodded, his eyes widening.

"Well, she makes those girls look sad, tired, and old."

"Now you're just braggin', boy," he said, in disbelief of her looks if not her nature.

"Tell ya what, old man. I got a fifty spot here in my wallet that says you'll eat those words later this evening. Whatta ya say?"

Gramps takes betting seriously, so he thought it through, nodded, and pulled a crisp portrait of Ulysses Grant from his fat, worn wallet, plunking it down on top of mine in the center of the coffee table.

"You're on, boy."

I grinned and stood up to stretch.

Another thought lit up in his eyes. "You're faster?"

I understood. He wanted a demonstration. I motioned him up from his chair, and he stood up warily.

"Take out your knife," I said, pointing at the three-and-a-half-inch hunting knife that was guaranteed to be on his person if he was wearing pants.

Looking even more wary, he pulled the blade from its well-used leather sheath and held it out to me, handle first.

I shook my head. "Hold it point down over the floor. Whenever you're ready, drop it and say 'now'," I directed, turning my back on him. I didn't have to see him to know that a furrow would be forming between his eyes as he got ready to participate in my little exhibition.

At his crisp, "Now!" I felt everything slow down as I turned around. I found the blade dropping as if in zero gravity, leaving me plenty of time to pluck it from the air. Time resumed its normal flow as I handed it back to him, handle first. He started as my abrupt motions stopped blurring.

Eyes wide, he looked at the knife and then me, pausing to scratch his chin stubble before taking back his blade. "Er... yeah. That's pretty fast. And your girl... Tanya is it?"

I nodded, knowing he damn well remembered her name but was stalling for time to process what he had just witnessed. "Tanya is even faster?"

I nodded. "Quite a bit faster, if she's really motivated," I said, thinking of her fight with Vadim.

He cleared his throat. "And you're stronger now, as well?"

I didn't say anything, just reached both arms and lifted him by his armpits, like he had done to me when I was a kid. I held his one ninety pounds out at arm's length long enough to make my point, then set him back down, gently. This time he coughed, his system agitated by the reality of what I had done.

"Tanya is stronger as well?"

"I could lift your truck's front end off the ground. Tanya could throw the whole damn thing. But, remember, she's unique, one of a kind. She is equal to the oldest of vampires."

"And that's because she's full blood, as you say?" he asked.

"Yup," I said, yawning heavily.

Now he noted my evident tiredness. "Hey, you gotta get some sleep. I grabbed a nap at a truck stop on the trip down last night, so I'm good. Why don't you crash, and I'll just go get a paper and do the cross word or sumthin'?" he suggested.

"You'll be all right if I snooze?" I asked.

"Yup, right as rain. Got a lot of food for thought. You get some shut-eye."

"All right, but leave that cannon here. I don't want you getting picked up by some of the Sixty-Eighth boys while I'm snoozing."

He agreed, and I racked out right where I was, the hospital scrubs making pretty good sleep wear.

I slept till just before noon, waking from one of the soundest sleeps I'd had in forever. It might have been because of my total exhaustion, but I think it had more to do with the steadying presence of my grandfather in the apartment. I opened my eyes, looking directly at where my brain had already told me Gramps was: sitting at my table. He was humming to himself, softly, while he worked his way through the *New York Times*, a paper he loved to hate. A staunch conservative, like many Northern New Yorkers, he had railed against the NYT and other mainstream media sources for his whole life. My father's .44 was lying on the table in front of him, holstered, with a wooden box next to it. I recognized the box as one of Gramp's handmade ammunition boxes. Next to the box was a short, two foot black nylon case. "You goin' to war?" I asked from my nest on the futon.

He glanced over at me and smiled.

"Actually, those are for you. Don't want you relying on that puny nine millimeter they make you carry." He shuddered at the thought of carrying what was to him a mouse gun.

"Well, it's not my ten millimeter, but my newest Glock is kinda special."

His eyes lit up with interest. Having spent his impressionable years in the Marine Corps, Gramps was a tried and true .45 caliber man, favoring John Browning's classic Model 19ll. He thoroughly respected my personal Glock model 29 in hard hitting ten millimeter, though. That gun was locked in the gun safe back at the farm. Dad's .44 was more of a woods gun, but would certainly do double duty as a personal defender. I retrieved the Glock 18 from the pistol safe under my futon and, after clearing the chamber, handed it butt first to my grandfather.

"Full auto, you say?"

He handled the gun expertly, admiring its balance, then slipped the thirty-three-round magazine into the grip and, leaving the chamber empty, tested its balance some more.

"Can you control it?" At my nod, he looked thoughtful and then handed it back.

"Well, I'll allow as that might get the job done pretty well," he said. "I still want to leave your dad's gun here as back up, as well as the shorty Remington.

Never can have enough backups, and you seem to be knee deep in alligators, son."

"Gramps, I don't want to leave you short."

"Aww, I don't need much, and I've got my .45s, the Mossberg, and the whole rest of the gun safe. Hell, if I had to, I could make do with that newfangled one-centimeter Glock of yours," he said with a sly grin.

After a moment, I nodded. He was right: it never hurt to have extra, plus the twelve gauge Remington 870 pump shotgun that was tucked into the black case was a terrific weapon at close quarters. The barrel was a thoroughly illegal fourteen inches long, the gun a gift from a skilled sheriff's department armorer who cared more that we had effective firepower than the letter of the law. As a NYPD officer, and particularly a member of Special Situations, I could get away with possessing the short-barreled weapon.

"I'll see about getting some silver buckshot made for it," he said.

"Don't bother. My team's armorer already has a huge supply of commercially made stuff."

He nodded, reminded that my team was well aware of what prowled the dark.

The sun was streaming through the window, and my stomach was calling attention to itself. "Hey, what say we grab some subs or something, and head over to Owls Head Park. Might not get another nice day like this for a while."

He agreed and after I showered—I still wasn't feeling clean enough—and threw on some jeans and a tee shirt, we headed out.

We got to the park by twelve thirty, bag of subs in hand and a big soda for each. He had complained when I ordered two seafood subs until he realized they were both for me. I ordered him his regular Italian meat combo.

"You really do eat a lot more now," he said, a little amazed.

I swallowed a mouthful of seafood salad and replied, "You should have seen me a few days ago. I'm actually slowing down, but I had to heal from some bumps and bruises, and my body is craving the zinc in this imitation crabmeat."

He snorted at that and took a bite of his own sandwich. About then, I noticed a swirl of leaves about twenty feet behind him.

"Ah, Gramps, I want you to stay real still. Don't do any jumping around and don't have a heart attack, but you're about to meet one of my new friends I told you about."

He froze in mid-chew for a moment, then swallowed.

"I thought they slept during the day."

"They do. You're about to meet Okwari."

His eyes widened at the mention of the giant bear spirit I had filled him in on. An image of me and Lydia, followed by one of me and Tanya, and finally me and Okwari, flashed through my mind's eye. I spoke quietly to the blurry mass that was forming directly behind my grandfather. "Okwari, this is my Gramps."

I played a series of memories through my head, figuring that would be the easiest way to convey my relationship to the man in front of me. A soft woof sounded just over Gramps' shoulder, and with eyes as wide as silver dollars, he turned to stare into nothing.

"Where is...?" he started to ask, but a big puff of moist bear breath blew back his hair as the giant made his presence known.

"Holy Mother of God, Jesus, Mary, and Joseph," my grandfather intoned. He wasn't cursing, but was calling on his religion protectively. I took his right hand and gently set it on Okwari's barrel of a head, the images in my head telling me Gramps had nothing to fear. After a time, the big beast folded himself onto the ground by our feet. Even lying down, his back was at least as high as the picnic table. He was sending me a series of messages about his neck and the awful itching it was causing him. I studied his neck with my Sight and when I looked real close, I could see little spots of greasy black deep down, below the spot where his collar had been. I told my grandfather about it while experimentally using my left hand to draw one inky spot out.

"Probably residue from years of wearing the demon collar," he speculated.

Gramps and I had spent years discussing the nature of the Hellbourne. I nodded my agreement.

"I wonder if it would grow back on its own?" he continued.

I looked at him, thoroughly alarmed. The next forty minutes was spent painstakingly finding and removing every minuscule speck of black. Okwari would have purred if he had been feline in nature, rather than ursine. The images I was getting now were telling me we had a very sleepy and contented bear at our feet. By now, my adaptable grandfather had grown secure enough to rest his arm on the big, furry—if invisible— back that was sitting next to him. Luckily, we were far enough away from any other park goers to avoid arousing suspicions.

We spent the afternoon that way, Gramps filling me in on the news from home, Okwari curled up next to us. It was oddly satisfying to hear such vanilla happenings as tractor breakdowns, who was caught sleeping with whose wife, and so on. A little after four, my cell buzzed with a text.

T: How's it going?

C: Great! I just introduced Gramps to the big, clear furry dude. We're at the park but heading back soon. Want to come over and meet him?

T: Is it safe?

C: Haha! He can't wait to meet you and Lydia.

T: Okay. See you in say twenty... thirty?

C: Thirty it is.

"Hey, now I'm nervous. What if your girl doesn't like me?"

"Plleeease! Like that could happen."

Okwari woke up from his nap and, after snuffling both Gramps and myself, slipped away in a column of air. We headed home, arriving back in only fifteen minutes. I was amused to see my grandfather sprucing up to meet Tanya.

Forty-two minutes after our text session, I felt Tanya's presence in the building. I looked at my grandfather and said softly, "They're here."

He gave me a look that said *how do you know*, and I said, "I got a Tanya sense. Hers for me is even stronger."

He looked a little wide eyed at that, and then shrugged. What was one more piece of strange among so many others?

I answered the door before they could knock, and ushered them in.

It took Tanya about four milliseconds to win my grandfather over. She entered wearing a blue sweater-dress over black tights, a smile on her beautiful face, but also a hint of vulnerability. Game, set, and match.

"Grandfather, may I introduce Tatiana Demidova and Lydia Chapman. Ladies, this is my grandfather, Alex Gordon."

Lydia was wearing a green sweater and black slacks. She stepped forward to shake Gramps' hand as Tanya gave her room. He looked stricken for just a moment, then collected himself and welcomed them.

"Miss Demidova, Miss Chapman, it's a pleasure to meet you both."

"Please, Mr. Gordon, call me Tanya."

"Yes and call me Lydia, although Chris calls me Pain in the Ass."

"Christian!" he rounded on me, instantly won to their side.

I held up both hands. "Give her some time, Gramps. You'll see what I mean."

"Oh please, Northern, like anyone of his obvious class will believe you," Lydia snorted.

I gave up, realizing I couldn't win this one. There was a moment of awkward silence, then I spoke up. "Ladies, I was thinking of taking my grandfather out for dinner. We could do that or order in, whatever you want."

Tanya smiled, which had the immediate effect of causing my grandfather to have an erratic heartbeat.

"So, ladies, how goes the first day on the job?" I asked.

Lydia laughed and Tanya gave her a look, then answered.

"It's going well. Arkady is doing a great job and no one has raised any problems."

"That's because they're all too scared to blink. Every time our girl here says jump, we gotta talk them down off the ceiling. And when the regular hangers-on heard we were coming to meet you, they evaporated."

Gramps had recovered enough to look puzzled, so Lydia answered his unasked question. "Your grandson is fast acquiring a reputation in the supernatural world. It seems like all manner of bad things can happen to bad monsters when he's around."

He asked why, and Lydia started to tell much more detailed versions of the events of the last week. Tanya and I picked a restaurant after only a little haggling. While they would only drink wine or water, the girls had definite ideas on the kind of ambiance they wanted. I offered to call a cab, but Lydia said it wouldn't be necessary, and Tanya looked chagrined.

"Why not?" I asked.

"You don't think Arkady would let the Young Queen, as she is now known, to travel unescorted, would you? The limo is waiting out front."

So we took the big Mercedes limo to a trendy restaurant, one that I couldn't have gotten into without a SWAT team, but that magically had a prime table available at the mention of the Demidova name. Dinner was amazing—actually, dinners because I ate three by myself, which provided great cover for the girls, who only sipped wine. But it was watching my grandfather talk with Lydia that suddenly sunk home the reality of vampire lifespans. Lydia is only about sixty in vampire years, a mere child. But she was close to twenty when she was Turned, and the combined total made her a few years older than Gramps. They had a ton in common and could talk about events and experiences that left Tanya and I out. Which was fine by us; it gave us more time to be together. Finally, about nine o'clock, my grandfather, who had been up for over eighteen hours, started yawning.

"Ladies, my grandson's apartment is smaller than a shoebox. Do you think you could keep him overnight, so I can have the place to myself. He's really kind of a pain."

Lydia laughed. "That's funny. I always compared his place to a litterbox."

So we dropped him off and I got to spend the night with Tanya. And oddly enough, when we walked in the door of the brownstone, the three vampires waiting to talk to Tanya took one look at me and decided their problems could wait.

"Cool, Tanya. Now we know how to get a night off whenever we want to," Lydia said, just before she disappeared into her own suite.

Chapter 22

When I woke the next morning, it was with a contented sigh and not a pain or bruise anywhere on my body. So this was what it was like to wake up happy. I rolled over and snuggled close to the warm female form, savoring the novelty of her presence. Tanya was deep asleep, as thoroughly sated as I, and tranquilized by daybreak. I lay there until nature called, then padded to her bathroom, which was about the size of my apartment. After a quick shower, I dressed, kissed my snoozing vampire goodbye, left her a little love note, and headed out. Mr. Deckert was waiting for me at the bottom of the stairs, a travel mug that smelled of coffee in one hand and an aluminum-foil-wrapped bundle in the other.

"Morning, Officer Gordon," he rumbled.

"Morning, Mr. Deckert," I replied, my eyebrow arched in question as I looked at the coffee mug.

"Sensors indicated someone awake in the Young Queen's suite. Figured it had to be you. Thought you might like some coffee, and the morning cook made you an egg sandwich. The limo is waiting out front to take you wherever you need to go."

He paused for a moment, as I had frozen on the stairs two steps from the bottom, stunned by his speech. He waited for me to make a response, obviously enjoying my surprise.

"Young Queen?" I asked.

"That's what they're all calling her now," he shrugged.

"Limo?" I asked.

"Both Arkady and Lydia were very clear about your status in this household."

Great, now if someone would just let me know what my status was.

There didn't seem to be anything to do but to accept the breakfast and free ride with as much good grace as I could muster.

The giant behind the wheel seemed vaguely familiar, then I realized he had been the guard in the garden when I had been wrestling the Hellbourne on the patio. We didn't speak, other than me giving him my address.

Heading into my building, I no sooner hit the stairwell then I could hear familiar voices on the second floor. I found Gramps chatting with Paige in the hallway outside my apartment, him with a paper under his arm and a Styrofoam cup of coffee, Paige in her running clothes.

"Hi, Chris. I just met your grandfather," she said with a smile.

The old man turned and arched one bushy gray eyebrow at me before adding, "Your delightful young neighbor was telling me all about the show you put on at that vampire club... what was it called?"

"Plasma. Yeah, Chris, we didn't get to see you much that night, but Kathy and I had the best time! The table you got us, our own hunky vampire to wait on us, the celebrities, and that fight scene! It was amazing! It looked so real," she said. "But it was too fast. Next time you need to have them slow the effects down or whatever. That part looked a little fake. But when the people at our table found out you are our neighbor, they started treating us like celebrities!"

"Well, I'm glad you two had a good time. You got home okay? No problems?" I asked.

"The little spiky-haired girl who seems to run things insisted that we ride home in your girlfriend's limo! It was unreal."

Gramps was looking at me in a bemused manner, and I smiled and shrugged at her excitement.

Paige blushed a little, then excused herself. "It was very nice to meet you Mr. Gordon. I need to get out on my run. Chris, thanks again for Halloween. I asked the spiky-haired girl what we should do to thank you, and she laughed and said we should feed you? Anyway, so we'll be making you some homemade ziti and bread some night this week, as a start."

"That sounds great. Lydia knows I like to eat, so she definitely steered you right. Have a good run."

With a last goodbye, she headed down the hallway while Gramps opened the apartment door. The futon was back in its couch position and the apartment looked tidy, so he had been up awhile. Farmers tend to rise with the sun, pretty much the natural opposite of vampires.

"So what do you want to do today?" I asked.

He looked at me with a gleam in his eye that warned of trouble.

"Well, Chris, the thing I want to do the very most is attend Mass at the Queen of All Saints church here in Brooklyn."

I groaned. I may have mentioned it before, but I really don't like church. I've got so many issues with God that I want to avoid all of his houses. Being in the demon-bashing business requires a certain amount of contact with clergy, but most of them know my views. Still, he had phrased his response in such a way that I pretty much had to comply. Not without a fight, though, however small.

"Why?" I asked

"Well Chris, I've heard a great deal about that particular church and its stained glass windows from Father Davis back home. This may be my only remaining chance to see it."

He was healthy as a horse, but whenever he wanted to fight dirty, he brought up his eminent demise.

I sighed. "All right. But I'm not getting dressed up."

"Khakis and a polo?" he asked.

"I suppose. Hey! What about our bet?"

Without another word, he handed me the two fifties from the table.

The Church of All Saints on Vanderbilt Avenue is spectacular. Modeled after the Sainte Chapelle in Paris, it has fourteen great stained glass windows, which contain two hundred and sixty biblical subjects from both the Old and New Testaments. Sitting in a pew and staring at the profusion of stained glass scenes, I felt fairly insignificant. That people would put such love and passion, not to mention money, into the creation of a place of worship was a little humbling. My reverie was cut short by a call of nature. The Mass wouldn't start for fifteen minutes, so I excused myself, leaving Gramps in silent contemplation.

It took a few minutes, but I finally found the facilities. After accomplishing my task, I opened the door to leave and stopped in my tracks. A man was leaning against the wall, his ankles and arms crossed, one foot tapping impatiently.

"About time!" he said.

He was about six feet tall, and had an athletic build, short, curly blond hair, and vivid blue eyes.

"Hey, I wasn't that long. And it was all business, not like I was reading in there or anything," I said, just a touch defensive.

He looked confused for a moment, then shook his head in annoyance.

"No, not that. I've just been waiting for eons for you to step into a church. It's bad enough that I had to be the one to talk to you, but then it takes you like forever to show up."

He stood up and I noticed he was wearing dark pants and a dark button-down shirt, untucked. I'm not one to notice another man's looks or even begin to judge what women find attractive, but I had a real strong idea that this guy was the type that caused women to swoon. However, I had no idea what he was talking about, or what he wanted. He didn't seem dangerous, but I was learning swiftly not to prejudge these things.

"Look, buddy, I don't know who you think I am, but whoever he is, I'm not him." I started to slide by him, but he was suddenly in front of me, which was troubling, because my enhanced eyesight could see old vampires moving at speed.

He hadn't made even a blur. He frowned at me.

"Of course you are he. I mean, you are certainly the him that I think you are." He shook his head again. "I'm making a mess of this. But it's all very frustrating. I told Michael that I was the wrong choice. Briathos or Eae would have been better choices. They're both big fans of yours, what with all the demon bashing and all. But no, he says, 'You're guardian of Scorpios, Barbiel. You have to talk to him.'"

I was thoroughly alarmed by his mention of demons and bashing, so I risked a quick view of him with my Sight. What I saw shocked me. His aura was almost equal parts silver and gold, colors I had never seen in an aura before. And bright, so bright I could barely look at him. Stunned by the sight, not knowing what else to do, I just stared at him.

"So anyway, you're stuck with me," he said with a sigh. "But maybe you could stop into a church a little more often?"

I answered with the first thing that popped into mind, still completely bewildered by this exchange. "I was just in a church the other day," I said.

He wagged one elegant finger at me. "Uh-uh! Funerals don't count. Particularly a police officer's. Michael would have my head if I had interfered with Officer Sanchez's service."

My brain was reeling from his casual knowledge of my recent whereabouts.

"But anyway, you're here. Sooo... I'm supposed to tell you that you're doing a great job, but you need to be careful. Your powers and abilities will serve the Dark as easily as the Light. You mustn't let yourself get drawn down the Dark path. Also, you need to explore your powers. They can do so much more than you are using them for. For instance, they will heal as well as hurt, although you have been helping the bear. Oh, and congratulations on finding your other self. Well, that's about it." He looked immensely pleased with himself.

"Wait, what are you talking about? Who the hell are you?"

He instantly frowned. "Hey, that's not even remotely funny! I didn't say anything about you and Hell. Why would you insult me that way?" He was pretty mad.

"I'm sorry, I didn't mean to say that. It's just that I don't have any idea of what you're telling me."

"Oh, don't be so obtuse. You understand it. And if you need to do something, you'll know how. Look, I've got to be going. You're not my only assignment, you know. Sure, you're all important and everything, but I do have other responsibilities."

He brushed past me and I spun to try to get some answers, but he was gone. Vanished from one step to the next. No noise, no poof, nothing. Even Tatiana at her fastest would have left a breeze in her wake. And he had felt solid as he brushed by me.

I stood staring down the hall when suddenly his voice spoke from behind me.

"Don't forget to come back soon!"

I spun again, but there was nothing and no one in the hall behind me.

I slid into the spot next to Gramps, still stunned by my encounter. He was chatting amiably with the older couple next to him and he pretty much ignored me, which gave me an opportunity to sit and ponder my visitor's odd words and actions. The Mass started and I went through the motions until a word, spoken during the sermon, caught my attention. " -- The Archangel Michael and the other led by Satan," the Pastor said. Wait, what had he been saying? Something about armies, squaring off or something. My visitor had used the name Michael twice. I listened to the rest of the sermon, which had to do with Satan being thrown out of Heaven. The priest wove it into a general discussion of angels and humans and their interactions.

After Mass, Gramps and I stood in line, waiting our turn to meet and be greeted by the pastor. Gramps was giving me sidelong glances, no doubt, wondering at my patience. I usually tear ass getting out of church as quick as I can, but here I was, standing in line like everyone else. When our turn arrived, Gramps thanked Father Turnick for an excellent sermon and complimented the church's beauty and magnificence. Then the stout little priest was shaking my hand and looking me in the eye.

"Father, I have a question if I may?"

"Certainly."

"Have you ever heard the names Barbiel, Briathos, and Eae?"

His eyes widened and he nodded. "Of course. Barbiel is the angel of October. Briathos is an angel who fights demons. I'm not so sure about Eae, but that one may also be a demon fighter. Why do you ask?"

"Well I heard the names mentioned in passing and wondered about them, that's all. But can you tell me what Michael's charge is?"

He nodded again. "He is the Angel of Protection and Courage. Patron angel of law enforcement and military. You have a look of one or the other about you, so he may well be your Patron."

"Thank you, Father."

I took advantage of the long line behind us to move past him, although I could tell he was curious about my questions.

"What was all that about?" Gramps asked when we were fully outside.

I gave him a quick rundown of my strange encounter with the confused and possibly angelic young man who called himself Barbiel.

Epilogue

We remained mostly quiet on the way home. Any attempts to discuss my odd experience at the church petered off as we each struggled with the implications. Instead, by mutual, if silent consent, we ignored it and spent the rest of the day roaming about Brooklyn, shopping for some things that Gramps was interested in (mostly books), and sampling the international foods. Gramps went home to the farm the next day, and I returned to work. I was waylaid by Briana Duclair right after seeing Gramps off. His Ford pickup had no sooner pulled away when a black government SUV pulled up in front of me and the head of D.O.A.A. popped the rear door.

"Hey, Gordon, let me give you a ride to work. Our introduction last week seemed too short." She smiled as she said it, but her eyes were hard and the two beefy guys in the front looked ready to try to force the issue. I actually contemplated letting them have a go at it, but decided it was early in the week for a charge of assaulting federal agents. So I paused long enough to let the tension ramp up, then shrugged.

"Sure, it'll give me a chance to ride on the government's dime."

I climbed into the back seat next to her, and the door no sooner closed then we were pulling into traffic.

"So, Gordon, you're pretty tricky for being just a tracker. But then, you're not just a tracker, are you?"

It was apparently a rhetorical question because she continued without waiting for answer. "Took me a while to track down the specifics on you."

She was smiling and it reached her eyes, but there was a harshness to her that set me on edge. She was brassy and aggressive, the kind of woman who really enjoyed going head to head with men and trying

327

to dominate them. Me, I'm not that big into the whole pack dominance and status thing. To many school bullies had tried to use my outcast self as a social step stool over the years. It never worked out well for them and left me with a bad taste for the human social structure. I would make a lousy werewolf.

"So, I find out that you're not only a demon exorcist, but, if the reports are to be believed, an incredibly effective one at that. Then I'm told you're the individual who stopped the 'Thing in the Pit', as your brothers in blue are calling it." She shook her head. "And your talents are being wasted in Roma's outfit."

I was starting to actively dislike her, some of which she must have read on my face.

"Oh, don't get me wrong. He's done okay for what he has to deal with, but he just doesn't have the full resources of the federal government behind him. Chris, I would like to bring you by our offices sometime and show you what we have to work with, the kind of cases we handle, and the kind of perks I can offer someone of your talents."

The muscle head in the front passenger seat was watching me throughout her spiel, and a grimace of anger flashed across his features. He was a guy who wouldn't approve of my coming aboard. He caught my eye and made a little show of tapping the dashboard with the law enforcement grade Taser he was holding in his right hand. Did he know that Tasers weren't effective on vampires and weres? I'm not sure what effect they would have on me, but he might be in for a surprise, if he ever zapped me with it. Briana caught our stare down and immediately rapped the back of his seat.

"Simmons, stay the hell out of this!"

Like a scolded school kid, he turned back to the front, his shoulders and the stub that passed for his neck rigid with anger.

"Well, Briana, maybe I'll drop by some time and check it out. Sounds interesting." I would have said no right off the bat, but I was thoroughly enjoying taunting meathead Simmons.

"Oh, we'll make it happen. You really need to see what you're missing out on. Right guys?" she asked the two in front. Simmons grunted, but the big black guy driving smiled into the rearview and gave a hearty, "Hell Yeah!"

His sly glance at his partner told me that he also enjoyed baiting the Neanderthal next to him.

I tuned out much of her speech on the rest of the ride. It mainly consisted of telling me what a great leader she was and how much better her team was than anyone else's. For all her vaunted prowess, her sources hadn't linked me to the New York Coven, club Plasma, and certainly not the New York Pack.

When I finally got to work, I was feeling pretty pissed off. Roma held a morning meeting and update, wherein Fran announced a veritable flood of visiting vampires leaving the city, Chet reported a break in and container theft at a certain dockside container yard, and I told them the reasons for both, conveniently ignoring my own role in the events of Friday night and Saturday morning.

"So let me see if I got this right," Roma said. "A faction of the vampires was in league with the Hellbourne to spread chaos and Hance throughout the world, then step up as rulers. You stomped the demon at Plasma, and your girlfriend and an Elder named Senka stomped the others?"

"Pretty much."

"Now Senka is on her way to Europe to take charge of the vacuum left by Fedor's death, taking Galina with her. Your girlfriend is in charge of the New York Coven. The other North and South American covens have their own division heads, all of whom will report long distance to Senka, is that right?" he asked.

"Anything else to report? Anyone? Okay, I'm going to brief the Commissioner. For once, we are ahead of Duclair."

He dismissed us and rushed off to his office to fill in his boss. The rest of us broke up, but Gina pulled me aside and asked if we could talk in her office. "Chris, I noticed you grimace when the Inspector mentioned Briana's name. Has she been in touch with you?"

I gave her my annoyed look, which slid off her pretty features without effect. "You seem to spend a lot of time watching me, you know that?" I asked, noticing that she was wearing a wedding band. The other times I had seen her, it had been missing, but a lot of police officers took off rings when working. They don't always mix well with the street.

"Actually, you are right. You are my pet project, per the Commissioner's orders. He feels that you're too valuable and your abilities are not well understood, so I'm your handler for want of a better term," she said. "But back to my question. When did you see Briana?"

"She ambushed me this morning and insisted on giving me a ride to work."

Gina just nodded, so I continued. "She is aware of my demon-banishing abilities, at least the exorcism ones. She also knows I had a hand in the Hancer lab debacle, but didn't elaborate. She never mentioned the Demidovas or Plasma, the Hellbourne, or anything about weres."

"Knowing Briana, she would most likely say something if she had that information. What about your physical speed, strength, or senses? Or your rapid healing and excessive metabolism?" she asked.

I just stared at her. To my knowledge, I had never divulged any of that. After a moment, she smiled.

"Bingo! We're not stupid, Chris. Brian told me you were holding back during his evaluation, a lot. We all saw you save Jacobella from falling. I've seen you with cuts and minor wounds on several occasions that were gone hours later. In the pit, you ran down two flights of stairs in the pitch darkness, without night vision goggles, avoided all the cops down there, and located the Damnedthing and the demon. Most of what I said was an educated guess, but your responses tell me I'm right."

She smiled again, but it wasn't a smug smile. "I can understand your reluctance to talk about this with anyone. But I have to ask you: are you becoming a vampire?"

I was still stunned by her perception, but I managed a head shake. She frowned.

"A were?" she asked.

I shook my head again, then managed to find words. "We don't know what I am."

She frowned at the word we, asking a silent question.

"The vampires have their own doctor. He's the one who recognized the base origin of the Hance molecule. Anyway, he has a theory that I inherited a mutated version of the viruses that cause both vampirism and lycanthropy. When I was exposed to the virus in Tanya's blood, my own mutated again, leaving me with attributes of both vamps and weres. It's all very complicated and I don't have the science to understand much of it, but it seems to fit. My demon abilities are all tied to it as well."

I waited for her to push for additional information, but she changed directions. "Chris, has the Damnedthing left or have you encountered it since?"

I sighed, figuring lying wasn't worth the effort. "He's still around. I think he's kind of adopted me. He's a bit... protective."

Her eyes got big as she wrestled with the idea of an ancient elemental animal spirit with godlike powers following me around.

"I don't think he will cause trouble. He doesn't seem to eat anything that I can figure out. He won't attack my friends," I assured her.

She looked a little dubious.

"You're not going to tell me that he's not dangerous are you?" she asked, one eyebrow raised.

"Oh, he's incredibly dangerous. He's the one who killed Fedor. Crushed him like a caterpillar. But he is intelligent, hates demons, and has declared himself to be my friend."

She picked up a pencil and tapped it on her desk top. "You know, I used to think this was an interesting job. Then you showed up, and I'm only just starting to find out the meaning of the word interesting."

She shook herself a little, then pinned me with a look. "Now, what did Briana offer you?"

"Well, I can pretty much expect the sun, moon, and stars, plus I'll have the daily privilege of basking in her glory and wisdom. Did you know that if Al Gore hadn't invented the Internet, Briana Duclair would have?" I asked with a straight face.

She laughed, reassured that I wasn't jumping ship immediately.

After that, my life started to settle into a pattern of sorts. By day, I worked for the Special Situations group, keeping hours as I saw fit. By night, I helped, dated, hung around with and generally continued my fall into love with the future queen of the vampires. And she insisted that I begin training with her, learning the vampire way of combat. I needed every bit of accelerated healing I could get, as she was by far the toughest instructor I ever met. But she made up for it in ways none of my old instructors could have, not that I would ever want them to.

Thanksgiving was fast approaching, which Gramps was coming down for, and the skies stayed mostly gunmetal gray. I was helping Chet with setting up a new piece of equipment that was supposed to measure neutrinos. He was working on particle physics, a direction first hinted at by Dr. Singh, when Olivia appeared in the doorway, excited and bearing news. "The Inspector just called. He and Fran have confirmed a demonic haunting in the Bronx."

She handed me a slip of paper with the address on it, then stepped back, a little breathless. It took me a second to realize that she was watching me for a reaction. I turned to Chet, and he was doing the same thing.

"What? It's just a demon," I said.

Chet snorted. "Just a demon, he says. You hear that 'Liv, 'just a demon'? Dude, this is our first chance to see you in action."

"Whoa there, cowboy. No one is going in with me. It doesn't work that way," I said.

"Yeah, but you can wear that new Chris Cam I put together. And I can send my little robot in to measure EMF, radiation, and all kinda stuff!"

"Yeah, I suppose."

Sooner than I anticipated we were at the scene. The entire team was assembled and, as Chet wired me up for video and sound, Fran and Roma gave me the run down.

"Family just moved in." He pointed to a black couple holding two kids. "Landlord offered them a hell of a deal on rent. They were no sooner in when all hell broke loose. Both kids scratched, bedroom doors shutting themselves and resisting all efforts to open them, you know, that kinda thing."

Roma was almost as excited as Chet, who was now sending in his little tracked remote-controlled robot with a complete sensor suite.

"Fran, tell him what you sensed."

"It's mean, maybe a six on the scale." Her voice dropped to a whisper. "And I think it knows you are here."

"Good. Makes things easier. Did you get a name?" I asked in a normal voice.

She nodded and handed me a slip of paper with the word *magottus* on it. I grimaced at the name.

"What's the matter, is it a bad one?" Fran asked.

"Nah, its name sounds like squished maggots! Can't these things ever sound normal?" I smiled to let her see I was joking. "All right, let me chat with the kids a minute, and let's get this party started!"

The boys were four and six, and quick to jump in with names for the mountain lion fetish I pulled from my rollout bag. The four-year old was in favor of Big

Kitty but the six-year old was heavily lobbying for Alex, after the lion character in Madagascar.

I tried for a compromise. "How about Big Alex?" I asked.

Something in my voice must have conveyed my diminishing patience, because they both agreed. "All right. I'm heading in. Don't get too comfortable; this shouldn't take long."

As I climbed the steps, I could feel a chill emanating from the house, a chill that had nothing to do with the deepening gloom of the November evening. A hostile presence awaited me within. Suddenly, I felt another presence arriving behind me, to the high-pitched howl of a German motorcycle, and, turning, I looked at the lithe form riding it. She pulled off her helmet, and her electric blue eyes sparked in the darkness. From the corner of my eye, I could see the team looking at her in surprise. But her gaze never strayed from mine. I smiled and winked, then spoke softly, knowing she would hear me above the noises of the city.

"Don't go anywhere. I'll be right back."

For the first time in my life, as I did what I was born to do, I had friends behind me and a girl waiting for me. I smiled to myself as I walked through the open door.

"Hey Magottus! Get your greeeeasy ass out here!"

The door slammed itself behind me.

The End

Look for Chris and Tanya in book 2, Demon Driven.

73809714R00201